PRAISE FOR *Salt Dancers*

"Hegi's book is a recognizable relative of her award-winning *Stones from the River,* in that her gift for interiors—of people, places, politics—is everywhere evident. The book is beautifully written, and Julia's discoveries are both entirely startling and completely plausible."
—Roz Spafford, *San Jose Mercury News*

"Hegi's exploration of consciousness pushes the limits of the novel, and the book succeeds brilliantly in portraying the narrator's doubts, fears, memories, and fantasies. *Salt Dancers* is a fine and complex novel."
—Susan Greiger, *Minneapolis Star-Tribune*

"With exceptional narrative authority, Ursula Hegi takes us into the labyrinth of adult memory. . . . She has a gift for recreating images from our own childhoods."
—*Winston-Salem Journal*

"Hegi has created an engrossing, potent story, well wrought with original, evocative description. In *Salt Dancers,* Hegi . . . has spoken the unspeakable, powerfully."
—*The Bookwoman*

"A masterly effort rich in mood and implication, *Salt Dancers* is at once a heartrending chronicle of a family's undoing and a journey of self-discovery and redemption."
—*The Washington Square News*

"In [*Salt Dancers*], Ms. Hegi weaves a finely textured tale of the enduring, yet frustrating, bond of love between parents and children."
—*The Dallas Morning News*

# Salt Dancers

■

## Ursula Hegi

Scribner Paperback Fiction
*Published by Simon & Schuster*

SCRIBNER PAPERBACK FICTION
Simon & Schuster Inc.
Rockefeller Center
1230 Avenue of the Americas
New York, NY 10020

First Scribner Paperback Fiction edition 1996
SCRIBNER PAPERBACK FICTION and design are trademarks of Simon & Schuster Inc.
Designed by Edith Fowler
Manufactured in the United States of America

1  3  5  7  9  10  8  6  4  2

The Library of Congress has cataloged the Simon & Schuster edition as follows:
Hegi, Ursula.
Salt dancers / Ursula Hegi.
p.   cm.
I. Title.
PR9110.9.H43S25     1995
823—dc20  95-13246
CIP
ISBN 0-684-80209-0
0-684-82530-9 (Pbk)

*Excerpts from* Salt Dancers *have appeared in* Prairie Schooner *and* Spokane Woman.

# Acknowledgments

I want to thank the National Endowment for the Arts and Eastern Washington University for grants I received while working on early drafts of *Salt Dancers*.

*For my women's group*

# 1

∎

WHEN I TURNED FOUR, MY father taught me the salt dance: he sprinkled a line of salt on the living room floor, positioned my bare feet on top of his shoes, and told me to leave everything I feared or no longer wanted behind that line. His gold-flecked eyes high above me, he walked me across that salt border into my brand-new year—he backward, I forward—my chin tilted against the buttons of his silk vest.

I would like to believe that the salt dance was a ritual he and my mother had seen on one of their journeys—in a mountain village in South America, say, or in Sicily—but my father simply made it up the day I turned four, and from then on it became a tradition in our family on birthdays as if backed by generations. Though I no longer recall what I left behind the salt line that day or chose to take with me, I can still evoke the tingling in my arms as they encircled my father's lanky waist. Below his right eyebrow curved the moon-sliver scar where a dog had bitten him when he was a boy. Rooted to his feet, I didn't slip off as we danced, careful at first—"Two steps to the right, Julia, one to the left"—then spinning through the rooms, past the radiant faces of my mother and brother.

When I was nine years old, I stopped loving my father. Of course it didn't happen all at once: it was rather a waning of trust until it became safer to believe that I ceased loving him altogether that one summer evening when he brought me chocolate with hazelnuts and lifted me from the windowsill and forced me to say I loved him.

Somewhere between those two images that continue to haunt me, things twisted, turned on themselves, and when I finally crossed the country and returned home to Spokane—forty-one, pregnant, and unmarried—it was because I was afraid I'd mess up my child's life if I didn't sort out before her birth why things had gone so terribly wrong with my family.

I STILL hadn't told my father I was pregnant when I walked with him down the path that led to our lake cottage. Old tracks had settled into deep, overgrown ruts; I walked barefoot in the furrow, my father above me on the wide band of grass that grew on the right. From time to time his bare elbow rubbed against me. I had to hold back to match his shuffle. He was slighter than I remembered him as if, as a girl, I had painted his younger version on a balloon and, in the years since, had let out some air, shrinking his likeness just enough to shift the edges of his body inward, render him harmless. It was ironic—now that the edges of my body were being pushed out, though not enough yet to proclaim my secret. My breasts were fuller—I felt their weight when I walked—and my clothes had grown tight, but the choice to tell was still mine.

Until two summers ago I'd known for certain that I didn't want a child, but a few months before I'd turned forty, an absurd yearning for a baby had attached itself to me. I could banish it as long as I didn't swim, but whenever I did my laps in the pool at the Y or floated in one of the lakes near my house in Vermont, the water rocked me into images of myself holding an infant. A girl child. What made it even more absurd was that I didn't have a lover at the time and felt content without one. My friend Claudia and I laughed about it: I didn't long for a man—I wanted a child.

Claudia, who also was my dentist, speculated on biological urges, internal time clocks, and finally resorted to the prescription: "Just stay out of the water, for Christ's sakes, before you trap yourself into having a midlife baby."

But her Aunt Edith, who'd recently moved in with Claudia and her family, eagerly offered to take care of any midlife baby I'd trap myself into having. A girdle fitter by profession, Aunt Edith had retired from Alexander's department store in the Bronx, where—as she liked to put it—she "used to stuff fat tochises into girdles for forty-five years." Taking care of a baby, she said, would be a vacation.

"A daughter," the doctor had told me during the ultrasound, and I'd nodded because I already knew. "Everything looks fine."

Until I'd seen the landscape of my child—delicate threads of shadow and light racing across the cone-shaped field on the gray computer screen—I had thought of my pregnancy as a condition, surprising and unsettling, but when the sound waves traveled through my flesh and bounced off the fetus, I saw translucent bubbles, stalactites and stalagmites, a harp even. My child initiated me into a world that existed already within me, oddly familiar yet foreign, as though I were looking through a kaleidoscope that didn't detain shapes but, in the shifting of threads, created a fluid impression, movement.

Claudia was with me, one of her large hands on my arm as the technician guided the transducer across the warm gel she'd squirted on my belly. "They didn't do this when I was pregnant." Her round face leaned closer to the screen. "So tiny," she whispered. In her family everyone, including Claudia, was exactly six feet tall. Both of her sons were already in college, young men with wide wrists and shoulders like their parents'.

I felt awed that the intricacy of what filled the screen

would come together to form my child. Sometimes the land-scape seemed surreal until the technician would point to the stomach, the labia, the femur. The heart pulsed like a tiny dark mouth opening and closing. A circle with a slender gap at the top turned out to be my child's thumb and fingers, about to touch. As I recognized the contour of my daughter's chin and mouth, she yawned. Her tongue stretched. And that's when she became real to me.

Though her shape was immediately lost to me in the over-play of swift threads, I waited for her to emerge from that canvas, a prelude to her birth. I wanted to see her in color— not just in gray through the practiced eyes of the techni-cian—wanted to recognize the sum of her lines and movements as they merged, wanted to guide my hand along the elaborate bridge of her spine that arched across the screen—a far more complex structure than I or any other ar-chitect could possibly design.

MY FATHER'S leather shoes loosened fragments of dried weeds that drifted around our legs like new mosquitoes. The rich scent of sun-warmed grass filled my head. High above us soared a redtail hawk; through its tail feathers the sun broke in splinters of fire. The sky was vast and streaked with salmon-colored clouds—the western sky of my childhood—so differ-ent from the fragments of sky among the mountains and trees where I'd lived since college.

When my father stumbled across a root, I caught his arm, and he sagged against me. "Thank you, Julia," he wheezed. Creases gathered themselves around his lips and below his ears; his full hair had turned bone-white in the years I'd been away.

*I'm stronger than my father.* I used to take his strength for granted—the kind of strength that flings you across the room, knocks you to the floor, burns imprints of his hand on your face. *If I want to, I can shove him aside. Beat him. Abandon him to rot on this path like a deer shot out of season . . . his legs at odd angles in his chinos . . . his shirt stained with blood—* My heart raced as if I'd walked for hours. Those pictures I saw inside my head—they couldn't be mine; yet, I kept staring, wishing, right to the details of him *lying twisted among decaying pine needles and new moss, shielding his face from my blows.* The sky tightened around me, tilted, swerved, snaring me there on that hillside in an orange-red haze of rage, both hands on my father's arm.

I let go of him, dazed that such cruelty was within me. How would it come out—against my child? As a girl I'd promised myself that I'd never slap my children, and from there another promise had grown—that I'd never have children. *Too many chances to botch things up.* I'd lost my husband, Andreas, over that. "We're not like your parents, Julia," he'd say, but I knew more reasons for not having a child than he could name for having one.

My father stood looking at me as if waiting for something, and I jammed my hands into the pockets of my shorts. "Are you all right?"

He nodded. Slowly, he pulled a handkerchief from his pocket and dabbed at his throat, his forehead. As he climbed back out of the furrow, the binoculars he'd brought along for bird-watching swung against his chest on their leather strap. Though we were the same height, he seemed taller than I as he ambled along the strip of grass above me. Anyone watching us from a distance—too far to make out our features— could mistake us for a man and a small child.

The path to the lake coiled downhill for nearly half a mile from the road where we'd parked my rental car. A long time ago my parents had considered graveling the path, but the estimate had been higher than the cost of the cottage on six acres of lakefront. On weekends we used to make several trips back to our car, lugging toys and clothes and books and food and, occasionally, one of those trashy tabloids from the grocery store which my family only read at the cottage and burned in the fireplace after we took turns reciting them to each other, laughing over headlines like, *Nun Kills Herself in Convent's Washing Machine . . . Three-headed Cow Saves Boy Scout from Drowning . . . New Jersey Dentist Does Root Canal on Space Alien. . . .*

Since my father and I were only staying overnight, we brought what we needed in one trip: he carried a plastic shopping bag with fresh fruit, two cotton blankets, and his TV guide; I carried a large backpack with food, oil for the lamps, towels, swimsuits, and my canvas shoes. Even with my thin arms, I was stronger than my father. I felt that seed of cruelty ripening inside me along with my child.

"JULIA, LOOK." My father pointed ahead. His short sleeve fell back, exposing the pasty skin on the underside of his arm. "The lake. You can see it from here." His voice was excited, and he raised the binoculars to his eyes.

Below us Lake Coeur d'Alene spread like blue ice. This was where I'd learned to swim when I was four, where my mother had taken me out into the bay in her inflatable yellow raft, each time a little further, staying next to me while I swam back, calling me her brave swimmer; this was where Travis and I had hauled the picnic table to the end of the dock when my father was at his office—where we'd practiced somersaults and reckless leaps into the deepest water that summer my brother caught up with me in height; this was where I had taken a razor blade into the woods late one night when I was eleven and set it against the inside of my wrist, but as soon as the cold metal had touched my skin, I'd known I didn't have to die to get away from my father.

"Isn't it beautiful?" My father's right hand swept across the view of the lake as if presenting it to me as a gift.

He'd always been a generous man, buying orchids for my mother, stuffed animals and comic books for Travis and me. And when we'd thanked and hugged him, he'd sometimes held on a little too tight. He was the one who'd given Travis the stuffed bear that would come to be named One-eyed

Teddy because its left glass eye fell out a week after Travis got it; he also was the one who'd pulled the hole together with brown yarn and embroidered an eye with long lashes.

Or was it my mother who'd sewn the new eye? As I tried to sort out that which had happened from that which could have happened, I was lured into the maze of memories that tricks us with distorted reflections of what we commit to its safekeeping; and what we wrest from it changes each time we hold it against the light, depending on the slant of the light and its intensity. And so we embellish our stories. Protect ourselves with gaps. And take all of that for truth. All of it. Until it might as well have been observed through the eye that someone embroidered on the face of a stuffed animal.

But I did remember that it was my father who'd brought me the wooden box with the trouble people from a trip to Guatemala. I still have it at my house in Vermont: it's oval, decorated with red dots surrounded by green rings, and the trouble people are sealed within, together, safe. The box is small enough to close my fingers around; but when my father gave it to me, I was five, and it filled my palm as though it had been made for it. Inside lay eleven tiny fairy dolls with painted smiles, their wire limbs wrapped with wax-coated, orange threads; scraps of colorful fabric were tied around them to simulate clothes.

"If you take out one of the trouble people," my father told me, "and whisper your problems to it, it will solve them while you sleep. That's what the Maya Quiché Indians of Totonicapán believe."

Six of the trouble people were men, five women. I was scared they'd grow at night and burst through the lid, just as I was scared of the dark because wicked spirits waited till the sun was down before they came out. Light turned them to dust. That's why I always slept with the closet bulb on. When I asked my father to keep the trouble people in his desk at the office, he took the box with him.

The following night my mother woke me up, whispered for

me to get dressed, and brought me along on her moon-walk which she usually took alone when the moon was at its brightest. Our house was halfway between two ponds—Manito and Cannon Hill—and we circled both that night as if following the pattern of a figure eight that held our house at the intersection of the two loops. We hiked up the South Hill behind our stucco house to Manito Park, where my father had asked my mother to marry him, and when my legs grew tired, my mother swirled me into the air and propped me on her shoulders in one fluid motion; her hands spanned my ankles—light, yet secure—and as she took steps longer than any I could have managed, I was rocked by the motion of her body.

"Someday," she said, "you'll be tall too."

My hands in her hair, I smiled to myself, knowing better than to believe that old story which most adults seemed compelled to tell children. I'd figured out a long time ago that children didn't grow up—they stayed children, just as adults stayed adults.

In the gauzy clouds that spun across the moonlit sky like cotton batting, we divined shapes of castles and trees and rivers—no monsters. When my mother told me that while we slept, we lived another life someplace else, I imagined a different existence for myself on the other side of the earth and envisioned a girl with my features sleeping there while I was awake in Spokane, stirring through the girl's dreams.

It started that night, my awareness that—each time we come up against choices—the unlived strands of our lives trail behind us, splitting again and again, likely to become tangled, and that we can will ourselves into those strands and experience the lives we could have chosen. There, time does not limit us to the familiar sequence of hours and days: we can soar through years in one instant, propel ourselves from the future into the past, grow old beyond our years, and return to the moment *before* that original strand separated as we seized our first breath.

And though I was far too young that night to name these words, I felt the strands of my mother's and my lives, splendid and intricate, touching yet separate as they stirred and settled into each other on the empty sidewalks. In Cannon Hill Park we stopped below one of the old weeping willows that dug its half-exposed roots into the earth where it sloped into the pond, and we searched for the ivory silhouettes of the swans.

"Where do *you* go when you sleep?" I asked my mother.

She laughed—a warm, throaty laugh I could feel as it vibrated from her skull into my hands. On the hazy skin of water, the reflection of the tree shivered as the swans passed through it. "To the Gypsies," my mother said. Enraptured by their legends and customs, she collected books with pictures of snake charmers and fortune-tellers, gaudy street dancers and wise crones, gilded caravans and fiery horses. One of her treasures was a rolled-up parchment map of the world with ocher veins that traced the wanderings of Gypsies over a thousand years, veins that originated in India and curved through Afghanistan and Africa and Hungary and France, even America.

When we got back to Shoshone Street, the porch light of the brick house next door illuminated the *For Sale* sign. In the last year, it had been bought and sold by three different families.

Inside my room the monsters had vanished, and my mother tucked me in. As she bent to kiss me, I asked, "Can I come with you tomorrow night?"

"Maybe some other time."

But I wanted to look forward to our next moon-walk. "When?" I probed, though I knew she didn't like to plan ahead.

She started for the door. "I don't know yet."

"You didn't say 'Pleasant dreams,' " I called after her.

"I'm sorry. I forgot." She turned. With a small, impatient frown she touched her nose to mine—four times—once for each word: "Pleasant—dreams—my—Julia." Her hair, straight and brown like mine, fell around my face. "Okay now?"

"Pleasant dreams." I tried to think up something to keep her with me, but I already knew she wouldn't stay. It was easier to get my father to do things he didn't feel like doing—like tell me stories though it was past my bedtime or buy me ice cream half an hour before dinner.

"I don't need the closet light on tonight," I told her.

For a moment there—when she closed the door and the dark curved itself around me—my tongue filled my mouth. Taking deep breaths through my nose, I pretended: *I'm still riding on my mother's shoulders, her hands warm braces around my ankles, linking me to her, to the ground, to the moon. . . . And in my dream my sleep-self joins my mother's sleep-self, wherever she is—* Yet, in the morning I couldn't remember where I had traveled in my sleep, and though I couldn't recall a reality beyond the one I knew with my family, I felt certain that I'd touched colors far more vivid than any I'd encountered before.

I told my father I was ready to have the trouble people box in my room. After keeping a fairy doll on top of the closed lid overnight, I found my favorite pen, which had been lost for weeks, and when I had a scratchy throat one evening and left one doll out, my throat felt fine in the morning. Sometimes I thought of the dolls all living together inside the people box—just as my parents and Travis and I lived together inside our house—and I wondered if the other dolls missed the one I took out. But I always replaced it in the morning.

It wasn't as though it was gone forever.

"WE ARE almost there, Julia." My father shifted the blankets to his other arm.

Ever since I'd arrived three days ago, we hadn't talked beyond words that kept us safe. He acted as if this were just another family visit, though I hadn't seen him since I'd left for college twenty-three years ago. We'd sent Christmas presents to each other as if we were like other fathers and daughters. But I couldn't pretend any longer because last week my pregnancy had turned into a child, prodding me to take my questions out of the silence where they'd kept growing. I'd struggled against the sudden urgency that pressed me to visit my father—terrified to return, terrified not to return.

It was far more natural to run away from him: I had done it a hundred times, a hundred different ways, and for many years I'd thought I could choose to forget. I'd believed I could leave my pain behind and be rid of it, but instead it had rooted itself inside me, a vine with countless runners.

What I had wanted was to take myself—from the hour I'd seen my father for the last time—and start my life anew from there like a salt dancer, inventing myself, counting only on myself. And it seemed to work: I graduated at the top of my class; liked my work as an architect; traveled to the Far East and Europe; involved myself in a mentor network for women entering architecture, where our numbers—though still low—had increased fivefold since I'd graduated. And even if sometimes I felt furious that I wasn't happier, I figured it had to be like that for most people. But with this pregnancy my old memories had begun to swell within me, rising through the fabric of my adult life which I'd woven so soundly, and I had no idea what would be left of me once all those memories broke through.

"Almost there," my father mumbled.

I adjusted my step to his slowing pace. His cheeks looked drawn, and the cleft in his chin had blurred with age. I didn't have any pictures of him looking like this. Only those from years ago which showed him in control of the body that now had betrayed him, slowing him down.

He used to wear tailored suits with white shirts. Italian leather shoes. Silk vests and ties. His hair had been a weave of silver and golden strands, the same shade of blond, he'd told me, as his Norwegian grandmother's who had immigrated as a bride. He'd grown up on Cape Cod but had moved to the Northwest as a young man. Though he was a banker, he acted in the plays at the Spokane Theatre Ensemble. He'd reserve front row seats for my mother, Travis, and me, and I'd watch his agile face, mesmerized by the imagined lives he inhabited so convincingly—as vibrant and passionate on stage as he was with us, who knew how to block our moves within the boundaries of his love.

After the performance he'd take *the four of us*—that's how he used to talk about our family: *"the four of us"*—to the Rooftop Restaurant, where he'd order butterscotch sundaes for Travis and me, Singapore slings for my mother and himself.

My mother's friends talked about him as flamboyant and, in hushed voices, as beautiful, as if embarrassed to assign that word to a man. Yet, it was a word that suited him better than my mother, though she was stunning and had a way of moving that was different from anyone else's: her tall body was either perfectly still or moved very quickly—not abruptly but with a sudden grace. When my parents danced, it was as if she enfolded him into that grace, and others would recede from the center of the floor, unwilling to disturb their pattern. He'd draw her close, real close, one hand pressed flat on the small of her back. Together, they'd generate a magic that neither of them could sustain alone. His eyes at the same level with hers, he'd look at her as they danced as if she were the only woman on earth.

At my Uncle Jake and Aunt Marlene's second wedding—they were divorced the winter I was six and remarried each other the following spring in our house—I ran from the edge of the dance floor and did what I'd been aching to do for a long time—break into my parents' dancing embrace to remind them of my existence. Their bodies parted to let me in as they both reached down to lift me, my father balancing a glass of champagne.

Feet dangling high above the floor, I whirled with them across the parquet of the living room, through the kitchen and sunroom, and onto the stone veranda, where Japanese paper lanterns bobbed in the April breeze. For several glorious minutes I danced with my parents, one side of my face against my mother's hair, the other against my father's smooth-shaven cheek, giddy with the scent of champagne and my mother's perfume. Had I known that I'd only have her with me for a few more years, I would have held on to her—no, to both of them—in that dance with all the power I could have invoked.

BEAUTIFUL, they called my father, beautiful and elegant. "Calven, you have elegant toes," my Aunt Marlene declared at one of our lake parties. "If I had toes like you, I'd wear sandals even in winter." Her thick braid hung past the sash of her swimsuit, and I caught it and made it swing like a pendulum toward my brother, who caught it and tossed it back to me.

My father, who'd spent all morning preparing his famous barbecue, sat with us on the dock, his tanned legs stretched out in front of him, the hairs on his shins and thighs bleached white from the sun. "I thank you, Marlene," he said gravely and studied his long toes as if they were the map to a buried treasure.

"She's right." Nancy Berger, who taught with my mother at Lewis & Clark High School, shielded her eyes against the sun. "Calven's toes are elegant."

One of my father's toes twitched, then another, and soon they were wiggling like wild. He tilted his face toward my mother and grinned. "I'll never be able to look at my feet the same way again."

She held her floppy hat with one hand and bent to kiss him; when she raised her head, the sun was in his eyes and the amber flecks around his pupils seemed even brighter than usual. I felt their love inside me as if I'd blotted it, so hot and sudden it was too much for me to contain—an odd, sharp rapture that makes you want to cry but you don't because it would be sappy.

I leapt up. "Come on," I shouted and hoisted my brother onto my back. His chest warm against my back, his wiry legs

slung across my bent arms, I gave him a mad piggyback ride
down the sandy slope of the beach.

"Not so fast, Julia." He screamed and giggled and held on
tight.

With only ten months between us, we were more alike than
different, both of us with long, wiry bodies and limbs, with
skin that didn't burn but turned nut-brown, with straight,
dark hair that had a way of retaining flecks of sun after it
dried; except that Travis flickered between moods, and that
the soles of my feet were tougher than his since I stayed barefoot until late every fall and had trained myself to walk on
rocks and twigs, hot sand even.

As we galloped into the lake like one tall body, I couldn't
tell any longer where his arms and legs ended and where
mine began, and I felt that fierce jolt of my parents' love, felt
it for Travis—for both of us—but then the water closed above
our heads and rushed between us, leaving my body cold and
separate.

When I climbed onto the dock, I flopped down on the hot
planks, my hair on the edge of my father's towel, my limbs
heavy as if I'd run all day.

"Listen, Marlene," he said and pointed to the wind chimes
I'd assembled from twigs, green yarn, and chicken bones.
They hung in the trees between the dock and the cottage,
and their hollow wail sounded like the ghosts of a thousand
chickens. "Julia can build anything. Last Christmas she made
us a deer feeder."

I grimaced at Travis, who sat on the far end of the dock,
but his eyes had turned sullen.

"Look what the sea brought in." My father squeezed the
water from the ends of my hair. "One thing I can always
count on with Julia . . ." he was telling Uncle Jake, "is that she
knows about people."

"She has good instincts," Uncle Jake agreed.

Travis was pulling at his fingers, making the joints snap.
His hands seemed too big for his wrists because his thumbs

grew at a wide angle from the sides of his hands and allowed him to pick up things far larger than I could get my fingers around.

My father's face was right above mine. "I often take my clues from Julia." The scar above his right eye stretched shiny-silver, the only evidence from the long-ago attack of a sleek, gray dog. As though the dog had been searching for him, it had singled him out among hundreds of other children who'd played at the Provincetown beach, lunging for his face, toppling him over and biting into the salty waves as if devouring him.

In the blurred sheen of the water fusing above him, my father must have felt the dark shape converging upon him and receding in a pink wash of blood that rose from his face in the shape of a paper fan. Three times he surfaced to screams that were not his own, surfaced to a searing pain on his face and a sun blinding him through a veil of red, so that he welcomed the sinewy paw that guided him back under the waves to the silence and the velvet-pink absence of pain.

His mother, who pulled the dog from him, had teeth marks on both arms and a chunk of flesh torn from her left thigh when the dog finally ran off into the dunes, never to be captured though the police hunted for it, as if it had materialized for that one feat and had vanished after marking my father with only one external scar, while the real injury was the fear of dogs that nested itself within him and the hunch that, somewhere, that gray shape was still waiting to claim him.

## 2

■

THE DOG'S ATTACK DIDN'T SURprise my grandmother. She had anticipated protecting her son against this and much less dangerous claims on his life ever since nine months before his birth when his only sibling—a brother named Calven—had suffocated one Monday afternoon. She'd found him with his temples wedged between the slats of his crib, his open mouth flattened against the sheet, which would remain damp with a bracelet of his saliva hours after she'd free him. When the tiny, white coffin was lowered into the earth, she allowed herself one long, exquisite pace toward the grave as if to follow her child in a cotillion.

It was her husband, a fisherman, who caught her with one arm around her waist, and she leaned into him as he led her toward the spiked iron gates of the cemetery. They kept walking until they reached the front hall of their house, where she brushed the black crepe dress—which still carried the new store smell—from her freckled shoulders, her hips. Her wrists sank to her sides as the crepe ringed her feet like a useless life preserver, and she stood motionless as if too weary to step from it. Her husband, a man accustomed to wearing spacious rubber boots, unlaced his stiff leather shoes, but he didn't take time to fling his borrowed black suit across the banister before the two proceeded to couple there on the mourning dress without any sound, not even a sob, in a blind yearning to resurrect their son, to give shape to his body through their mating, which left them pale and chilled and famished for something tangy—say, pickled beets and smoked herring—in the early evening hours.

And when, four weeks later, a midwife confirmed that my grandmother was pregnant, the sorrow in her eyes was displaced by the certainty that her son *had* returned to her. She thought of her pregnancy as an extension of Calven's last sleep from which he would finally awake, a sleep that made it possible to prepare herself to do everything right this time—to watch over him every moment, to pick him up as soon as he cried, to protect him from drafts with blankets and closed drapes, but most of all to keep him safe in the spacious crib without slats which her husband would build with his chapped hands from a sketch she made. Of course the child was a boy when he emerged from her, and of course the labor was effortless because she had already given birth to Calven once before.

When my father turned his head inside his crib, his eyes must have slid from the solid white partitions that blocked his view of his room; perhaps his attention would have been drawn to a knothole, the one irregularity on the smooth surface. He must have heard his mother approach but would not have seen her until she stood right above him and looked down on him, a sparse-bodied woman with gray-penciled eyebrow arches and white-blonde braids pinned on top of her head, her arms amazingly sturdy as if made for yanking her loved ones away from catastrophe.

My grandmother was a woman who attracted catastrophe. It didn't begin with the loss of her first child and wouldn't end with the gruesome death of her husband soon after the

second Calven was born. There had already been a childhood friend who'd vanished on the way to school when both
girls were seven, an older sister who'd lost one arm in a har-
vesting accident, a melancholy suitor who'd escaped into suicide when she'd chosen to marry the fisherman.

The morning after this fisherman brought her and the second Calven home from the hospital, he set out to sea with his
partner, and when his boat failed to return that night, she began to grieve his death though the wife of his partner insisted
the men would come back. Three weeks after the capsized
boat had washed ashore, a fishing crew gutted an eleven-foot
mako shark near Martha's Vineyard and found a pair of rubber boots, covering partially decomposed feet. The boots
were ordinary—brown rubber with black, ribbed soles—but
the tortoiseshell-colored orthopedic inserts helped my grandmother identify the feet as belonging to her husband.

Catastrophe courted my grandmother, enveloping her
with its offerings: an intricate scar on her thigh; an old
suitor's despondent love letters; an infant's crib in the attic;
brown rubber boots torn by a shark; her sister's copper ring.
Her tragedies were not modest; they bordered on the extrav-
agant, the lavish, as if to pledge to her that catastrophe was
rehearsing for its final union with her. And so she braced
herself for an end far more dramatic than anything that had
befallen those she loved, but as she grew into an old woman,
catastrophe deserted her as if bored with her. She was too
willing, too prepared. There was nothing else to take from
her, nothing to maim, to ravage. She would stay remarkably
fit, still riding her bicycle to the cemetery, still waiting for
that death which would trick her with its uneventfulness,
molding itself to her deepest fear—to die peacefully and un-
aware in her sleep.

MY FATHER would grow up surrounded by models of British
steamships with glossy black hulls and bright orange smokestacks which my grandfather had patiently built from balsa

wood and pine: the magnificent *Lusitania,* which had sunk off Ireland in 1915; her sister ship, the *Mauretania,* which would not sink; the *Titanic,* with her grand staircase and the skylights on the top deck, which had sunk off Labrador in 1912; and her sister ship, the *Olympic,* which also would not sink. If my father learned anything from this heritage, it was that sister ships were safer, and he would take those two models—the *Mauretania* and the *Olympic*—with him when he'd move west, as far away as he could from the cemetery where he and his mother used to carry fresh flowers every Sunday to the family plot, where the name *Calven Ives* had been chiseled into the granite stone.

When my father first told me about his brother, I was in second grade and kept wondering what it would be like to grow up knowing there was already a gravestone with your name. We flew to Cape Cod for our summer vacation that year and stayed with my grandmother in her house of weathered shingles, where my father had slept the first eighteen months of his life in an oblong white box, before his mother had bought him high-sided bunk beds as if to furnish his room for both Calvens. When I asked him to bring me to the cemetery, he said no, but my grandmother buttoned her black raincoat over her cotton dress, covered her silvery braids with a scarf, and cut a bouquet of blue hydrangeas from the bush next to her porch. Flowers bobbing in one arm, I rode on the back of her wide-framed bicycle through the spiked gates of the cemetery. Although the gravestone was partially overgrown with glossy vines, it brandished my father's name as if it knew more than any of us, and I wished I hadn't asked to see it.

That evening I climbed on my father's knees on the porch swing, and he laughed as if surprised and rocked me back and forth while I held on to the front of his sweater, thinking how hard it would be for me to move forward into the next day and the day after that, if that were my name on the stone. When it occurred to me that I hadn't sat on anyone's lap for a long time and that I was far too old for that, I tried to slide off, but my father folded his arms around me and kissed my cheek. I didn't know how to get away without making him feel sad and was relieved when my mother said it was time for Travis and me to go to bed.

In my father's old room, we fought over who'd get to sleep in the top bunk. When we wouldn't listen to my mother about taking turns, my father dismantled the structure, and we ended up with twin beds at opposite walls of the room, further apart than Travis and I would have liked to be. That's how my father usually solved our conflicts: if we couldn't compromise quickly, he'd take whatever we might be quarreling about—a toy, a book, a trip to a fair—entirely away from us.

It so happened that we spent far more time in that room than expected because, for two days, we had to stay in bed with the flu. My mother urged us to drink lots of water to bring down our temperature, and I emptied the glass she held out to me; but Travis pressed his lips shut, and when she kept the glass in front of him and insisted that she wanted to see half of the water gone, he grabbed the glass and—as I watched with admiration and horror—poured exactly half of the water on the rug in front of my mother's feet, his eyes bright as if he were electrified with what he could get away with. After a long moment of silence, he slipped his index finger into his mouth. His eyelids dropped as he began to suck.

ONE MORNING all of us crowded into my grandmother's car and drove to the pier where she had arranged for the charter of a sailboat. She knew the skipper who was to take us to a sandbank where the wreck of an ancient ship pierced the surface of the sea. But the instant the engine started, I felt certain that something—too dreadful to name or envision—lay waiting for us below the waves, and that I had to get my family off the boat. I cried out, yanked at my father's hand, my mother's sleeve.

My grandmother caught me in an embrace, crouched next

to me, and pointed to the deck where my shadow stretched as though it belonged to a giant. "Fear," she said, "is like that—out of proportion depending on the angle of light. What is meant to happen, will happen."

My father whispered in my ear, "It's all right to cry. I was afraid of crocodiles in the toilet when I was your age. I used to leap from the toilet seat as soon as I was done, certain they'd snap at my butt."

I had to laugh and that only made me cry louder.

"Why don't the rest of you go sailing and have a grand time," my father suggested. "I'll stay behind with Julia."

But when I refused to disembark without my family intact, he persuaded my mother and grandmother that all of us should go ashore. He had already paid for the charter—our vacation splurge, he'd called it—and when he validated my premonition, I believed he knew what really awaited us below the surface. And perhaps he did. Perhaps what I feared that day was not something beneath the water but beneath the surface of my parents' marriage, something that would contain itself at a tenuous distance for only one more year.

IT WAS toward the end of that year when the dream started, a dream that would follow me into my adult years. The sequence of images was always the same, and so was my panic: *I chase down an endless corridor after a tall figure. I run as fast as I can, my breath a rattle in my throat that blocks all other sounds. The walls narrow, and the distance between us decreases, but when the figure finally turns, the face is blank. Just skin. No features.* I'd wake up with that panic, shivering in a clammy sweat. After my mother vanished, I would come to believe she was the figure in that dream—a warning I had failed to understand.

The first time I'd come out of that dream, I'd sat up straight in my bed, my face hot with tears. From the living room came my parents' voices, and I got up quickly, already taking comfort from imagining my father taking me by the hand and asking me why I was crying, my mother pouring me a glass of apple juice, but when I reached the stairs, they were fighting about love with ugly words that turned the air hazy-gray, words like "slut" and "pompous ass" and "bitch" that made me feel as though something even worse was about to happen. Squatting on the second step from the top, I wound the hem of my nightgown around my ankles.

When my father accused my mother of not loving him, she said he was choking her with his love.

"That's why you go to him?" he shouted.

And she shouted back, "You don't check with me on everything you do either."

I kept my breath steady and cool and light in my throat to hold the air in my body separate from theirs. I couldn't see my parents from the steps; yet, whenever I think of that night, I see my family as if through the roof of the trouble people box: *my mother on the sofa with her arms clasped around herself as if freezing, my father in front of the unlit fireplace with a bottle of beer, my brother asleep in his room with his arm around One-eyed Teddy, and myself—there on top of the steps, afraid to move since they'll hear me and come to the bottom of the staircase.*

To be discovered by them would have been more dangerous than their fight—by exposing myself as witness, I would have taken all of us out of that safe frame of secrecy. And that frame was crucial—it held together the portrait of our family, especially when things did not fit into that picture, like the night my mother had taken Travis and me out of bed and ridden with us in a taxi all the way to Uncle Jake's farm, or that Halloween Travis had worn the bumblebee costume and my father had tossed him into the air until my mother screamed at him.

I must have fallen asleep on the stairs, because I woke up when my father carried me to my bed. As he straightened himself to leave, I grabbed the sleeve of his chalky shirt in the dark, afraid I'd be sucked back into the dream. I had to make him stay there, with me, and the one thing I could think of was to ask him for a Julia-story. That's what he called the stories he liked to tell me: Julia-stories. They were about things I'd said and done when I was little, things I'd forgotten until he would recount them to me. From then on I'd remember them as my own.

He hesitated but didn't remove his sleeve from my grip. I felt him listening for my mother. "Just one," I pleaded.

As he sat on the edge of my bed, I couldn't see his face, only the outline of his shirt. For a few minutes he sat quietly, thinking. "You had long, jagged fingernails when you were born. . . ." His voice startled me. It was louder than usual, as though he were telling the story for my mother as much as for me. "Several of the babies in the nursery had long fingernails, and no one did anything about it. One little boy had scratched his wrists. . . ."

I rotated my wrists. Tested them against my lips. They were smooth and salty when I grazed them with my tongue. Through my gauze curtains pressed the shadow of the haunted house next door, and I felt as though the cranky old woman who used to live there were watching us. Her husband used to fuss around the garden and sweep the sidewalk every morning, while she'd argue with him through the open window from her hospital bed which had been set up in the living room, or yell at children who would run across her lawn. Late one night an ambulance took her away, but she complained about the nursing home until the old man brought her back in his car. The day she returned she spit up blood and died in the living room. After her funeral the old man stayed inside the house with the shades drawn. My mother tried to invite him to eat dinner with us, but he wouldn't open the door. His lawn turned dry and yellow, and one Tuesday, exactly five weeks after the old woman, he died.

The house was bought by a salesman, who slept there only one night before he went on a business trip from which he didn't return. Though one of the neighbors said he'd been transferred to Chicago, I was sure the ghost of the old woman had chased him out. The next owners were newlyweds who kissed and ate ice cream on their front stoop the day they carried their furniture into the house, but within a month they both looked gloomy. From the window of Travis' room, I saw the man kiss the throat of another woman in the kitchen, and soon after that, a stake with a new *For Sale* sign was pounded into the front lawn. The brick house always sold faster than any other place in the neighborhood. A week ago, when two sisters from Oregon had moved in, I'd warned them about the old woman, but they'd only smiled at each other the knowing way adults do when they don't believe kids.

My father settled one arm around my shoulders and kissed my forehead. "When the nurse brought you for the first time to your mother's room," he said, "I asked if she could please trim your fingernails. She refused and wouldn't even lend me scissors—some foolish hospital regulation." His voice rose as though he were still annoyed with the nurse. "I finally took the elevator down to the pharmacy and bought those small, curved scissors. Your mother held you while I cut your fingernails. . . ."

From somewhere on the first floor I felt my mother listening, connected to my father through the sound of his voice, and I thought, if I can only keep them like this, both of them, their breaths will form a bridge to span the night and get *the four of us* across to the other side.

Throughout my childhood my father used those rounded scissors to cut my toenails—toefangs, he called them—as if he'd pledged himself to that task of protecting me the day I was born. But of course they weren't enough, couldn't be enough, to protect me from him. He'd lament about the state of my fingernails, which I'd chew off as soon as they had enough of an edge to grasp with my teeth, but my toenails belonged to him. That's what he'd say in his best vampire voice: "Your toefangs are mine, *Dschoulia.*"

Once a month, after a bath, he'd prop me on the kitchen table, pull a stool close, and hum while he'd guide the curved blades with gentle precision. In the warm kitchen I'd sit wrapped into a fluffy towel, while crescents of my softened nail clippings drifted to the newspaper he had spread across his legs.

His stories would develop gaps after my mother left: none of them would contain her name anymore, giving them the same eerie feeling of void as our house had without her. *The four of us* became *the three of us*. Listening to him, I'd feel as though he were telling me about someone else's life, about a girl and her brother who'd been brought up by their father.

As a banker he was successful, well put together—his suits stylish and immaculate, his hair in place—and he stayed that way during the day. But in the evenings all of that changed. Came apart. The transition was so gradual, at first only a loosening which—if I hadn't known—would have been something to like: he became the father who hummed, who tried to swirl me in a crazy dance through the house. But he'd bump into furniture, step on my toes, and when I'd break away from his hands, he'd bicker and wheedle, demand confidences and services, speak of himself in the third person.

"Make a sandwich for your poor little father, Julia. . . ."

"What are you and Travis whispering about?"

"Where is that bottle your poor little father bought yesterday?"

Though he didn't beat me every time he drank, I could feel the tension, the possibility: the dog might get in his way; he might kick a toy he'd brought home for me; he might call me ugly names. And even when nothing happened, it felt as though something were happening. Because I felt the danger, the fear. If I was lucky, he'd crumble into sleep at the table, his face half turned into the angle of one arm, and I'd take the bottles and hide them, hoping he wouldn't wake up and stagger into his car to buy more.

For years I believed that if only I could hide every bottle he brought into the house, we'd be all right again; but he became adept at concealing them, and we'd circle each other in a contest of hide-and-seek where the stakes surpass the threat or solace of the bottle. And that sound of a car, any car, start-ing late at night still makes my limbs go stiff, makes me want to climb into a locked place deep within myself.

BUT ON my father's thirty-fifth birthday it was still the four of us. The month before, my mother had begun to hint about his present. None of his guesses came even close, and he was left with the clues that it was "bigger than a milk bottle and smaller than a bread box." He didn't have any idea—for good reasons, it turned out, because he would have never allowed a dog into the house. I'd seen him cross the street to avoid dogs, had smelled the sudden sweat on him if a dog came close.

"You don't have to be afraid of this one, Calven," my mother said when he shrank from the dachshund puppy I'd already claimed in my arms.

"Keep it away from me. Please."

"It won't get much bigger. See? Show your father, Julia."

He backed against the living room wall, his face pasty.

The puppy stirred against my chest, nudging its wet snout against my neck. It smelled of soap and piss. "The salt dance," I reminded my father. "You haven't done the salt dance yet."

But he kept staring across the room at my mother. "Why would you get me a dog?"

"I thought it would help you get over that fear."

"You better get it out of here."

"What if I take care of the puppy?" I offered.

He turned to me, that sweat scent all around him. "I'm sorry your mother is putting me into this position, Julia."

"Don't try to make me look like a bitch. I was trying to—"

"I wish you hadn't bothered."

"Please?" I said. To stop them. To keep the dog. "Please?"

"I can't." My father shook his head. "Just the thought of having a dog in the house with me—"

"It's too late to take it back tonight," my mother said.

"Tomorrow morning then."

She didn't look at me when she nodded. "All right then." And it wouldn't be until weeks later that she'd say to him, "I guess I should have talked with you first about the dog."

I don't remember what kind of birthday cake she'd ordered for my father from his favorite German bakery—only that I threw up what little I ate of it and woke during the night to the persistent whimpering of the dog. Downstairs in the kitchen, I sat on the tiled floor next to the basket which my mother had padded with a frayed towel. As I stroked the silky brown fur, the puppy snorted, gulped for air, and shifted into a hush.

"You'll catch cold, Julia." My father stood in the doorframe, his travel alarm clock in one hand.

"It was crying."

"Maybe it misses its mother." He wound the clock and handed it to me. "Tuck it into the towel," he said. "The puppy may think it's the mother's heart."

But it was my father's heart that won out that night, transcending his fear of the dog, which would come to choose him as its favorite person as if playing the part my mother had chosen it for—to gradually heal my father from his fear. Despite my jealous bids for its undivided loyalty—including letting it lick my spit from my fingers—the dog would desert me if my father was near, following him with its nose so close to his heels that, often, it would get bumped. Obviously, the thing with the spit didn't work even though my best friend, Lynne, assured me that savages trained their dogs to be faithful—to them alone and no one else—by feeding them their saliva. But she didn't know which savages, and she wasn't sure how often you had to repeat the ritual.

My father's last resistance to the dog was to confine it to the closed kitchen at night. We decided to call it Zeck, but it never became accustomed to the name because it ignored all commands except my father's: "In the kitchen!" Then it would give him a persecuted look and slink off to my old baby quilt next to the refrigerator. Since the kitchen in our cottage didn't have a door, my father carried the dog to my room. "Kitchen. Kitchen," he announced and set it down on a corduroy pillow under my dresser.

"You're confusing the poor animal," Uncle Jake told us. "He'll think that's his name." But eventually we called the dog just that—Kitchen or Kitchendog. Said in a firm voice, "Kitchen" could mean anything from "Get away from me" to "You chewed up the wallpaper." In a friendly voice, it signified "Come here" or "Let's go for a walk."

The dog would escort my father to his car in the mornings and wait for him in the driveway, as if already preparing itself for that night—eight years away—when the sick crunch of its bones under the tires of the car would be the one thing powerful enough to stop my father from driving to the liquor store.

My FATHER'S feet resumed their slow pattern through the high grass. There was something fragile about him, cautious. He walked as if he had to decide about each step. Linking my hands beneath the bottom of the pack, I shifted its weight. I hadn't seen the cottage since he'd hired a builder to renovate it, but over the years he'd sent me photographs documenting each change as if he wanted me to approve of his choices: the breezeway off to the side, the skylight in the living room, the deck that wrapped itself around three sides of the building. *"Julia can build anything."* At first he'd mailed the photos to Carnegie-Mellon, where I'd studied architecture, then, after I'd married Andreas, to Vermont, both places a good three thousand miles away from him. "And when you get home, we'll spend a few days at the cottage," he'd added to most of his letters, as if refusing to believe what I'd told him—that I would not return.

Perhaps his refusal had pulled me back home after all these years. But if I believed in the power of that, I would have pulled my mother back a thousand times over, yanking her to me with the sheer force of my refusal to accept that she'd left me, eliminating the terrible distance she'd seduced me with.

My memory of her was luminous and gauzy, like an old black-and-white movie that had been run too many times; in places it was faded or too bright, yet it kept reeling over the same impressions without a sense of conclusion: *She tries on a floppy hat in front of our hallway mirror, tipping her chin so she can see her profile; she runs next to me with my kite, letting it soar high above us; she sits between Travis and me in Mr. Pascholidis' speedboat, her hair flying around her face, her mouth open with laughter; she peels an orange for me, leaving one ribbon of fragrant peel.*

Had she died, I could have grieved for her. But she disappeared when I was nine—as clearly as if she'd drawn a border of salt and migrated to the other side of it. I subsisted on fantasies that I was traveling with her in exotic countries, riding hotel elevators and chasing bottle-green waves. Certainly, she must have wanted to take me with her. Certainly, she would come back to claim Travis and me. I learned to will myself into her imagination, forcing her to see me, to look at me, that moment, and sometimes I would transcend the distance between us and merge with her—inside her skin and mine at once.

The first time it happened by accident: I was afraid to jump from the brick wall behind the apartments where my friend Lynne lived with her mother and brother. One arm around a birch trunk, my weight on my left leg, with my right leg crossed over in front of it, I waited for the fear to go away. That's when I closed my eyes and wished my mother would catch me. *She comes to me easily, her face and shoulders tan against an embroidered dress I've never seen before, but when she opens her arms, I cling tighter to the tree and look down at the wall, which has become a different wall, wider and even higher, piled up of gray stones with patches of lichen. And the tree, it has turned into an evergreen with glossy, oval leaves.* Years later in a biology class, I would identify it as an orange tree. *I feel the grain of its* bark, feel the hem of her dress as it billows around her knees, feel the sun hot on our shoulders.

Behind my mother the hill drops down to houses whose roofs look like steps to the blue-green harbor, where masts jab the sky like matchsticks. Breathing in the scent of the tree's white blossoms, I watch my mother and, at the same time, look through her eyes at me as she studies me, somberly, and when I abandon my fear in one bold leap, I feel the impact of both our bodies as she catches me. We tumble into the grass whose long blades release a tart green smell— and I want to bury my face into the earth and taste its rich grains to prolong the moment before I'll have to open my eyes and find myself back within the isolation of my body.

# 3

■

$J$ CAN'T REMEMBER IF I LEAPT
from Lynne's brick wall that day. What matters is that it was
real when I soared through the sun-drenched air into my
mother's arms. And it was like that with the countless stories I
made up about her: they fused with my memories. Like the
story I kept coming back to when all the others failed to
soothe me: *She's become the Gypsy woman in the Rousseau painting she's shown me in one of her books, sleeping next to her mandolin in the desert while a lion waits to nudge her awake. I am that
lion. Waiting. Certain that, somehow, she has shifted herself into
that other life strand, her Gypsy life. Time has reversed itself for her,
letting her only be with me while I sleep and live the life of that foreign girl somewhere else.*

Many nights I'd sit up in my bed to guard myself against
sleep. If our times overlapped I'd be able to catch my mother,
snag her back into my time, my family. *My father touches her
hair with both hands—lightly—as if to make sure she isn't an apparition, and then he pulls her into his arms and looks at me over
her shoulder, speechless with gratitude.*

After all, people came back together again. Uncle Jake and

Aunt Marlene had. *We have an even bigger celebration than they had for their second wedding. . . .* But inevitably I'd grow too exhausted to keep my eyes open, and when I'd startle myself awake, I'd feel weakened by an immeasurable regret that I'd missed her again.

"My mother——" I had told Coop last September after we'd made love in his cabin, where he lived with four parrots, "probably became a Gypsy. Maybe she still roams all over the world. When she was eight, she saw her first Gypsies. They were brown-skinned women and men, she told me, and her life was never the same after that. . . ." The Gypsies had invaded the schoolyard in Rosalia one night in early June with their tents and horse-drawn wagons, and when my mother arrived in the morning, she was one of the few farm children not afraid of them. Dazzled by the splendor of their garments and the brilliant whites of their eyes, she stretched out her fingers and touched the glittering belt of their leader, who howled his refusal at the principal's request to evacuate immediately.

"Ah——" As if it were a precious bird, the Gypsy man trapped my mother's hand in his and grew silent. A fine hoop of gold glinted in his left nostril. Tilting her palm toward the sun, he piloted the scarlet stone of his ring across the creases in her skin as if to decipher them. Then he nodded and let out a long sigh as if relieved and pleased all at once. "And you—— You wish to come with us." It didn't sound like a question but rather like something he already knew, and without hesitating my mother said, "Yes."

A child of the Palouse—that vast region of amber wheat fields that roll like dunes in every direction as far as you can see—my mother loved the endless horizon that was only shortened to the east where the mountains of Idaho rose in their shadowy hue; yet, she was ready to follow those Gypsies into a world of lustrous colors that lay beyond her sculpted hills, which turned from green to sun gold as the rigid stalks of wheat ripened and bowed into the dusty gales of summer.

And perhaps the Gypsy man saw that landscape in my mother's hand and felt she had summoned him there. He would have known all about horizons and could have shown her real dunes and the oceans beyond them.

I have seen them so clearly, the two of them, standing in that schoolyard, that sometimes I felt as though it were my hand the Gypsy was holding in his, and I wanted to believe that even if I couldn't find my mother, it would be enough to locate him—this man with the scarlet ring, who had to know how to chart his way back to her and might be persuaded to lead me.

"Would you have gone with them?" I'd asked my mother when she'd first told me about the Gypsies, and she'd smiled at a place far off in the distance. "That day. That day I would have."

But the principal wrenched her away from the Gypsy man; by her wrist he led her into the dim building where the somber colors of the teachers' clothes sapped the smears of sun that strained through the closed windows. Though my mother wanted to push those windows far open, she sat in class, her hands obedient on the varnished top of her desk. By the time the bell rang for recess and she rushed down the wide stone steps into the schoolyard, the Gypsies had departed without leaving any evidence of their visit, as though she had invented them.

Her eyes sieved the horizon for a string of horses and wagons, but there were only the familiar silos and farmhouses, ringed by clumps of trees. Beyond rose Steptoe Butte, the highest rock formation in the Palouse. That night she listened to the chant of the coyotes in a different way—as if their high-pitched ballad held the secret to the Gypsies' whereabouts.

Coop stroked my temples as I told him how my mother had searched the streets of Rosalia, the shallow valleys between the hills, and her favorite hiding place—the cavelike impression on the side of the town's highest slope, where it was impossible to harvest wheat. Weeds and blue flowers and odd seeds, cast there by formidable winds, molded fragrant cushions where she liked to read, and where I, too, would bring my favorite books as a girl and scan the distant open terrain for my mother. It wasn't hard to imagine that all this used to be covered by water. My mother had told me about the Spokane Flood—"rushing across this land a hundred feet high, Julia, more powerful than all the rivers in the world together"—which had shaped these gentle hills about fifteen thousand years ago, and about fields of black lava—"hundreds and hundreds of feet thick, just think of it"—that lay beneath this rich soil with its traces of volcanic ash.

Lying back against Coop's chest, I described to him the lopsided tent she'd assembled that day after school in front of her family's round barn: she pushed the ends of rake handles and broomsticks into the ground, pulled their tops together with a length of bleached washing line, and draped two checkered tablecloths and her mother's red and white piano shawl with the silk fringes across the frame in anticipation of the Gypsies' return. In the creek behind the church she found glittering stones and, like a sorceress, arranged them in peculiar configurations, that came to her as she touched them in the sun in front of her tent to lure the Gypsies back to her. Every afternoon she climbed into the bright red turret of the barn, which stood far higher than her stone house, and stayed there until her eyes stung. It would have been impossible not to see the Gypsies, had they been near.

She wouldn't find them again until three years later in the pages of a book in the main library of the closest city, Spokane. In the book the Gypsies would be called the Romany people, and of course their faces would be different, but that wouldn't discourage my mother because the blaze in their eyes would be the same. Perhaps it would have amused her had she known that, one day, she would give birth to a daughter who'd prefer solid walls to the flapping sides of a tent and who'd design permanent dwellings that kept people together in one place.

■

THROUGH MY mother's absence, her myth grew. She was the perfect mother, the mother I could imagine whatever way I chose to when I blamed my father for her leaving. Travis speculated that she was teaching school someplace else, that she had tried to call us. Sometimes I felt certain she had disguised herself and was watching us, close enough to touch. All I had to do was figure out who she was, and she'd reveal herself. I'd walk up to strangers and peer into their faces, ask them what time it was so I could test their voices. "Little girl, it's rude to stare at people like that," a thin man with a beard admonished me once, but most simply walked away from my stare.

Six months after my mother vanished, I found her ski hat behind the bookcase in the living room. Specks of lint clung to it, but when I held it against my face it still gave off the faint scent of her shampoo and sweat, and suddenly the house seemed even emptier than before and the hat lifeless, a flimsy substitute. I felt an icy-hot rope snap between my chest and throat, but even then I didn't cry—I made my mother reach for the hat, willed both of us onto skis, and retreated into another mirage, racing next to her down a slope of powder snow, the brisk sun on our faces.

When I was thirteen, my mother's high-heel shoes began to fit me. Most of them were made of fabric, dyed to match the colors of her dresses that my father had given to Goodwill: deep blue, bright red, vibrant yellow. For some reason—perhaps because he'd forgotten about them—he'd left her shoes on the shelves in the cabinet in our hallway, and I began to wear them with my plaid skirts and corduroy jumpers and jeans, tottering to school, feeling far older than the other girls—a woman, almost; and yet, I felt at a disadvantage because I wasn't coached by a mother like other girls, who seemed to have an easier time with fashion and hairstyles. How I envied them for being able to buy their first bra with a mother instead of having to follow a father who'd center himself in the lingerie department as if it were a stage, attracting an immediate audience as he proclaimed, "I want to buy a bra for my daughter."

I wouldn't cry for my mother until that afternoon when Andreas took our apartment key from his key ring and handed it to me, awkwardly, on his way to stack the last of his belongings in his car. Once I started crying for him, I felt my mother's loss all over again. I sat at my desk, my face wet with tears, then crouched on the floor. But the room around me felt so vast that I finally crawled into the knee space under the desk and cried. Cried over Andreas. Over my mother. Kitchendog. My brother. Even my father. Over everyone whose love I'd counted on until it had been taken away.

But what if I was the one who hadn't loved enough? What if my father was right and I was incapable of love? I felt sick with grief. It sliced itself between my ribs and took my breath. Because I hadn't loved my father enough, he'd lashed out at me, had begun his down spiral. *"Children are supposed to love their parents." "You'll never be able to love a man."* And my mother—if my love had been strong enough to hold her, she would have stayed. Andreas too. And Travis. I saw all of them, my daughter too, attached to me with long gossamer cords the way moon walkers were stabilized; yet, when their cords were severed or too weak, they spun into nothingness, danger, destruction, while I was left with the frayed ends of that love, stretching my body huge in all the directions where I'd lost people.

I didn't want that power, that terrible power to destroy people with my love. With the absence of my love. And I didn't have that power. No one had. No one should. Not even my father. I knew what it was like to love—deeply, abundantly— but my love was not a lifeline. All at once I found it easier to breathe, and as I saw myself cutting those gossamer cords, I felt myself shrinking, contained within my body, separate.

THAT EVENING I postponed going to bed. I read the newspaper in the living room. Watered the plants. Paid bills that weren't due yet. When I walked into our bedroom, the light hurt my eyes, and I turned on the bulb in the closet instead and undressed by its weak glow. Andreas' half of the closet was empty. On the floor a faint layer of dust outlined where his shoes had stood. I moved the hangers with my clothes along the empty length of rod, leaving spaces between them, telling myself I liked the way they hung, uncluttered.

When I lay down, the bed felt too big. Too level. No longer was I drawn toward the center of the mattress by the familiar slope caused by the weight of Andreas' sturdy body. In the dark I felt too thin: My collarbone and hipbones jutted through my skin, through the sheet. My arms felt even skinnier than usual. I wished for a narrow bed to define where my body ended—not emphasize the space Andreas had left—wished that I'd been the one to move into a new place where not everything was a reminder of him.

To stop myself from thinking about him, I tried to picture details of the walk I'd taken that morning: the rich brown of the dirt path; the matted winter grass, now free of snow; the spider pattern of frost on the flat rocks next to Otter Creek. I could almost feel the wind blowing strands of my hair into my face, between my lips, and all at once—though I tried to stop it—I'd been back to another morning when my hair had fallen forward, catching between my lips, his lips while my legs had straddled his waist in the high stand of cattails and weeds next to the creek where we liked to hike. Arched toward him in a kiss, I'd tried to push back my hair with one hand, but he'd laughed, catching it between his lips, and I'd laughed too, and then he'd gathered my hair, holding it back from our faces as we kissed.

I wanted to hold on to that memory to keep from sliding deeper into my pain, but it no longer protected me. Alone in the wide bed, my body curved itself around my husband's absence like a drying leaf, absorbing the hollow of my ache. Despite what I told it: that I had agreed for the marriage to be over . . . that I respected his wish to have children. . . . But those were only words—*agree, respect*—and my body spoke a different language as I retraced the imprint of his shape on the cold sheet.

I finally got up and returned to the living room, where I turned on the television and lay on the sofa. With the flicker of the screen and the sounds of an old Western, I was able to drift asleep. A few times that night I twitched awake, startled; but reassured by the light and noise, I sank back and closed my eyes. In the early morning hours I had a dream in which I bent over an infant crying in the old-fashioned wicker carriage that used to be mine. As I lifted her out, she felt rigid at first, then clung to me. Her mouth instinctively searched for my breast. It felt weird at first; yet, I nursed her, stroking her cheek, her fine, reddish hair. She didn't ease up, afraid I'd pull away, and as I let her drink for as long as she wanted, I felt restored with a comfort that was still with me, a gift, when I woke to the stirring of my womb, rising and tightening ever so slightly as if preparing to release the child from my body. For an instant there, on that dusky rim between sleep and awareness, I believed I was about to give birth and—for the first time in my life—felt entirely ready to have a child, this child, but when I turned my head to tell Andreas, I was alone, and my belly was flat.

AT WORK I functioned—met with two clients, began a new project, even had some fun with the complaint of a retired math professor, who called at five-thirty with the observation that our roofers had to be pissing on his roof. He didn't say "pissing" of course—he used every euphemism from "voiding" to "eliminating"—and he only spoke with me after asking to talk to a man in the office and finding out that everyone else had left for the day.

"Has there been any . . . leakage?" I made my voice sound concerned, glad he couldn't see my face.

"Not yet," he said. "But they never climb from the roof in order to use the facilities. They even eat their lunch on the roof."

I couldn't resist. "They're young men with strong bladders."

"They have to respond to their . . . physical pressure sometime."

I pictured him sitting in his study, shoulders hunched, afraid of piss trickling through the ceiling. After I assured him the roofers were reputable and promised to speak with them, I called the foreman on his mobile.

"Listen, Jack. One of our clients tells me you have a special bonding agent for the roof tiles. . . . Some old family secret?"

"What the hell are you talking about, Julia?"

"Piss."

A silence.

"The professor has concluded that your crew must piss on his roof."

Jack roared. "The professor's conclusion is abso-fucking-lutely correct."

I was still laughing when I got into my car, but as soon as I pulled out of the parking lot, I felt like crying and drove to the store for ice cream I didn't want.

I found it easier to sleep on the sofa: it was narrow—just enough for one person—and it felt safe to lie in a place that didn't have room for anyone else. I wouldn't touch the bed again for months, and the first time I'd return to it would be with a man. It didn't matter that I'd only met him two hours before in the whirlpool at the Y and already knew I wouldn't sleep with him again—all that mattered was that I was able to bring myself back to my bed through him.

To keep from missing Andreas, I set myself the goal of meeting one new man a week.

"Impossible," Claudia said. "Not here in Vermont."

But it was amazingly easy—as if I'd slipped on a snug T-shirt with the logo *Available* silk-screened across my breasts. I encountered men at the blueprinter's, the pizza joint, the car wash, local AIA chapter meetings, the produce section in the grocery store, the post office, the city building and planning department. After Andreas, who'd been thoughtful and reliable, I chose lovers who were frivolous. We danced, we sailed, we made love, but soon I'd want to move back into my work, while they'd still want to dance and sail and make love.

Nights that I slept without a man, images of my mother would stalk me without warning, splintering my dreams. I'd wake with a sad, heavy feeling throughout my body. My pillow would be damp, and I wouldn't remember if I'd cried over the loss of my mother or Andreas. Some nights I slept in my clothes on the sofa: it was easier to trick myself into sleep if I told myself I was only resting and that, any moment, a friend might stop by. In the mornings my body would feel bruised, stiff.

Eventually those dreams of my mother receded, but never entirely: like a pulse, they'd pick up again. Though they grew fainter over the years, I kept looking for her in airports, on fairgrounds, in movie theaters. As long as there was a chance that I could still find her someday, I felt linked to her as if the strands of our lives had formed a weave. *I come across her someday, when I least expect it. A tall woman walking in front of me stops and turns around. I recognize my mother's features and her straight, brown hair which she wears parted on the side in one wave across her forehead.*

She would always be twenty-nine.

With each year younger than I.

Until I'd grow old enough to be *her* mother.


I HAD survived on longing—it was the most familiar feeling I knew. At times I had mistaken it for love. Certainly with Andreas, whose accent and aloof eyes suggested a mystique that had captivated me when I'd met him at a winter carnival in Killington, Vermont. I'd come there for a week during my last year of college, and one icy night, when the ski patrollers wound their way down the slopes with burning torches, I stood in a crowd at the base of the mountain, shivering in the wind.

"It's called a *Fackelparade*," a man's voice said in an accent that sounded soft and harsh at once.

"A what?"

He wore the red jacket and emblem of the ski school. About my height, he was built solidly, with muscular thighs and a strong neck. His face was so smooth that he looked as though he never had to shave. "*Fackel*—the German word for torch. A parade of *Fackeln*."

"Sounds dirty."

"In your language, *ja*."

"There must be English words that sound funny to you."

He smiled. "Most of them, actually."

"Like what?"

"Like—" He hesitated. "I don't mean to have a lewd conversation." He pronounced *lewd* like *lute*. "I might scare you away."

"We'll think of it as language research." I found myself wondering if his chest was as smooth as his face, and it would turn out to be just as I imagined it—hairless, with raised, small nipples that grow taut the instant I touch them. "International communications," I added.

"Foot," he said, looking embarrassed.

"Foot." I nodded.

"A not so good word. For a person's bottom."

"I promise to survive the shock. Where in Germany are you—"

"Not Germany," he protested. "Austria, I come from Austria."

It was something I would hear him clarify many times afterward upon initial meetings, disconnecting himself from anything German. Once, when I would try to ask him why, he'd say because of the terrible war and insist it didn't count that Hitler had come from Austria because, by nature, he'd been the worst of all Germans— "*der Schlimmste aller Deutschen*."

That night of the winter carnival Andreas had a flask of hot, sweet tea and a red blanket, and he shared both with me, first the tea—far stronger than I was used to—which lined my throat with warmth. Then he shook out the blanket, held it stretched between us like a curtain, and I surprised myself by turning into the span of his arms without hesitating. As he wrapped it around me, I felt on fire, alive, spinning—though I only turned once—spinning within the warmth of my breath, spinning under the stars and the ribbons of flame from the torches, spinning against the backdrop of this man's compact shape.

He would always stay outside that blanket—reserved and distant—though I yearned for him to spin with me, but I didn't suspect that the night of the *Fackelparade* when he walked me to the lodge where I stayed. After I returned to Pittsburgh and Carnegie-Mellon, he told me in his letters how oppressive it had been to grow up in one of those Austrian postcard villages, surrounded by mountain peaks, where the light was dim most of the day because the sun only passed across the village for a few hours before the mountains blocked it. "Winters especially are dark," he wrote. "Shadows all the time."

From the day he'd turned ten, Andreas had wanted to get away from his village, far away, and even after we were married, he still acted as if he were shut in by mountains, while I waited for the day when I wouldn't ache with longing for him.

"DO YOU NEED help with the pack?" my father asked as he struggled down the path with the plastic bag and blankets.

"No." I ran my thumbs beneath the padded straps. "How about you? I could take those blankets."

He frowned. Blinked as if he'd already forgotten what I'd said.

"The blankets . . . I'd be glad to carry them."

"You don't have to do that, Julia."

From time to time he stopped and pointed to birds: a gray heron heaving itself into the air as if it didn't belong there, two ospreys and their bulky nest in the fragile crown of a tree, the black and white wing flash of magpies rising from a clearing. Ever since he was a boy, he'd been enchanted by

birds, by their flights, their generous colors. He used to rescue injured birds, settle them in boxes which he lined with
dandelion puffs, and serve them water, birdseed, and dead
bugs.

Once he was almost hit by a milk truck as he snatched an
injured pigeon from its approaching wheels, and his mother,
from whose side he'd darted, kept screaming with the vision
of his funeral, a vision that took hold of her whenever the
puckered scar on her thigh chafed against her slip. She kept
screaming even after my father stood next to her, the fat pigeon squirming in his arms, and she slapped him twice,
hard, and then dragged him against herself in a fierce embrace that must have caused further harm to the bird, because the following morning—even though she helped my
father stabilize its leg with the stub of a gray eyebrow pencil—it lay in the box, claws extended, opaque membranes
clouding its eyes.

Despite the nature of my grandfather's death, my grandmother was not afraid to let my father swim in the ocean. She
believed you were safe from a catastrophe that had already
claimed someone close to you. The more bizarre a death, the
more certain you could be that it would not revisit your family. It was different with death caused by choking or pneumo-
nia—a death like that was ordinary and could easily revisit
your family unless you guarded against it.

And so my grandmother took my father to the doctor for
every cough, made him stay indoors when it rained, and bun-
dled him in so many layers of clothing that his movements
were restricted. He became accustomed to waking some
nights to his mother standing by the side of his bed, her
freckled wrists—he knew the pattern of the tiny copper
specks though it was too dark to make them out—crossed beneath her breasts as she watched over him, solemnly. His
chest heavy with the burden of having to breathe—not only
for himself but also for the brother who had failed his
mother with his death—he felt ashamed at being the son

who was alive, and certain his mother would have preferred
the first Calven.

By the time he was five, he sensed that he could afford to
be reckless, and he abandoned obedience and prudence,
confident his mother would form a barrier between him and
any peril. After all—the brother whose name he carried had
already passed through his death for him, and he felt invio-
lable, immortal.

As he entered his teens, it became easier to escape his
mother's concern for his safety, but he always felt his
brother's presence as though he carried him somewhere
within him. He thought he'd free himself from him once he
left for college in Seattle, three thousand miles away, but
even there he felt the first Calven close by.

As a young man, he picked up one of the tabloids he
adored while waiting in a checkout line and, intrigued by the
headline *Portuguese Priest Pregnant: Cannibalism or Miracle?*
read about a seventy-eight-year-old pastor, whose body must
have absorbed that of his twin long before birth. It wasn't discovered until the priest had a tumor removed which contained a finger bone, an eyeball, and bits of the twin's
body—not unlike the fragments of stories my father had
heard about his brother, who hadn't been alive long enough
for his parents to gather a whole impression, only those bits
which they passed along to my father and which lay still, em-
bedded in his awareness. And perhaps that concept of cannibalism would grow to become quite comforting to my father
after he had his own family—not in the grotesque way of
someone else's body parts swirling within him, but in a rather
abstract manner of folding himself around his wife and children to keep them safe, keep them forever.

As MY FATHER and I came around a bend, the gray cottage
with its fieldstone chimney lay below us. The roof had been
reshingled within the last few years, but the old tin drum
where we'd kept stale bread for the ducks was still propped

on logs next to the outside sink where my father used to clean fish. Near the dock an orderly file of ducklings trailed a black duck as if pulled along on a transparent string. For some reason I didn't understand, I wanted to scatter them, chase them to the other end of the vast lake.

The lumber of the new porch was still natural—it hadn't aged like the cedar shakes of the cottage. White geraniums overflowed the wooden planters by the front door—my father's work, no doubt. He used to plant two flower gardens every year, one in Spokane, the other at the lake; the first spring without my mother, he'd already bought seed packages with pictures of marigolds, zinnias, and asters, but he never opened them.

That day in May, when we woke up in the morning and my mother was gone, my father drove us to the cottage in Idaho, where he would sequester us until the end of summer. Travis was eight, and I'd just turned nine. My father kept us out of school and locked the house in Spokane as if he wanted to make it impossible for my mother to get back inside. With red letters I printed a note to let her know we'd be at the cottage and taped it beneath the three leaded-glass panes on our front door.

But my father tore my message from the door and said it wasn't a good idea to let everyone know where we were. "An invitation to thieves."

"When is she coming back?" I insisted.

He folded the note into a tiny square and pushed it into his jacket pocket. "She is gone." His voice was hoarse. "For good."

But I believed my mother would find us on her own. She knew things that happened without being there. Once, when Travis and I had stayed with Uncle Jake while our parents were in New York—Travis in our cousin Andy's room, I in the room with the blue Jesus picture—my mother had saved my brother's life from over three thousand miles away. It was a Saturday and she was sitting next to my father in the Mark

Hellinger Theatre during the first act of *My Fair Lady,* when she felt nauseous with the certainty that Travis was in danger and cried out his name. "We need to call Jake," she told my father. "Something's happening to Travis."

He didn't question her as they left the orchestra seats he'd reserved months before and found a phone. I was the one who answered, my hands still shaking since, only minutes ago, I'd been jolted by a sudden wash of panic when a voice—my mother's voice—had cried, *"Travis!"* inside my head, and I'd dashed from the blue room and up the stairs to grab his ankles before he could fall from the second-floor hall window.

Without my message she won't find us, I worried, as my father motioned us to his car. Travis' nose was runny, and a smear of snot had dried on one cheek where he'd wiped it with his wrist. While he claimed the front seat with One-eyed Teddy, Kitchendog jumped on the rear seat, and I knelt next to him, one arm around his neck. In my other hand I clutched my red purse which held my favorite belongings: my first baby picture taken two hours after my birth, foreign coins from my parents' many travels, the ring with the green pearl from the dentist, the magnifying glass Lynne had given me last Christmas, and my box with the trouble people.

That purse would grow increasingly valuable to me over the next years, and it would stimulate lengthy decisions as to which things were important enough to be stored inside, ready to bring with me as soon as my mother sent for me. "Bag lady," my father would tease me, but I kept collecting.

From the back window of the car I stared at the stucco house that already looked as if no one lived there: all windows, even those in the two gables, were blind with drapes, and the flagstone path, which led up through my father's rock garden, was no longer cluttered with our bicycles and gardening tools. For a moment, before we drove off, I heard my mother's voice again as if warning me, and I was afraid I would forget the house and afraid that—if I no longer remembered it—the house would really be gone, that nothing would be there if I ever got back, and that eventually I would doubt it had ever existed.

It was a fear that would envelop me from then on whenever we left the house with suitcases, and when we returned I'd dart from room to room, touching books and chairs and curtains—greedily—until I was certain everything was still the same. I was like that with my house in Vermont: reluctant to leave it for long trips, impatient to return.

Claudia was looking after it while I was in Washington. After my divorce from Andreas, I'd bought a run-down farm in Proctor with her and her husband, Matt. Built in 1820, the hip-roofed Federal had started out as a tavern and coach stop. We'd divided the ten acres of pastureland along the natural border, a brook that ran through the middle of the property, separating the tavern and barn. First I'd drawn up plans for the restoration of the brick house for Claudia, preserving the outer structure but enlarging the common spaces around the four chimneys by knocking out walls between some of the smaller rooms and enlarging several doorways to accommodate Claudia's tall family. Then I'd moved into her guest bedroom—which now belonged to Aunt Edith—and begun the design work on the thirty-eight-foot-high barn for myself, using the original wood framing to emphasize an open floor plan with skylights and vaulted ceilings and spaces that flowed into one another. I'd oriented the view and decks toward the brook and the stand of maples in back. My favorite room was my studio loft with its floor-to-ceiling bookshelves on one wall and a window seat that I'd upholstered with a woven shawl in shades of sun colors.

Claudia had been even younger than I when her parents' marriage had ended. They had told her together. She was to move with her mother to the Bronx, where they would live with her mother's sister, Edith. As she listened to her parents without blinking, tears streamed down her broad face. Late that night her father found the wall in the garage lacerated with countless slashes.

When he brought Claudia downstairs from her bedroom

to ask her about the damage, she showed him the circular saw blade she'd flung into the wall, again and again, miraculously without harming herself.

"I only wanted to make stars," Claudia said.

"It's not your fault—the divorce," her father assured her.

"It's not, you know." Her mother pulled her close. "It's something your father and I need to do for ourselves."

"You'll come back and visit me here," her father promised. "And I'll come to see you."

Claudia slipped from her mother's arms in her white nightgown, strangely calm. "I only wanted to make stars . . . just to see how they look on the wall."

How I envied my friend's passion to lash out at losing her family. If only I, too, had discharged my rage by carving a wall to ribbons—an entire house even—the day my mother left, but instead I'd forsaken that fierce side of myself—the side that was openly defiant and oblivious to consequences—and had climbed into the car and into an unfamiliar caution that would sometimes restrict me in the years to come despite my attempts to break through it. I was assertive when it came to things like choosing a school and the profession I wanted. And I was good at design, dealt well with clients and contractors, made sound decisions. Sometimes I laughed too loud—a sound that delighted me because it carried beyond the caution as the old side of me, the authentic me, strained to get out; yet, when everything was totaled up, I was still facing that wall—intact.

# 4

■

$\bigcup$ N HIS CLOSET AT THE COTTAGE
Travis began to hoard apples, salami slices, tiny bars of
soap from hotels, cheese, candy bars, peanuts in their
shells. . . . Some foods, he found out, spoiled—like bananas
and ham, whose stench would get into his clothes; other
foods dried out—bread and oranges and cheese, becoming
stone-hard and inedible; peanut shells got crushed and left a
mess of brown flakes. Restaurants were the best sources for
his supply: he collected sugar packets, crackers in cello-
phane, mustard and ketchup in plastic packs. Sometimes he
acted like a baby, afraid to be alone in his room.

I made sure not to lose my father: whenever we left our cottage, I'd walk or sit so close to him that his arm would touch
mine and I'd know without having to look that he was there.
After work he would empty his pockets and drop his loose
change into the Chinese bowl with inlaid grains of rice that
turned translucent when skimmed by light. While he'd pour
his first drink and begin to cook dinner, I'd sneak into his
room and take one or two coins from the Chinese bowl—
never more, so he wouldn't find out. If he disappeared too, I

planned to use the money to buy a giant box of chewing gum and sell it, stick by stick, in downtown Spokane.

With my mother I'd seen a movie in which a Gypsy boy stood on a busy street corner, selling gum to buy food for his family. I'd earn enough to feed Travis and myself till we'd find a Gypsy family to take us along. It shouldn't be too hard—after all, there were over five million Gypsies in the world, my mother had told me, people who wandered the earth and didn't stay anyplace for long: they preferred to live and eat in the open air. In some tribes the women gave birth outdoors.

COOP HAD SAID he wanted to be with me during birth, and he'd seemed startled when I'd said yes, even more startled than I had been when he'd come forth with his brave offer of marriage.

"Without this pregnancy," I'd said, pointing to my still-flat belly, "would it have occurred to you to *want* to get married?"

"But this changes everything." He sat down in front of me on the low table facing my sofa and placed his hands on my knees as if to keep both of us from running away.

"You've never had any desire to get married. To anyone. You told me so."

"Well, no— But that was theoretical. You too, you said you didn't want to get married again."

"And I still don't. Really."

"So you're not pissy?" He smiled at me. "Withdrawing? Doing the I-don't-need-anyone bit?"

"Listen, Orville Giuseppe Cooper—"

"You promised to forget those dreadful names the minute I encouraged you to drag them from me." Orville had been the name of his father, an accountant from Louisiana who'd died when Coop was in high school; Giuseppe had been added upon the insistence of Coop's mother, a concert pianist who'd come here from Italy as a girl.

"Coop, then," I said. "Listen, it may be a hell of a lot better for both of us and this child if we stay pals instead of doing the honorable thing."

"You really mean that?" He seemed relieved, perplexed.

I nodded and looked at him, steadily, this lapsed Catholic who was still subject to flare-ups of guilt. I had liked his lean face and quick, amused eyes the instant we'd met seven months ago at the clinic where he'd taken my blood for a routine checkup. While he bent over my arm, the syringe in his competent hands, he asked me about my work and if I liked what I did, and he listened as if genuinely interested in my answers. As the vial filled with my blood, I imagined tracing my free hand along his strong jaw to where his reddish blond hair—though thinning on top of his head—curled abundantly behind his ears. That evening he pulled his hair into a ponytail, and we rode fifty miles on his motorcycle to the last carnival of the summer, where he dragged me on every single ride with the enthusiasm of a boy.

He told me about his parrots, and the following Sunday I drove along a network of unpaved roads and crossed the rickety wooden bridge to his log cabin, where the brightly colored birds greeted me with Italian obscenities which Coop would refuse to translate for me until we'd know each other much better. They perched on dowels that Coop had fastened to rafters and walls, stretching their lush necks, shifting from one claw to the other like people waiting in line. Those parrots, along with a set of flamingo-pink dishes displayed on a shelf above the sink, lent an exotic quality to the austere cottage which contained only practical pieces of furniture.

"Julia, you are too serious," Uncle Jake used to tell me, and I wished he could see me with Coop. With him I'd learned to laugh more, to not consider everything so damn important. Though he was only five years younger than I, he often seemed half my age. Sometimes I wouldn't hear from him for weeks, and then he'd stop by when I didn't expect him; but that was all right with me because I didn't long for him and went about my own life. We'd never have anything permanent anyhow, I figured. He was Coop, after all—playful and eccentric, irresponsible when it came to making plans, ambitious enough to have finished medical school but content to work part-time as a nurse, comfortable in his cabin until a restlessness set in that made him deposit his parrots with his neighbor, get on his motorcycle, and take off without destination.

"I'm telling you, Julia, I am going to be part of the kid's life."

"Good. You and those parrots. She can visit you."

"We'll figure out a way."

I closed my eyes. It frightened me to have this child by myself, to be the one safety net between her and disaster. A child with two parents had to be far more secure in the world. But then again, I would have been safer with only my mother.

"What is it, Julia?"

"I—I don't even feel pregnant. It's more like the doctor slapped this diagnosis on me. Still . . . I did dream about her once. Years ago, when my marriage to Andreas was ending. She had your hair."

He waited, quietly.

"I nursed her. It was sort of weird. And . . . nice, I guess."

"What if it's not a girl?"

"I have a hunch it is."

"You may need time to think about this—" He hesitated. "But I'd like to be there . . . with you. During birth."

"All right."

He squinted at me.

"You can do all the breathing for me and rub my back or whatever else it is fathers do during labor."

He leaned forward and, lightly, kissed my forehead, my nose, both cheeks, then planted a quick sequence of feathery kisses around my lips, on my lips. "You're pretty terrific, you know that?"

"Because I'm not holding you to your rash proposal?"

"I'll reactivate it. Once a year, on the kid's birthday."

"To be valid for twenty seconds."

"Twenty-four hours. I guarantee."

As I drew him toward me and we made love—slowly, differently, as if our bodies were testing and validating the pregnancy—I didn't tell him that I'd raged against him just two days before when I'd left the doctor's office in Rutland. I'd gotten into my car and had kept driving north on back roads far beyond my house in Proctor. Along Otter Creek I stopped near a bridge, kicked off my shoes, and scrambled down to the water, where I screamed at the silver current. I felt trapped—I didn't want to be pregnant even though I had yearned for a child. When my period had been late, I'd even dug out that box with the trouble people from a trunk in the attic, but the dolls hadn't worked their magic—just as they'd failed me when Andreas had first talked about divorce.

"I didn't mean it," I yelled. I wanted to break something, anything—but I knew it couldn't be the baby, and that made me feel even more trapped.

Holes in the soles of my panty hose, I climbed back up to the car; from the dashboard I grabbed the flamingo mug Coop had filled for me with hot chocolate that morning, as always after I spent the night at his house. I hurled the mug against the closest bridge pillar and watched the shards fly. It was only then that I noticed big red letters—*Jesus Saves*—sprayed on the pillar as though about to club me with their message. Those letters must have been there all along, surrounded by other graffiti like *Dumb Fuck* and *Oprah Knows*. Choose your message, I thought, and had to laugh aloud. For the next ten minutes I picked up fragments of the mug and other debris from around the base of the pillar. I'll come through this all right, I promised myself, I will. Then I squatted by the edge of the creek and sobbed.

GYPSIES NEVER spoke the name of someone who had died. My father never spoke my mother's name after she vanished, and so she became a ghost—a lovely, elusive ghost. Travis and I whispered about her when we were sure my father couldn't hear us. To say her name in his presence felt cruel. Dangerous. I didn't know then that things you don't talk about—ghosts and secrets—feed on silence, that they grow massive and imposing until you divest them of their feast.

We were alone at the cottage for most of that spring and summer. Years later I would wonder why he'd left us there without an adult to look after us. Wasn't he afraid that our mother might come and take us away? After all, it was the obvious place for her to search if she couldn't find us in Spokane. Or did he know of something that would keep her away from us? At times we felt like prisoners; other times we thought we were getting away with something by not going to school. My father borrowed books from our teachers and assigned us homework every morning. His face, which used to convey so many expressions—on stage and off—was immobile, as if his jaw had stiffened on him. Before he'd depart for the bank in Spokane, he'd make us promise not to go near the lake, but as soon as he was gone, we'd strip off our pajamas, race to the end of the dock, and leap naked into the cold water. Damp swimsuits would have been evidence of our disobedience. We'd wrestle and push each other's heads under water till we'd shoot up, gasping, spitting arcs of water.

From our picnic table and a kitchen chair we built a diving tower which one of us steadied, while the other stood poised to dive. By four the table would be back in the grove of ponderosa pines, and we'd be sitting in the cottage, doing our homework and sucking black coffee through sugar cubes.

If it was hot when my father got home, he'd announce it was time to swim, and we'd have to pretend enthusiasm at struggling into our confining swimsuits and getting wet again. "You used to like to swim," he'd puzzle when we'd head back inside after ten minutes in the lake.

The last Friday in June he surprised me by bringing Lynne along after work. Her ears had been pierced, and her blonde hair was pulled into a ponytail to show off rhinestone studs.

She was starting to get breasts, and though she was shorter than I, she looked older—at least eleven. My father carried her suitcase, and she brought me two goldfish in a round tank like the one she had in her room. As we opened the box of fish food and scattered the white flakes across the water, the fish rose like bubbles, nibbling at the food from beneath. *What if I forget to feed them? What if I drop the tank? Their orange bodies squirm on the floor among the sharp fragments of glass, their scales dry, their eyes bulging.* Better not to give them names— there were too many ways they could die. Lynne had found dead goldfish in her tank. If one of mine died, I'd simply buy a new fish and pretend I still had the same one. With fish you could do that.

Monday morning when my father got ready to take Lynne back to Spokane, I asked if I could come along.

"You can walk us to the car," my father said.

Lynne and I took turns carrying her suitcase uphill, and when I returned along the path to the cottage, alone, I was sure she would find herself another best friend. But that evening, when my father found me sitting outside in the dark, he wrote down the area code I had to dial ahead of Lynne's phone number. When I called her, we talked until I felt sleepy. My father said I could phone her every day until we returned to school in September.

WE WENT a bit wild that summer, Travis and I, high on caffeine and freedom, but it was a wildness tempered by time because we made sure to settle down before my father appeared in the late afternoons. It was a summer of secrets and light and fear.

During our first days alone, Travis and I had searched for photos of my mother—they'd disappeared in the days after she'd left—and we hadn't found any. All summer we embellished our made-up stories about where she'd gone, but we didn't talk about the bruises on my skin. Travis told me about terrible and fantastic creatures that slithered into his dreams: they had octopus arms and walrus fangs and laughed such dreadful laughs that even One-eyed Teddy couldn't always keep them away. When Travis got scared like that, he'd lapse into baby talk: "sour eyes" instead of sleepy eyes, "blankie" instead of blanket.

Every night I'd line the contents of my red bag on my dresser, counting and arranging them in a diamond pattern—the trouble people in the middle—before I'd return everything to the bag. Afterward I'd brush my teeth with seventeen strokes and set my slippers beneath my bed, toes pointing out. If I followed my ritual, I'd feel as if I were inside a little box of my own that kept out turmoil, and if at times I didn't feel safe, I thought it was only because I wasn't doing it right, and I'd invent other details, like sleeping with my pillowcase turned inside out or alternating two large bites of food with three small bites. I had to focus hard, eating like that, and couldn't think of much else.

Our only other visitor that summer was my grandmother, who arrived uninvited from Provincetown, informing my father that Travis and I were far too young to be left unsupervised. She brought us pink and green saltwater taffy and cautioned us—while we chewed—that taffy was known to pull fillings from people's teeth. Painted gray arches rose above her pale, thick eyebrows, and when we stood close to her, it looked as though centipedes clung to her forehead with countless silvery legs. She baked Norwegian cookies for us and showed us how to cut long chains of paper dolls from newspaper.

My father evaded her whispered questions—about my mother, I was certain—by glancing at us and saying, "Shhh—the children . . ."

The one day my grandmother wore her skirted swimsuit, she showed us her scar—a jagged, pearly line high on her bony thigh—and told us we could only go into the water to our waists. She kept urging us to be cautious when we ran so we wouldn't break a leg, to eat slowly so we wouldn't choke, to go to sleep by eight so we wouldn't invite weakness and subsequent illness. She insisted we take naps—something I'd refused to do since I was two—and ignored our protests.

Her perpetual fretting provoked us into bothering the ducks: when they swam close to the dock, we'd leap into the middle of their flock and they'd scatter up, squawking, and land on the water with their feet skimming across it, pulling long V-shaped water ridges behind them. To defy my grandmother, we swung from the upper branches of trees though we scared ourselves with our recklessness.

As if to reward her fears for our safety, Travis sprained his wrist when he tried to lift the picnic table by himself, and I developed an earache which she diagnosed as swimmer's ear. When she ordered me to stay out of the water for a week, Travis and I sneaked from the cottage and snapped off two hollow reeds which we used like snorkels in the green water space below the dock. Submerged in the shallow end of the lake, we were breathing through the reeds, as we had many times before, when my grandmother darted from the cottage and along the edge of the water, screeching our names with such urgency that, almost immediately, it became too late to reveal our hiding spot. We hadn't meant to frighten her— we'd simply missed that moment when it would still have been all right to come out and laugh.

She didn't collapse on the dock or succumb to hysterical fits of crying—not my grandmother—though any of those responses would have been easier to take than her tragic-faced departure the following morning. "Too many terrible things happen in the world," she told us at the door, flanked by matching plaid suitcases. "To pretend disaster is heartless."

We didn't want to be heartless and we didn't want her to leave—we just wanted her to stop watching us every minute. But she was determined to return to Cape Cod, and we weren't even allowed to walk her to the car. Gloomily we watched her start up the trail with my father; but just before the first of the larger trees shielded her from our sight, she turned and waved to us.

■

IT WAS the last year I was taller than Travis. For a few weeks in July we were the same height, and I felt the power, which I used to take for granted as the oldest, diminish and balance itself out between us. It didn't only have to do with physical strength but also with influence because, sometimes, I became the one to follow my brother's ideas. Until then, he had been the follower, and though I hated losing that edge of being in charge, I liked the excitement that came with the challenge of not letting him take over entirely.

His moods shifted even quicker than they used to—from shy to daring, from cheerful to bleak, from silent to enthusiastic. Since I didn't know what to anticipate from him, I couldn't wait in the mornings to get up and be near him. Sometimes when I looked at him, I felt as though I were staring into a mirror.

I took him along when I assembled dams along the swampy fringe of the bay, proclaiming him my apprentice until we ended up pelting each other with globs of deliciously cool mud. He made up a new game, the diving game, racing me toward the center of the bay, where the water was dark and mysteriously deep; there he would dive underneath me, and I—knees bent—would plant my feet firmly on his shoulders and push him with all my force toward the cloudy lake bottom; then it would be my turn, and as Travis' feet would catapult me into the deeper, colder layers of water, bubbles would rise around me like a silver fishing net; sometimes I'd manage to touch the ground and grope for a rock or a slimy piece of wood before I'd shoot back up, the inside of my chest prickling.

Some nights I'd startle myself awake with the sound of my voice, calling out something I couldn't decipher, and I'd sit up in my bed, trying to grasp those lost words that still floated through my room; quite often Travis' voice, which hadn't deepened yet, would rise from his room, sleep-clogged as though it were the echo of mine, and then it would be still again and I'd ease myself back on my pillow, soothed by the notion of our voices drifting off toward some faraway chorus that still held imprints of our and our parents' voices.

As the green smells of early summer gave way to the yellow scents of August, we became more defiant and took the inflatable raft to the other side of the bay and around the point from where Mr. Pascholidis' speedboat had appeared many summer mornings to take my mother and us on a whirl-tour of the lake. A sturdy Greek man with laughing eyes and an untamed mustache, he used to own a resort on the other side of the lake. Rings had flashed on his hands when he'd steered his boat, which had been so fast that, sometimes, it had felt as though the wind would tear off my face.

Travis grew restless at the cottage and came up with most of the plans that would get us away for the day. While I'd make a sandwich for myself, he'd raid the stash in his closet and bring out bruised apples and candy bars in wrinkled wrappers. A few times we got back so late that my father almost caught us. We took Kitchendog up the huckleberry hill where we used to hike with my mother, ate berries till our fingertips were stained purple and our bellies taut. With the raft we explored the mouth of the St. Joe River and counted fourteen white mountain goats on the cliffs. We never told my father about our excursions but took turns feeding him stories of our days in the cottage. Amazed that he never seemed to doubt us, we competed and set each other off with details that became increasingly colorful.

Once we hitchhiked into Coeur d'Alene and bought cigarettes and comic books. The clerk in the store asked us if we were twins, though my mouth was wide like my mother's and too large for my face, while my brother's features were evenly proportioned.

"Yes, we are," Travis told her before I could protest.

"How far apart were you born?"

His eyes darted away from me. "Five minutes. I was born five minutes earlier than my sister."

I jabbed him with my elbow. "Liar."

He was giggling so hard he got hiccups.

I turned to the clerk. "It takes hours or days before the second baby comes out. . . . You must know that. My brother was born thirty-two hours after me."

"Not so." His face was red.

"Yes so."

"She believed me," he brought out between gasps of cigarette smoke behind the store.

The odd thing was that it felt as though we were twins; and from time to time we would embellish that story, announcing to strangers that we were twins and inviting them to guess who'd been born first.

THERE WERE hours that summer that felt so dazzling and bright and splendid that—when I suddenly remembered my mother—I was jolted into shame at the pleasure I'd felt despite her absence. That curious mix of shame and pleasure— I still recall it whenever I touch the veined, pear-shaped rock that now lies on the mantel of my fireplace in Vermont. Travis brought it up from the lake bottom during one of our diving games, and when I take it into my hands, it feels dry but smells damp like the bed of the lake it came from. It's as though it changed and yet remained the same, like my brother's thin boy-face that stayed narrow in adulthood though the bone structure—which used to create hollow planes which retained light and shadow—had receded as if blotted by his pale skin. With his immense eyes and wide, agile hands he looked like a sculptor or a pianist, not a perpetual yard sale organizer.

He lived with my father in our old stucco house on Shoshone Street. It was full of junk from other people's garage sales, which Travis resold on the front lawn once a month between March and October. From Uncle Jake and from my brother's infrequent letters I knew that he had worked in a pet store and fast-food restaurants, as a lifeguard and as a delivery driver for the newspaper—mostly in jobs kids would hold—as if he were reluctant to venture into the adult world.

I knew he'd been married at eighteen, a father at nineteen, and divorced at twenty; I knew he hadn't stayed in contact with his son after his ex-wife had married a man who lived in Florida; I knew he'd studied philosophy at the University of Oregon for two months before he'd moved back home with my father, while I'd stayed away like my mother—I didn't know him at all. The brother I had as a child had soft feet— sissy feet, we called them in comparison to my hardened soles—and giggled when he got anxious. The brother I had as a child was filled with mischief and daring, but this grown man, who wore long-sleeved flannel shirts even in summer and watched me as if worried I might do something shocking, unsettled me.

"Just take Dad to the cottage for a couple of days," he'd urged me the day I'd arrived in Spokane. "Summers are my busiest time of year."

He still hadn't learned to resist my father's needs: he drove him to the lake almost every week, except in winter, even though he'd come to loathe the cottage after our enforced summer there.

I didn't want to be alone with my father, but I finally gave in, figuring it might be simpler to talk to him without Travis protecting him. The two of them shopped and packed as if preparing for a gourmet expedition: fresh salmon from the fish market; croissants from the French bakery; artichoke hearts and Sicilian olives from the deli.

"Your visit means so much to Dad," Travis told me, and I wanted to scream, *What happened to you?*

But then he used to be safe with my father. He did not go into Travis' room at night, did not shine the light into his eyes until he woke up. And when Travis became ill with the croup the year after my mother disappeared, my father car- ried him into the bathroom, turned on the shower and aimed the stream of scalding water toward the back corner. When he asked me to shut the door, his voice sounded fuzzy, as though the steam were wrapping itself around each word.

I sat on the closed toilet lid, safe from the crocodiles of my father's stories, while he lowered himself on the edge of the tub with Travis on his lap, his chin resting on Travis' hair, his face flushed. Travis hadn't had the croup since he was two. I wished he'd stop crying. It made the coughs worse, like barks almost. His body shook in my father's arms as he strained for air, each breath a long-drawn whistle. Opening my mouth, I sucked in deep breaths for my brother.

Our dog scratched on the door, and I flinched as my father shouted, "Kitchen, no." But then he smiled at me and it was silent, except for the jets of water hitting the white tub. It was odd to have water and steam spout from the shower without anyone standing beneath it. Swirls of moisture drifted up and changed shapes as they circled the globe of the lamp. The fine, long crack in the ceiling faded, and the mirror transformed itself into a milky square. Hot mist tugged at the hem of the eyelet curtain, filled our chests, and gradually melted whatever had made breathing so difficult for my brother. As the side of his face dropped against my father's chest, his finger slid into his mouth.

My father pulled at his collar until it came open; his shirt looked damp where it clung to his chest. "How are you holding out, Julia?"

With the back of my hand, I wiped the moisture off my forehead. "Okay."

He rested his chin once more on Travis' hair, and I reached across to him but touched my brother's leg instead: it felt feverish through the thin cotton pajamas, and I was confused by the sudden wish that I were the one sitting there with my father on the edge of the tub, encircled by his arms.

WHEN WE reached the steps that led to the deck, my father set down his plastic bag, shuffled over to the sink, where he filled an empty coffee can, and watered the geraniums. Without opening the front door, I knew what it would look like inside the cottage: the brown velvet couch with its back against the smaller window; three deep chairs around the fireplace; the oak table in the kitchen; red-bellied oil lamps on the mantel and table. I knew the pattern of the Persian rug would have worn deeper, but didn't know—couldn't know—how the place would enfold me until my father unlocked the door and we stepped inside and I couldn't breathe in the familiar smell of dried lake water and cold ponderosa ashes.

I shook the pack from my shoulders, dropped it on a chair, and dashed past my father toward my old room.

"Julia?" he called out.

I shut the door behind me. It still had the holes from the latch hook I'd bought and installed when I was fourteen, the one he'd yanked out that same night. The skin across my cheeks felt tight, cold. On the dresser next to the empty fish-tank sat the porcelain clock my parents had brought me from France one summer. They'd gone to Europe for a whole month, and when soon after their return enormous crates stamped with foreign words began to arrive at our house, we scattered nails and shredded newspapers all over the living room as we unpacked the furniture they'd bought in Spain and Italy and France.

"Once you're older, you can travel with us," they told Travis and me, and when I wanted to know how old, they said, "Eleven or twelve," a promise that never got fulfilled because by then, of course, my mother had long since vanished.

My bed still stood in the same space, covered with a quilt I'd never seen. Someone had taken down the drapes and installed bamboo shades instead; sun spooled through the gaps between the slats and twined itself through the room in luminous bands. Beneath the window stood the wooden trunk; I raised its lid though I knew what was inside: a blue yo-yo, stuffed animals, a spin top—things my father had bought for me on days after he'd been drinking, things I'd never played with.

Leaning against the wide windowsill, I forced myself to

take long, even breaths. It was warm inside my room, warm and dry—yet, I shivered. Until it stopped being safe, I used to like sitting on the windowsill, legs drawn up, feeling invisible in my favorite hiding spot between the drapes and the cool glass. I'd watch the lake, its surface a mixture of grays, levels ranging from pearl to charcoal as the wind rippled the waves from one slaty layer of gray into the next. In the darker zones the waves would become as invisible as I longed to be.

The third Sunday without my mother—after we'd eaten the veal cutlets and scalloped potatoes my father had prepared, after Travis was asleep in his room and the dog had curled up on his pillow beneath my dresser—I sat on my windowsill and opened the oval box with the trouble people. I took out the most colorful doll, the one who looked like a Gypsy with her black hair and the purple scrap of fabric tied around her like a long skirt. Her feet and hands were sharp points, and she held her arms extended as though greeting me. As I positioned her on top of the closed lid, just as I had every night since we'd arrived at the cottage, I willed her to travel through night and time to my mother and bring her to me.

Twice already, my father had asked why I kept leaving the same doll out, but I hadn't told him because I was afraid he'd make her vanish too. He'd touched my chin and raised it toward him, gently. "Some problems take longer than others to solve, Julia, and some are solved in different ways than we might wish."

And yet it was that very doll which would disappear—not at the cottage or at our house, but much later when I married Andreas and moved with him into our first apartment. I'd find the oval box packed in a huge carton with dozens of other things, but the Gypsy doll would be gone, as though she'd become fed up with being confined and, like an escape artist, had wriggled free to set out on her own quest.

But that evening on the windowsill she lay with her orange arms wide open. "Bring back my mother," I whispered to her as I set the box down and watched the lake for a rowboat that would carry my mother toward the shore. From the living room came the sounds of a chair moving, glass clicking. *My mother ties the boat to the dock, walks up the slope of lawn to my window. She presses her hand against the glass where my hand is so that it surrounds mine like a radiant shadow and—*

"Where . . . Julia?" My father's voice—thick and slurred. His steps halted outside my door.

I squeezed my eyes shut and made myself invisible.

"Julia?" He turned on the light.

*I'm invisible. Invisible.*

But his strong arms lifted me from the windowsill. "Here you are. Hiding from your Daddy." He laughed. "Don't you have a kiss for your Daddy?"

I had to turn my face from his sour breath.

"One little kiss?" One hand around the back of my head, he guided it until I had to—had to look at his face. It was flushed.

My feet felt miles above the floor, dangerously high. "I want to get down."

"I brought you some chocolate." He let go of my head and dug one hand into the pocket of his gray pants. "For my favorite girl. See?" he whispered. "You don't have to share with your brother."

"I'm not hungry."

He laughed and let me down on the floor. "It's the kind you like best. With hazelnuts."

"Can I go to sleep?"

His yellow eyes filled with tears. "Don't you love your poor little father anymore?"

I couldn't answer. I locked my fingers behind my back and held myself still, separate, though his hands seized my shoulders, shaking me, back and forth and back and forth until I thought my neck was going to snap.

"Say you love me."

The damp nose of the dog prodded my heel.

"You—" My father raised one foot and Kitchen skittered

across the wooden floor with an outraged yelp. "Stay where
you are."

"Don't hurt him."

"Say you love me." He kept shaking me.

The window was barren, and the dark beyond it empty.
There was no boat, and my mother felt further away than she
could have traveled in three weeks. All at once I felt a rage at
her for leaving me with my father, a rage that frightened me
so much that I had to imagine her back on the lake *in that
boat, about to tie it to the dock and walk up the slope of lawn to my
window where she presses her hand against the glass and*—

"Say you love me." My father slapped my face and pulled
me across his knees. His thighs dug into my stomach. His
hand stung my bottom.

It had to be an accident, a dreadful mistake. I saw him with
me at the fair *high up on the Ferris wheel high up and then he
hands me an airy web of cotton candy cotton candy cot*— but what
I tasted was not the pink spun sugar but the iron tang of
blood where I'd bitten into my lower lip. Pressing my eyes
closed, I willed the Gypsy doll with the purple skirt to get
back into the people box. I saw myself taking out the man
doll with the white shirt instead, leaving it on top of the box,
instructing it to kill my father.

"I'm sure he loved you," Andreas would say many years
later when I'd tell him about that night, and I would cry, "But
it's the wrong kind of love. How can you defend him?" I
couldn't understand a parent who could beat you and love
you at the same time. Those things didn't belong together.
And I didn't want to pass that kind of love on to a child. I
won't repeat this, I promised myself. And I would try to convince Andreas that I could only be certain not to make those
mistakes if we didn't have children.

"Say you love me." One arm across my back, my father
held me while the other hand kept coming down.

"Yes," I whispered.

"Yes what?" His hand didn't let up.

"Yes, I love you." He felt even further from me than my mother, but he was all I had left, and I shouted it then—shouted it to bring him back: "I love you, Daddy!" And that moment, that one dreadful moment that still tightens the skin on my arms whenever I think of it, I wanted to convince myself that I loved my father.

His hand came to a halt on the small of my back, where it lay, warm and heavy. He let out a slow breath as if exhausted. "I love you too, Julia."

My body felt numb and bulky as I crawled off his knees and into my bed.

"Here—" He bent across me and pulled the covers to my chest the way he did most evenings. "Let me tuck you in." His light-colored hair fell across his eyebrows. His palm cupped my cheek.

My heart thudded in my ears, my throat, a sound much darker than any night—*an accident, a dreadful mistake*—

As he raised himself from my bed, his eyes lost their focus. "Slut." He stumbled away from me, toward the hall. "Slut, you."

"JULIA? JULIA?" He knocked at my door, opened it without waiting for my answer, and stepped next to me, hunched over with the weight of my backpack which he carried in his arms. "What are you doing?"

"Nothing." I took the pack from him and leaned it against the wall below the window.

He looked at me as if concerned.

"Remembering things," I said and quickly retreated into, "Looking at the lake."

"It has changed a lot." In one theatrical motion he waved toward the shoreline across the bay as though the scenery were his stage. "All built up now . . . Not like this area." His words were isolated by pauses. "The best investment I ever made . . . lakefront. Not like Spokane. Property values there—" He rubbed his chin and looked at me, waiting for what I didn't know. Suddenly he smiled. "There are some good programs on tonight. If you want to, we can bring the TV from my room into the living room after dinner."

"Not for me."

"Travis gave me a Zenith last Christmas. Almost like new. He bought it from a bus driver who retired to Ritzville. Are you hungry, Julia?"

I shook my head.

"Ask—" he said, his voice gentle, "ask if you need anything."

All at once my eyes stung with tears, and I turned my face from him. The questions I had to start with were: *Why—why did you beat me all those times? What was it about me?* But I didn't know how to make my questions as real for him as they were for me, and so I stayed silent, trapped in that caution I despised, my eyes fixed on his hands as they rested on the windowsill, veins raising the creased skin. His fingers were long, his fingernails manicured. I wanted to bolt, wanted to stay and hear him say the words—what words I wasn't even sure— that would acknowledge my pain. Erase my pain.

# 5

HAD WANTED TO BOLT EVER since I'd arrived at the airport and had seen my father next to Travis at the gate. As he moved toward me, I was stunned by the slowness of his movements, his glazed look. He raised his right hand, hesitated, then waved. His wrists looked shrunken. He still wore expensive clothes—a beige tailored suit, white shirt, and paisley silk vest—and had about him a remnant of that old assurance of being the most attractive man in any crowd; but it seemed to take effort to convince himself of that. I'd imagined our first meeting so many times that I'd expected to feel angry, frightened even, but instead I was sorry for him.

As he opened his arms, I dodged his embrace by grasping his hands. He smelled of mouthwash. And cologne. "How are you, Father?" It sounded stiff. Cold. And yet I knew it was all I could give to him. After I dropped his hands, it was impossible, of course, to hug Travis, and I tried to make up for it by touching the sleeve of his worn flannel shirt. "It's good to see you."

"You too, Julia," my brother said, but he was looking at my

father as if worried that I had hurt his feelings again. It was that look which had come between us after that night on the windowsill. Travis didn't know what I'd figured out: Someone you don't love can't destroy you. He didn't understand the danger that was only a nightfall away, and though he must have heard my father's voice in my room, he'd see his attempts at being friendly to me the next day while I'd keep my face averted; he'd see my father's sadness when I'd refuse to eat my favorite dishes which he'd cook for me; he'd see the presents my father would buy me, presents I couldn't bring myself to accept. And I—I didn't know how to tell my brother that the harm went far deeper than the surface bruises on my skin, and it wouldn't be until I'd been away from both of them for years that I would find the words to name the rage and shame that stayed inside my gut long after the bruises had faded.

Once, I'd thought, Travis had almost understood—that winter night he'd slipped into my room. At first, when the door opened, I was afraid my father was coming back, but the shape blocking the light from the hallway was slighter and carried the peculiar scent of stashed-away food.

Softly he closed the door. I felt him coming closer, stopping next to my bed. "Julia?" he whispered.

My face felt hot, swollen.

"Are you asleep, Julia?"

"No."

"Did he—did he hurt you?" When I didn't answer, he reached over and patted me awkwardly on the shoulder. He was shivering.

"He'll be mad if he finds you here."

"He's sleeping." Travis sat on the edge of my bed. "I'll put this on your face." Something damp brushed against my nose. A washcloth.

"I hate him."

He held the washcloth against the side of my face. "Does that hurt?"

I nodded. With my tongue I pushed a strand of my hair from my lips.

"I brought you some crackers."

In the dark I found his hand and ate the three stale crackers. "You want some of my blanket?"

He pulled up his legs into bed next to me, and I held the washcloth while he covered himself up. Our heads lay side by side on my pillow, and our elbows touched. His feet were icy, and I felt the trembling of his body through his pajamas. The ceiling of my room looked lower than during the day, as if someone had gradually pulled it down, and I thought, if it keeps coming lower it'll squash us. But I wasn't worried: I was glad the ceiling was too low for my father to come back into my room, and I figured Travis and I would be able to suspend the ceiling if we both raised our arms and braced our palms against the white swirls of paint.

But just as I was about to suggest that, Travis whispered, "He didn't mean it."

The ceiling snapped back into place. I lay still. Very still. Though I hadn't moved, my elbow no longer touched my brother's. "You better go."

"Can't I stay?" His voice was small.

"No." I closed my eyes while he stole from my room.

It wasn't the first time he had defended my father. He must have believed things would get better if I let my father make up to me. After all, we were all Travis had left of *his* family—a father and a sister. That's why he sneaked my father's presents into the wooden trunk in my room. That's why he flitted between my father and me with a strained expression on his angular face, trying to fabricate peace between us. Eventually he became protective of the wrong person. And so I lost my brother too, and what rushed between us was much cooler than the water that had separated us that day when I'd carried him piggyback and we'd leapt into the lake as one body.

It took a few years to completely pry us apart—the same

years that the differences in our bodies became increasingly apparent and we reacted toward each other with an unfamiliar modesty. One afternoon, when I sat on the front steps of the cottage with a book and he walked toward me from the lake, sunlight cast his body golden, revealing the swelling of his chest and the new width of his shoulders, making him look so startlingly beautiful that I couldn't shift my eyes from him and felt struck with an odd joy and embarrassment. That moment I loved him with an outrage for changing so.

During those years I felt cold most of the time, even during the summers. I'd wear two or three sweaters and put on wool socks before going to bed. Instead of taking my first swim the beginning of May, I'd lie on the dock and imagine the sun burning through me. It couldn't get hot enough for me, and it was only on sweltering July afternoons that I'd race my brother to the center of the bay. But we no longer played the diving game; each of us would try to reach the lake bottom alone, though we couldn't get deep enough to bring anything to the surface. When we'd head back to shore, our arms and legs churning the lake, we'd keep a break of water between us.

"IT MEANS a lot to Dad to have the three of us in the house," Travis had said in the airport garage as I'd climbed into his battered truck and slid to the center of the vinyl seat. As he helped my father onto the seat next to me, he added, "If you change your mind, you're welcome to your old room."

"Thanks, but I thought it would be easier for everyone if I stayed at the Ridpath. I've made reservations and—"

"No pressure. As long as you remember that it's your home too." He started the engine, and the truck shuddered into life. "All I have to do is get a couple of boxes out of your closet and from under the bed."

My father's breath was warm against the side of my face. "Did you have a good trip, Julia?"

"Yes." Wedged between him and Travis, I stared at the dusty dashboard with slips of papers taped to it, each containing an address and a circled word like *tent* or *furniture* or *bicycle* or *rug.*

"Are you comfortable, Julia?" my father asked.

I nodded, curved my shoulders around myself, and remembered another time my father and I had been in a car next to each other—just the two of us—driving through a deeply wooded area. As I'd watched his hands on the steering wheel, I'd suddenly felt certain he was taking me somewhere to kill me. It was cold in the car and he was silent and drove fast, one arm resting in the open window. Two schoolgirls had been murdered in Spokane that last month. Looking at my father's hands, I believed he was the murderer and would kill me next.

A week later the police arrested a heavy man with a mustache. His picture was on the front page of the *Spokane Chronicle.* I didn't know him, but I'd seen his mother, Mrs. Berg, who rented the top floor of the house where Mandy Paulson lived. Mandy was in my fifth-grade class. No one liked to play with Mandy because everyone knew her mother had let her drink milk from her tits until she was seven. Mandy's mother still picked her up from school, and I couldn't help staring at her breasts under her white blouses. Big breasts, jug-tits, filled with milk. I felt sick at the thought of Mandy coming home from school and sucking on them. Even though Mandy was eleven and hadn't sucked on them since she was seven. Still, I couldn't stop the pictures: *Mandy's mother opens the buttons of her blouse, lifts one jug-tit toward Mandy and—*

My mother's breasts were smaller; she used to undress in her room with the door closed. But five times I saw her breasts, nights when my father beat her, and I came down the stairs and saw my mother trying to get away from him as he lunged for her, tearing her nightgown.

Five times I saw him beat my mother. Other times I heard him beat my mother, but I didn't open my door. I stayed in bed and pulled the blanket over my head and hummed— faster and faster—until my ears vibrated in the dark.

■

IF I HADN'T recognized our old neighborhood, I wouldn't have known the house when Travis parked the truck. The stucco looked splotchy, and most of the grass had turned brown. My father's rock garden was clogged with weeds. Two old men in jogging shorts pounced along the sloped brick street toward Cannon Hill Park in a determined rhythm that would have left my father far behind. If my mother were returning with me, she'd stare at the piles of junk in the yard: old washing machines and car parts, broken chairs and stacks of plastic flowerpots. For her it was thirty-two years since she'd been here, for me just twenty-three. I felt her walking next to me, this woman who was younger than I, entering the house which had taken on the stale smell of Travis' closet. Except for the furniture in the living room, nothing felt familiar: the wallpaper was peeling and the rooms were filled with unfinished projects, as if my father and brother had given up on the house after I had left.

"A lot of this will be cleared out in a few weeks," Travis said without much conviction.

"Travis is getting ready for another yard sale," my father explained.

"You'd be amazed how much you can net," Travis said as he led me through the house. He had converted the sunroom next to the kitchen into a workshop where he glued legs back onto chairs and stripped paint from dressers. "If the zoning allowed for it," he said, "I'd open an antique shop. But the neighbors already give me hell. They keep calling the city on me."

He told me he liked to buy sealed boxes for a few dollars without knowing their contents, and then sort them out and resell the items. "Once I found a pocket watch worth eighty bucks," he said.

"And that figurine," my father reminded him. "Don't forget that porcelain figurine you found. . . . And don't forget to call back that minister with the dishwasher."

"I'm not calling him back. What does he want? Warranties on used appliances?"

"Travis sold a broken dishwasher to the Lutherans," my father told me. "Now the minister says he is going to small claims court and—"

"That dishwasher was working just fine when I delivered it to the church hall."

"When can we eat, Travis?" my father asked.

"I'll get it now. Julia, if you want to wash your hands while I set the table. . . ." My brother motioned toward the bathroom door. His hands were still huge in proportion to his slender body. "Plenty of towels. Be careful though—I'm renovating."

Relieved to have a few minutes away from both of them, I locked the door behind me. Where the sink used to be, gaped a hole, half filled with chips of tiles and rotting wood. Lined up on the toilet tank were a Burger King glass with about a dozen matted toothbrushes, a hammer, a sand dollar, green mouthwash, two new peach-colored guest towels, and a wrapped bar of peach-scented soap. After I bent over the tub faucet to wash my hands and face, I almost opened the medicine cabinet—a leftover habit from those years when I'd snooped through everything that belonged to my father, hoping to find evidence of my mother's whereabouts.

The window framed a section of the haunted brick house next door and—a block and a half downhill—one of the weeping willows that surrounded the Cannon Hill pond. In the scummy water Lynne and I used to catch turtles. After giving them names and printing them on their shells with red paint, we'd release them. *Star* we caught three times. *Wing* twice. For hours we'd sit and talk beneath one of the stone bridges or in the branches of the willows that leaned across the edge of the pond. We climbed most of the trees in that park—the higher, the better.

One evening when I was thirteen, Lynne's brother, Scott, who was already a college student, pedaled his bike past the park and stopped when he saw us. He let me ride on the handlebars, and we rode around the pond, faster and faster, his arms like a hundred fireflies on either side of me, until we toppled into the grass. When I leapt up, he chased me to the playground and tickled me. This happened exactly one week after I'd been passed a chain letter in my math class, scribbled on a page torn from a notepad: *This letter is a test of romance since 1802. Copy by hand and give it to four other girls. Do this within four days of receiving the letter. On the fourth day drink a glass of water and say the name of the boy you love. This is no joke. Within the next four days he'll either kiss you or ask you out. If you break the chain you'll have four years bad luck in your life.*

I had followed all the instructions, except that I'd drunk two glasses of water—large glasses to make extra sure—saying Scott's name aloud between each gulp and keeping his round face with its shadow of a mustache suspended in my mind. And I knew the test of romance had worked that evening when he hoisted me on the handlebars of his bike, and though he didn't kiss me, that ride with him was as good as if he'd asked me out.

Whenever I'd fallen in love since then—even as an adult—I'd increased my water consumption, whispering my beloved's name between gulps. I'd done it after I'd met Andreas at the *Fackelparade,* after Gil sat down next to me in my structural design class, after I was introduced to Jeff who restored churches, after Coop had taken my blood at the clinic, and I'd kissed each of them on exactly the fourth day after the ritual.

WHEN I opened the bathroom door, I followed the sound of my brother's voice to the living room, where the gold-framed enlargement of my wedding photo above the large-screen TV stopped me. I hadn't seen Andreas since our divorce seven years ago. He'd moved to Denver where he'd taken a job as assistant ski school director and had found himself a woman who didn't think it was too risky to have children—three so far. Occasionally we wrote or phoned each other: he'd called me the day before he'd married his second wife, who was born in the Austrian village he'd left; I'd talked with him after I'd quit my job with Sunders & May to open an office with Bob Elling; he'd sent me birth announcements of his children.

As I touched the edge of the ornate frame, I was stunned by a sudden longing for Andreas, something I hadn't felt in years. He'd never minded that, sometimes, I laughed too loud or that I could get stubborn in going after what I wanted—at least not until what he wanted was in direct conflict with what I was afraid of wanting: a child. Once he knew I was about to go through with having a child—would he feel betrayed? Confused? Too late, I thought and closed my eyes. I felt his hands on my shoulders, pulling me into the strand of life I would have been in had we stayed together. *We hike up the trail behind his village, bend over the crib of the child we could have had. He waves to me at the airport when I arrive home from this trip. We trim each other's hair, make love, argue, stack firewood, grow old. We sit in a waiting room, both with gray hair, though I don't know what we're waiting for, and I remember my disbelief when my mother told me that I, too, would grow up.*

I wondered what had happened to the mirror that used to be in this picture frame. My mother had found the frame in one of the junk shops she'd liked to explore. After removing the faded print of three cats in topcoats, she'd painted it golden. The afternoon we'd taken the frame downtown to have a mirror inserted, we'd worn our matching green dresses. In the restaurant of the Davenport Hotel we ordered fresh strawberry sundaes, but just as they arrived—festive in silver goblets and garnished with lacy wafers—the Greek man from the lake strolled past the window, and my mother picked up her spoon and laid it back down. Shielding his eyes with one hand, he brought his brown face close to the glass and waved.

My mother smiled and motioned for him to come in. "Mr. Pascholidis," she said as if tasting his name.

I crammed a spoon with ice cream into my mouth, dug for the biggest strawberry.

"What a surprise—Lily and Julia." He had the whitest teeth I'd ever seen.

When my mother asked him if he'd like to sit with us, he

slid into the seat next to her. She didn't move her arm; it rested against his, thinner but nearly as dark from being at the lake. Where the dense hairs on his arm touched her skin, they looked as if they were trying to climb across.

ALL OF the living room walls were covered with framed photos—none of my mother, only a few of Travis, most of them of me with Andreas: holding hands on the balcony of our first apartment; taking riding lessons at the Chittenden Inn; getting on the ski lift at Killington; picking apples at his grandfather's orchard in Austria. . . . My throat ached. Those early years with Andreas I'd sometimes woken up at night, my love for him stretching every cell of my body with fear because so many accidents and illnesses could claim him from me. Those nights I couldn't imagine how I could possibly continue without him.

But he didn't know that. "You look like you don't need anyone," he'd said to me on our honeymoon when he'd watched me run up the hill to our tent, barefoot, my hair tangled, my clothes stained with sweat. His voice had been filled with awe. "You're so incredibly strong. It makes me love you even more." It was only after our divorce that he would admit to having been afraid that instant of being superfluous in my life.

I shook my head and walked to the fireplace where another group of photos hung, all of them showing me smiling. Like being inside a bloody shrine. Some of the pictures I'd forgotten—I'd slipped them into envelopes to compensate for letters that had felt too brief. A few times my father had written about wanting to visit me, and I'd stalled him with lies—*We're renovating the apartment. . . . We're about to go on a trip, but we thought you'd enjoy these photos. . . .* Eventually he'd stopped asking.

He still had most of the furniture he'd bought with my mother on their trip to Europe: massive wooden chairs with leather upholstery and matching footstools, a brass wall hanging that looked like a huge antique coin, dark red woven rugs, wrought-iron lamps with amber glass, and the heavy round dining room table—half of it set with a beige lace tablecloth, odd pieces of china, and two new candles, while the other half was covered with a jumble of knick-knacks and unopened mail.

While my father sat with his palms touching the edge of his plate as if impatient to eat, Travis insisted on serving me first. He cut pink slices of roast beef, spooned broccoli and scalloped potatoes on our plates, poured red wine into the crystal goblets.

"Just water for me," I said and stood up to get it from the kitchen. Though I missed the occasional glass of wine I enjoyed, I'd gone along with my doctor's suggestion to cut out any alcohol till after the baby was born.

As I sat back down, my brother asked, "You don't drink at all?"

"Sometimes."

He raised his glass. "To my sister's return." His eyes were guarded.

My father emptied half of his glass in one gulp and beamed at me. "And that she may stay forever."

Fat chance, I thought. "Who lives in the haunted house now?"

My father adjusted the gold fountain pen in his shirt pocket. "That house was never haunted."

"It still is," Travis said. "Someone from Pullman just bought it but hasn't moved in yet. A graphic artist, from what I hear."

"Remember that nasty old woman?"

"She chased me once when my soccer ball rolled into her garden."

"I don't remember her ever being outside. Just behind that window . . . in her hospital bed."

"You didn't give us much warning," Travis said. "I would have liked to get the house ready for you."

"Don't worry about it."

"It was awfully sudden."

I nodded. It was too soon to tell him I was pregnant. In time I would let him know.

My father cut a small triangle of beef and chewed it slowly. Though I'd been hungrier those past few weeks, I found it difficult to eat. I wished I had some of the bland crackers I'd subsided on during the first three months of nausea.

"It seemed rather . . . urgent when you called." Travis sounded suspicious.

"The timing at work was good."

"Timing . . ." He nodded, but I could tell he wasn't convinced.

My father emptied his glass, and I tried to stall him as he reached for the bottle. "Those scalloped potatoes—they are very good."

"Travis cooked this morning," he said haltingly. "Travis is a good cook. But he did not—" He frowned. Shook his head as if the rest of the sentence had become stuck and he had to jiggle it loose.

"I just warmed everything up," Travis said.

My father ate slowly, his face flushed, content. Suddenly he raised his eyebrows as if he'd made an important discovery. "Why didn't your husband come with you, Julia?"

"We're no longer married."

"But you sent me postcards from Austria."

"That was quite a few years ago . . . when we made trips to the village where Andreas grew up."

As a boy, Andreas had never understood why all those tourists kept coming to his town. He had to leave the stark mountains before he could see their beauty, and it wasn't until he brought me there that he began to love them though my eyes. From that time on, though, he no longer felt at home in either place. While in Austria, he'd long for Vermont, but as soon as he'd arrive back in the States, he'd want to return to Austria.

"You're lucky you can travel." Travis' mouth looked pinched. It was as though behind that one sentence were years of words he hadn't said. He rubbed one finger back and forth across the band of his wristwatch.

My father's eyes followed the movement of the finger.

"I can't even go away for a weekend," my brother said.

A piece of beef slid from my father's fork and left a trail of gravy on his tie and shirt. He tried to stop it with his fork but only ended up wiping the prongs on his shirt.

"Jesus— Look at you, Dad." Travis leapt up and bent across him with his napkin. "Just look at you. Sitting that far from the table . . . Come now, move closer." He wiped the gravy from my father's chest. It was absurd. Here he was—in his old clothes, surrounded by clutter, getting upset over a gravy stain.

"I am sorry, Travis," my father mumbled and shifted his chair closer.

"You have to be more careful." A circle of crimson was widening on each cheek as though something hot were burning its way through Travis' pale skin. He reminded me of a teenage mother I'd seen at the grocery store last week, hair stringy, shorts wrinkled, while her baby was immaculate in a white dress and patent leather shoes.

Travis leaned toward me. "It's impossible to keep him in a clean suit beyond a meal."

"No wonder if you treat him like a child," I whispered.

"I haven't seen you express any willingness to step in and look after him." Though my brother's voice was low, it had a frantic sound to it. "You don't know what it's like."

He motioned with his chin to my father, who was trying to eat carefully, though it only increased his awkwardness. And yet, he had a certain craftiness about him, as if he were pretending to know less than he did. I had a sudden fantasy of kidnapping him, letting him eat a hot fudge sundae in his best suit, and then taking him to a movie that ended hours after the curfew Travis had probably set for him.

"I can't even go on a vacation. Who would take care of him? Tell me."

My father lifted one arm as if to claim that right for himself, but his hand only veered to his hair, and he patted it as if to make sure it lay in place. "You let me know if you need some money, Travis," he said and gave me a conspirator's grin that made me wonder if his question about Andreas had really been as innocent as I'd assumed, or if he was playing some role in a script of his own. If Travis was letting himself be supported, that was his concern.

"I cook his meals, do his laundry . . ." The skin along my brother's throat stretched and contracted as if he were trying to swallow words before they could escape him. ". . . take him to doctor appointments, to the barber . . ."

My teeth worked along the edge of my thumbnail, pulling off tiny shreds. I wanted Travis to stop it. For himself. For all of us. It felt ugly. Ugly and deceitful. As if he'd tricked himself and my father into this situation and had been waiting for years to recite for me the litany of burdens he had taken on—the dutiful son—for this old man he had inherited when I'd left. His inventory was endless, his voice as urgent as those last weeks before my mother had disappeared. "Look at me, Mama," he would shout, leaping high or running fast or lifting heavy objects, "look at me, Mama," performing for her as if he sensed she would leave us and was trying to keep her there with his stunts.

". . . his ironing, write his checks, make sure he gets some exercise . . ." His eyes brilliant with tears, Travis stared at me as if he wanted me to recognize that I couldn't just surface in my father's life without listening to him first, that I owed him something I hadn't figured out yet, and all at once I envied him for getting to it so quickly, while I hadn't even started. The least I could do for him was listen. And let him finish.

Through all of this my father kept eating, his movements fuzzy, as if the wine was affecting him faster than it used to. When he was finished, he got up and stood next to my chair, beaming at me as if delighted to have me back in the house. "Do you want to watch TV with me, Julia? *Taxi* is on."

"No, thank you," I said and leaned toward my brother. "I'm sorry, Travis."

He turned his face aside as if impatient with me.

My father sauntered over to a reclining chair, cleared newspapers and a box of nails from it, and pushed the remote control. The faces of Danny DeVito and Judd Hirsch bobbed on the large screen.

"Not so loud, Dad. Please," my brother said.

"Sorry, Travis." He clicked the volume button, but the TV only got louder. "Sorry, Travis." He fumbled with the control until the voices receded. "Now everyone is saying 'Sorry Travis,' " he mumbled.

"Uncle Jake and Aunt Marlene want to see you," Travis told me. "I called them right away after I heard from you."

"I want to visit them real soon." As a girl, I used to ask my uncle if he'd heard from my mother, and he'd fix his blue eyes on me until I'd see myself deep inside his pupils. "If there were anything I could tell you, I would." After I left for school, we kept writing to each other. He and Aunt Marlene flew out for my wedding and brought me a woven shawl. They sent me a framed print of Klimt's woman with the golden harp, *Music I,* when I graduated from college, and they came to stay with me for a week after the divorce. Although we still mailed gifts to each other at Christmas, we'd written less in the last few years.

"For a while he was in remission," Travis said. "But lately—"

I felt a hot catch at the base of my stomach. "I didn't even know he was ill."

"I'm sorry. It's his prostate, Julia. I thought they'd told you."

"No," I said. "No."

He reached across and, briefly, touched my hand. "Sometimes he feels all right, but then he has stretches of looking awful. Since Andy's still teaching in Alaska, Aunt Marlene is the only one who looks after him. It's hell on her. He gets so depressed. Sometimes I take Dad over for a visit."

"That's nice of you," I said, wishing immediately I'd said something else.

"It has nothing to do with being nice. I like Uncle Jake."

"I— It was an insipid thing to say."

He looked at me as if trying to settle if I meant it. "It was insipid," he finally said, "but we'll let it go." He started to laugh, and then I did too, and for an instant I forgot what we were laughing about, and when we stopped, I only felt worse about my uncle.

"He talks about you," Travis said. "A lot."

"I want to see him tomorrow."

My father turned in his chair. "Can I come along, Julia?"

I didn't want him there, but before I could think of an excuse, my brother stood up. "We'll all go," he concluded as if daring me to contradict him.

HE WAS silent when he drove me to the hotel. At the front desk the clerk handed me a key and two phone messages, one from my friend Lynne—*Will stop by after school tomorrow at 3:30 if she doesn't hear from you*—the other from Bob Elling—*We have the library.*

"Great." I showed the message to Travis. "So far, it's the biggest job we've submitted a proposal for. What makes it even sweeter is that we've beaten Sunders and May, where Bob and I used to work."

"Congratulations."

As we got on the elevator, I told him about Stupid Ike—officially Ike Sunders—who'd been so difficult to work with that he'd inspired Bob and me to quit together. "His partner, Peter May, he's terrific—I still respect him—but Stupid Ike . . . he went over budget with each single project. He'd generate unnecessary work for consultants . . . have me or Bob or one of the other architects hand-deliver his field notes at our billing rates. . . ."

"He sounds wasteful."

"That's what Nattie said about him. She was the office manager there, meticulous, so patient . . . and Stupid Ike would infuriate her, dictating verbose letters that he'd scribble over with red and then double in length."

"Sounds like you're glad to be out of there. What's your favorite project so far?"

"A restaurant opposite a waterfall. Three gables. Lots of glass. When the sun hits those windows, it reflects the waterfalls like one tidal wave . . . one split Red Sea."

"I hope you'll show me someday."

In the mirror of the elevator there was something so familiar about my brother's face that I put one arm around him and drew him against me in a quick half-hug. He nodded, blushed a little, and kissed my cheek. My eyes stung.

"You took the wrong side, Travis." I whispered it, the thing I'd wanted to shout at him all those years.

A sudden glint came in his eyes. Then his eyelids closed for an instant, and when he looked at me, his face was without expression. His eyes on the numbers that lit up above the door, he rode up, silently. I'd only arrived a few hours ago, and already things with my brother felt botched. I wanted the magic back, the kind of magic we'd lived as children, that easy magic we'd taken for granted, but the man next to me felt far away.

"It is getting late," he said as the elevator stopped.

We unlocked my door and carried my luggage into the room. *Stay awhile*, I wanted to say, but I was afraid he'd say no.

"Do you need help with anything before I—"

"I'm all right. Thank you."

He started for the door. Turned around and said, "Julia . . . Julia . . ."

I let my arms drop along my sides and grimaced at him. "Travis . . . Travis . . ." I said in the same tone.

He shut the door and came toward me. "Dammit, I *am* glad you're here."

"It's so hard to come back." I had to swallow twice before I could say anything else. "But I am glad I'm with you."

He wrapped his long arms around me, and though I felt confused by this sudden switch in mood, I held on to his angular body, grateful to have him back, afraid that the old link between us had become so frayed that it would tear apart if we made a single mistake.

"Spend some time with Dad, Julia." He stepped away from me. "You could take him to the lake. He doesn't get out there often enough."

"Why not?"

"His license . . . he's had it taken away a few times. Minor accidents, mostly. But this last judge was tough with him."

"Drinking?"

"Nobody got hurt." He scratched the back of his neck. "Dad misses the cottage, Julia."

"He has changed a lot . . . much slower, not only physically—almost like he blanks out at times."

"I know. Other times he is all there, clear and everything. What it basically is—Dad's getting old. . . . He doesn't talk on the phone anymore, simply refuses to answer it or make calls. . . . And then the drinking, of course." Travis walked over to the dresser and stared at the picture of two horses galloping across a food-color-green meadow toward an unnaturally large sun that took up half the picture; set in the orange sun was a clock with Roman numerals. "Pretty disgusting, isn't it?"

"Huh?"

"This clock." He faced me. "Why don't you spend a couple of days with him at the cottage?"

"You're still trying to make peace between us, Travis."

"I'm not trying anything."

"It may be too much." I crossed my arms. "Not just for me. For him, too."

"That cottage means more to him than anything else. TV's become a close second. He's become a regular TV-junkie, watching every piece of trash that's on. . . . Better for him to be outdoors, move around. I take him along to sales and auctions as much as I can, but he gets in the way, wants to buy expensive stuff I could never resell." He shrugged. "Once he bid on a set of silver we almost got stuck with. The thing is, he looks so distinguished with the white hair and the dark suits. . . . He even dresses like that for the garage sales at our house. And then he pouts when I don't let him accept every measly offer. Once in a while I leave him home alone and Mr. Curtiss from across the street—he's a retired piano teacher—stops by to make sure Dad's all right. But I don't like to ask him too often."

"Maybe I will take him to the lake. Let me think about it."

My brother smiled as though he took my answer for yes. I looked through the picture window at the lights of Spokane far below us, thinning in irregular patterns away from the core of the city, except for two blazing rows which darted north and east, far beyond the boundaries of downtown—Division Street and Sprague Avenue. Even twenty-five years ago these two streets had been ugly, lined with most of the city's fast-food restaurants and discount stores. Saturday nights Lynne and I would cruise in her mother's green Corvair up and down Riverside, where other kids with cars caused solid traffic jams with blaring music, shouts, and laughter. At the corner of Howard and Riverside, Rickie Janowitz had yelled from his truck to ask me to the prom though he saw me at school every day, and I'd yelled back: "Yes yes."

"When are you due?" Travis asked behind me.

I swung around. "What makes you think—"

"With my wife I could tell before she knew. I usually can."

My face was hot. "I'm just older. Heavier. Once you're past forty—"

"It has nothing to do with age or weight. It's more—" He considered for a moment. "The way pregnant women move . . . different, you know? As if they had more light around them." For someone who hadn't stayed connected to his own child, he certainly had some nerve to probe like that.

I hit right back. "Your son . . . he must be close to twenty."

He flinched. "Just about."

"You miss him?"

"At first I did."

We stared at each other, silently.

"Five more months," I finally said. "All right? Don't tell *him* though."

My brother nodded.

"More light around them . . ."

"Also, their necks seem longer."

"You're amazing."

"How are you feeling?"

"I'm sorry I snapped at you."

"The pregnancy, I mean."

"I get tired a lot. And I puked some at first. Other than that—oh yes, my hair and fingernails are growing faster. . . ."

Travis nodded. Smiled. And then he asked something odd. He asked if I was happy. Andreas had asked me that same question a week before our wedding. Everything that day had been the best it could possibly be. We made love, ate blackberry muffins in bed, went for a long walk in the sun, swam naked in an isolated creek, and when he asked me if I was happy, we were lying in the deep grass next to the creek, our bodies still wet and wonderfully cool, and I thought that this was the kind of day I loved, and that it should make me feel happy; but his question pushed me toward that space deep inside me, that dim and flawed space that sucked up whatever happiness I should feel. My body felt rigid, and all at once I needed to cover myself up. I struggled into my shirt, my shorts, and evaded Andreas' hand when he reached for me, his eyes puzzled.

What I wanted was the happiness I'd known as a child *before* I'd found out that even if things were the best they could be, you were always right on the brink of that bone-chilling isolation because people who were the closest to you—like your mother or father or brother or lover—could turn on you, turn from you.

They had all proven me right. After Andreas divorced me, I either left men before they had a chance to leave me, or held on too tightly. "I feel like your hostage, not your lover," one of them told me. It didn't matter how a relationship ended—I knew it would anyhow, though some of the beginnings were so passionate that I could ignore the old wash of fear and lure myself into believing that, this time, it would be different.

At least I didn't have those illusions about Coop. I didn't know if he'd still be around in another year. He'd talked about being part of bringing our daughter up, just as he'd talked about meeting me at the hospital for the ultrasound, and he'd forgotten that. *He forgets to be there at her birth. On her third birthday. Arrives too late for a conference with her teacher. The day of her wedding she waits for him to walk her down the aisle—*

"Well—are you?" Travis asked.

I wanted to tell him how hard it was for me to be happy, and how scared I was of passing that on to my kid, and how I wished for her a world where things I had lost over the years—or thought I could cast off behind a line of salt—were no longer missing, but it would have been easier for me to balance naked on the rooftop than to admit that. I made a face at him and tried to joke him out of it by asking, "What kind of question is that supposed to be?"

But I could tell he didn't think it was funny. He was watching me, gravely, as if he knew. His face looked much more as it used to when he was a boy, and it was as though we had arrived at this moment directly from our childhood, as though all the uneasy silences of our teenage and adult years had been absorbed in the benevolent folds of time, granting us this unexpected reprieve.

# 6

■

$\mathcal{M}$Y FATHER SAUTÉED ONIONS
and bacon, sliced mushrooms and potatoes to make his famous fried potatoes. "No, I don't need help. Relax, Julia." A
towel tucked into the waistband of his trousers, he padded
barefoot around the kitchen of the cottage, checking on the
salmon he was broiling, humming a tune I recognized
though I couldn't remember the words.

He seemed more agile and confident than the old man
who'd waved to me at the airport, who'd soiled his shirt at the
dinner table; and I could picture him living here by himself,
surrounded by his fishing poles, his pots and pans, his out-
door magazines, and the framed collages of theater programs, ticket stubs, photos, and reviews. Travis' disarray had
not spread to the cottage, perhaps because he would have
found it impossible to hold a yard sale that far from people,
and the place had clearly remained my father's territory—
even the flowers in the planters outside proved that.

For an instant I was seized by a deep regret that I had to
break into my father's contentment with my questions, and I
wished I could somehow protect him from me, but the in-

stant he opened the refrigerator and pulled out a bottle of wine, he was not just this old man I could watch from a secure place—he was my father—and I wanted to snatch the bottle from him, stop him from pouring his fourth glass though he hadn't even uncorked the bottle yet.

He used to believe not drinking had to do with willpower. At least that's what he told me one Sunday evening when I was five and ill from eating too many French fries. "I stopped drinking the day I met your mother," he said as he laid his cool hand on my stomach.

I rested my hands on top of his and let out a long sigh.

"Does that feel better?"

My belly felt distended. "Not yet."

He knelt in front of my bed. "The first time I saw your mother," he said in the voice he used for his stories, "she was standing in the entrance to her father's barn. I was there to appraise the farm, since her father had applied for a loan at our bank. She wore a yellow dress without sleeves. . . ."

Both my parents had told me the story of their first meeting before, and it was as though I held the ribbons of their words and let them run from two spools which I could slow down whenever I wanted to fill in my favorite pictures—like that moment he stopped in front of her and they looked at each other, or when she took him to her shallow cave with its pillows of weeds and cornflowers. After a childhood among dunes, my father was drawn to the sculpted hills of the Palouse, but even more so to the recognition of something he used to feel when gazing across the vast sands of the Cape and the horizon beyond them, and it was that feeling—as much as the amber slopes of wheat—that made him fall in love with my mother that day he saw her in the entrance of the barn.

She would come to share his passion for faraway places. They both were accustomed to looking into the distance without seeing houses, and she—who had just finished high school and hadn't been further than fifty miles from Rosalia—would search for that expanse of landscape wherever she would travel with him, but she wouldn't reclaim it until the day after their wedding when they'd arrive on Cape Cod, where she'd see the ocean and sense that she'd returned to a place that had forever dwelled within her. Of course she'd seen pictures of oceans in books before, but they had been confined to the size of pages and couldn't possibly reveal this infinity.

It was there, in Provincetown, that my father taught her to swim, and when she took to it easily, he brought her out past the shorebound crests of waves. I slowed down my spools and let the ribbons touch as my parents rode the cool swells of the sea, their arms stretched out as they balanced themselves on the cusp of the earth.

My grandmother told my father his bride didn't look like a farm girl—too sophisticated, she said, too beautiful. But when he told my mother, expecting her to feel flattered, she became angry: "What did she expect? Someone who mucks stables all day?"

That evening, though, after her hair had dried—thicker with the sediment of salt—my mother held it back with both hands and brought her face close to the mirror, examining it as though it belonged to someone else: she saw a graceful woman who traveled, a woman who belonged in the world that she'd first encountered in the Gypsy's eyes.

While my father worked at the bank, she went to college in Spokane, even during those months after I was born. Some days she'd take me along to her classes, strapped to her front inside a large cotton scarf that she'd fasten around her neck and waist. By then she was pregnant again. Curved against her expanding body, connected to her and my brother's heartbeats, I'd sleep through tests and lectures. Soon after my third birthday, she had her teacher's certificate.

"The afternoon I met your mother," my father said, "I promised myself to stop drinking and to marry her someday." His hand rubbed my queasy stomach, lightly, and I would have gladly promised never to eat French fries again.

"Did you tell her right away?" I asked, though I knew the story.

"I waited until the weekend when I invited her to a concert in Manito Park."

And he had kept both promises.

And he had broken both promises.

It felt chilly in the cottage. *What happened to make you reach for that bottle you'd kept closed for so long? Don't blame it on her for leaving, because you started long before that.* I got up from the oak table, crumpled pages from an old fishing magazine in the fireplace, stacked kindling and split logs on top, ignited one of the long wooden matches. Perhaps the yearning for that first drink had ripened inside my father so that—when he finally surrendered—it must have become impossible to stop again.

I poured oil into the red bellies of the lamps, lit their flat wicks, and as the glow of their flames connected the dim spaces in the living room like dots in a constellation, I saw my father as a boy, *walking to school across the bridge near his house, battling another longing he'd told me about—the longing to toss his books into the water. He clutches the books against his chest, walking faster while daring himself to fling them from the bridge.* Though my father had told me this, I wondered how much of it had become mine. Where had I filled in the gaps? This was what must have happened on the bridge: *Some days he feels certain he won't succumb to this urge that intrigues and frightens him, but other days he has to cross that bridge three or four times, the collar of his corduroy jacket turned up against the wind, until he's proven his resistance to himself—even if it means arriving late at school and without a proper excuse.*

SCOOPING HANDFULS of onion skins and potato peels from the sink, my father dropped them into the trash. "Travis makes such a mess when he cooks . . . always fussing around my other kitchen." He rinsed the strainers and turned off the faucet. "It is dripping again."

"You have some washers around?"

"I don't know." He fiddled with the handle. "Washers . . . We should have some tools under the sink or in the shed—I am not sure, Julia."

Unlike the fathers of kids I'd grown up with, he'd never learned how to fix things. He knew the latest dance steps, wore the most stylish suits, and surprised us with gourmet meals; but for repairs he used to call Mr. Turgent, who'd arrive with a bulky tool belt slung around his scrawny hips, a bandanna in his black curls, and cowboy boots polished to an impossible luster. Mr. Turgent let me follow him around the house, and I held and steadied things for him as he worked on them and explained to me what he was doing. One December, when my father decided to surprise Travis and me by building bookshelves for us, it was Mr. Turgent who taught him to cut and fit the boards, and who completed the half-finished shelves with me the day after Christmas. He inherited an aunt's farm in Kentucky when I was eleven, and I took over the repair of leaky faucets and broken windows.

My father bent and retrieved a couple of screwdrivers and pliers from beneath the sink. "I think we have more tools in the shed."

"I'll check the faucet tomorrow."

"You've always been smart." He lifted two green-stemmed glasses from the cabinet and held them against the light. The back of his white hair was meticulously trimmed and styled, and I recalled another time when he'd stood here in this kitchen, just like this, reaching for something in the cupboard with his back to me, a young man still, his shoulders heaving as if a deep fissure were cleaving itself through the center of his body.

Though I sensed he was crying over my mother, whose name he hadn't spoken in two years, I didn't dare console him because it would hurt him even more if I reminded him of her. Something hot—a half-forgotten devotion to him, perhaps—soared within me, and in my heart I hurled at my mother the names he'd called her that long-ago night when

I'd listened to them from the top of the steps—"bitch" and "slut" and worse even—names that would make me ashamed for weeks to come; but that day, when I saw my father cry, I wanted to wrap him in whatever power I could call mine and shield him from his despair; instead I got sucked into its dark sheen though not one single word passed between us, and when he turned around, he wore the mask of a smile—my father the actor—while I was left feeling his sorrow as though he'd transfused it to me.

It was around that time, too, that a woman began to call him on the phone. Soon, I recognized her voice—like sticky perfume. "Oh . . . Calven Ives, please," she'd sigh, and when I'd tell her I'd get him, she'd murmur, "Oh . . . thanks a million, Julia," without telling me her name. She sounded like the kind of woman who'd wear beige lipstick and pile her hair high on top of her head.

"Who is that woman?" I'd ask my father.

"A business call," he'd mumble as he'd usher me to the door.

"Then how come she knows my name?"

He must have gone out with women during those years after my mother left, but Travis and I never met any of them, and when he received a phone call, he seemed flustered, as though he were doing something forbidden.

THE GREEN STEMS glinted in the light as my father polished the glasses with the towel that hung from his waistband. "I still miss that dog sometimes," he muttered to himself, and looked around as if half expecting the Kitchendog to appear. Carefully, he filled the glasses and set one of them on the table for me. "Skoal." He brought his glass to his lips, but hesitated as if waiting for me.

I opened my mouth to say the words that would release all my other questions—*What went wrong, Father?*—but the fear that gathered itself deep inside my gut was stronger than the fear of not asking, and for an instant I could no longer tell where I was, in Vermont or Spokane or Coeur d'Alene, in the past or the present or the future even, because every place I'd ever lived in fused in this room. I made my way to the table, sat down, and pressed both hands against its top. Much of the varnish had worn off, and the grain of the oak was rough.

My father smiled, an uncertain smile, as he nudged the air with his glass, encouraging me to pick mine up.

There was nothing he could do to me. Drunk or not drunk. *Nothing*. I raised my glass—"Skoal"—and set it back down again without drinking. Like a blind woman, I guided my fingertips beneath the tabletop until I found the gouges I had carved in here many years ago: *LI*, my mother's initials, my child-sorcery to bring her back. *Lily Ives*. I had printed her name in my notebooks, scratched her initials with ball-point pen into my left palm. After it became infected, I added an *E* to the two letters: *LIE*.

By then she'd been gone for a year, and when Travis found a snapshot of her tucked into the pages of the world atlas, she looked grave and unfamiliar with her hair parted in the middle. All summer I'd longed for a photo of her, but this one was inadequate—it left out too much: the sound of her laughter, low at first, then rising; the texture of her hair, heavy and tangled when wet, then drying to dark silk; the scent of her skin, warm and light. I stared at the photo until her face became no more than an arrangement of nose, mouth, eyes, chin, until I had to rely upon my memories of her moving—always moving—to recapture her.

Travis and I took turns keeping the photo in our rooms, swapping it every evening, then every week and every month until he forgot to ask for it back and I simply kept it. I still carried it in my wallet, encased in plastic across from my driver's license, though sometimes it struck me as preposterous that this woman, whose face showed fewer lines than mine, could possibly be my mother.

■

My FATHER prodded the salmon with a long fork. "Almost done."

Never again would I let him grab me and swirl me in one of his long-ago, crazy dances through the kitchen. Never again would I let him enter my room at night and bend over me. I was stronger than my father, who carried plates and flatware to the table, who filled a ceramic bowl with fresh fruit.

I arranged our place settings so that we both faced the picture window and the dark beyond it. My grandfather's models of the sister ships which had not sunk—the *Mauretania* and the *Olympic*—sat on wooden stands on either side of the window, each nearly four feet long and twelve inches high, including the masts. Once, when Travis had broken a mast of the *Mauretania,* I'd spliced the dowel back together with wood glue. Although the black of the hulls had grayed, and the white superstructures had taken on a yellowish hue, the orange of the smokestacks had held fast over the decades, and the metal trim and fittings gleamed as though my father had recently polished them.

Three fishing rods were mounted above the drawn-up bamboo shades. From the hook that secured the cord for the shades hung the binoculars through which my father used to watch the ducks and ospreys. One spring the ospreys had built their nest on a pole at the end of the dock, and my father had made sure we stayed away from them and swam from the sandy part of the beach instead.

"Look, Julia." He reached across the table to the windowsill and handed me a glass jar, half filled with gray powder. "Mount St. Helens ashes."

I unscrewed the lid. The ashes had the musty smell of old chalk.

"Some people thought it was the end of the world. Imagine that—the end of the world, Julia."

Ten years ago, in the spring of 1980 after Mount St. Helens had erupted, my father had sent me newspaper clippings with grainy photos of the lava stream that had killed people and torn away trees and houses. Though Spokane was nearly three hundred miles from the volcano, the sky had darkened in the middle of the day as ashes rained down and covered everything in heavy layers.

"Travis bought us surgical masks. . . . We wore them whenever we had to go outside." My father poured himself another glass of wine. Though he spoke slowly, his voice was lucid. "Those ashes got into everything, even our clothes and beds. A lot of car engines got wrecked. Travis changed the oil filter in our cars every couple of days."

I stuck one finger into the jar. "Like talcum powder . . . I saw ads in the *New York Times*, offering one ounce of 'genuine Mount St. Helens ash' for two dollars. American greed. Last fall there were ads for chunks from the Berlin wall."

My father sliced one hand through the air above his plate. "The explosion ripped the top off the volcano. Traffic stopped. Schools and businesses closed. They kept interrupting TV shows for news of the volcano." He pointed to the jar. "I have been saving it for you."

"Thank you. We can share it. I don't need all that."

"I have three other jars." He pointed to my fork. "Eat, Julia."

"Eat, Julia," my mother had told me that evening my father had been late. She didn't look at the empty chair across from her as she took Travis' plate and began to cut his lamb chop, though he was old enough to do it himself. When a car door slammed in the driveway, she blinked.

My father's face looked flushed when he dashed into the room. He was laughing. "I got the part, Lily— The lead, imagine." The top button of his white shirt was open, his throat tanned. He carried a cardboard box with red string around it.

Without glancing up, my mother continued cutting Travis' lamb chop into smaller and smaller squares.

"I bought us cheesecake to celebrate. With huckleberries." He winked at me and stumbled as he set the box next to my glass. "You should have seen me, Lily. I knew I had the part the moment I started. I could feel it, I tell you, I could touch it, it was like a gift, a—"

"Would you please take this off the table?" My mother's voice was cold-polite, and I felt so hollow inside my chest that a hundred echoes could have fit in there.

My father looked bewildered.

"I would love some cheesecake," I dared to say.

My mother cast me a warning glance, and I speared a pulpy carrot slice with my fork and slid it off with my teeth, careful not to let it touch my lips.

As my father bent forward to pick up the box, his breath skimmed my face; it had the evening smell it got whenever he came home late. "Why don't you let the children have a little piece at least?"

"You know perfectly well I don't want the children to eat too many sweets."

God, her voice could turn so cold, but perhaps that was the only way she knew to be when he drank while, deep within, she shook with the fear which I would come to inherit after she left. Yet, when I was seven, I felt angry at her for making my father look so sad as he stood there, the box in his hands, and I wanted to follow him as he stumbled from the house, wanted to stay awake to wait for him, but when I next heard his voice, it startled me out of sodden sleep, and I felt like a coward as I pressed both hands against my ears to shut out sounds of his shouting and my mother's crying.

"EAT, JULIA," my father said.

The salmon was tender, the potatoes spicy. We ate artichoke hearts, Sicilian olives. Above us, the skylight framed a segment of new moon and two dim stars. In the wind the ponderosas creaked, and the water slapped against the piling that supported the wooden planks of the dock—a steady, hypnotic sound. And all at once I felt an amazing contentment that I carried a child within my body, that I was no longer entirely alone. I could see her room in Vermont, *bright wall hangings and mobiles, a vaulted ceiling with a platform above so that she can have a tree house inside her room. . . .*

My father's and my reflections in the picture window made . it appear as if there were *the four of us* at the table. I squinted till I made the image blur enough to see my mother and Travis with us. *A young Travis. A father whose face is smooth.* "You look like your mother, Julia," Uncle Jake used to say. *Me. My mother. One.* There, in the mirror reflection that could change if I dared look at it with my eyes open. *Dark hair that ends above shoulders like a sculpted sheet; the wide mouth that needs a woman's face to grow into; long hands and fingers . . . We still have three years before she will disappear. He hasn't reached for a drink since the day he met her and won't resume his drinking for another year. Silences are comfortable because they are just that—silences—and give way to laughter and words. Sometimes, when she looks at him, a sudden light leaps into her eyes and she touches the cleft in his chin as if she can't stop herself. Mornings he rests his lips on her hair before he says good-bye. Often, while she reads, he watches her silently, intensely, waiting for her to glance up. . . .*

The essence of burning wood had woven itself into the aroma of my father's cooking as so many times when the four of us had sat around this table, and I felt content, sleepy almost. I had been here before, and I didn't want to leave. I could make this last—move all of us into that strand before my father yielded to that first drink, pilot us into a different direction where we'd stay together: *Though Travis and I still go away to college, we come home on vacations and holidays, gather around this table with our parents for countless meals, all of them begun and completed together, meals that grow to include our families.* I restored his wife and son to my brother, brought Andreas back, heard my mother laugh as she talked with him. . . .

And as that strand shaped itself, taking on its own momentum, it lured me into years where I was as old as my father, and he, of course, much older, *passing one of his famous dishes to my daughter who's already grown-up. She has strawberry-blonde*

*hair like Coop's, but her mouth and nose are just like Andreas', and
her feet—they're tough like mine; and before I know it, she has two
children of her own. As I peer into their faces—hard, so I'll remember
all of them after I return to my present*—my father's voice yanked
me back to the table where he and I sat, alone, and as I tried
to make out his words, I felt struck with grief at the loss of my
large family.

But he spoke them again, those words that had brought
me back before, said them as if he'd shared my vision of that
large family: "This is a good place to bring up children."

## 7

WOKE TO THE SOUND OF MY
father's steps. He was making his way down the hall. Outside
my room he slowed as if listening for me. My breath flattened
itself like a small animal in a dark space, and I felt the shape
of my spine against the mattress. My hands found my belly.
Cautiously I pressed against the sides of the small mound,
searching for my child's movements though I knew it was still
early for that. I heard the latch of the bathroom door, water
running. I kept listening for his steps, waiting for him to return to his room at the end of the hall.

But it was silent in the cottage. Too silent. I should have
never agreed to stay here with him. It was isolated, far away
from help. If only I could step up to the window and see the
familiar lights from Claudia's house. I felt a longing for my
bedroom in Vermont with its sloping ceiling, wanted to look
forward to the morning ritual of brewing a cup of espresso in
my blue-tiled kitchen, even though coffee had been making
me queasy ever since I'd gotten pregnant.

When Claudia had driven me to the airport, she'd still
been baffled by my decision to visit my father. "I thought you
never wanted to see him again."

"I need to talk with him about what happened . . . find out why."

"But it won't change what happened." Claudia had a wonderful bullshit detector and was practical when it came to sorting through confusion. Yet, she could be scattered about little things—like keeping the gas tank filled. Her husband, Matt, was a dentist too, and they shared an office in Rutland with a carved sign in the front window: *We Cater to Cowards.* Until my pregnancy, Claudia and I used to play racquetball once a week, getting embarrassingly competitive, and then laughing about it while we soaked in the hot tub afterward. Since both of those activities would have to wait until after the baby was born, we got together for early morning walks instead.

"It won't change what happened," I agreed as we checked my luggage at the airline counter, "but maybe how I am with it from now on. So I don't pass the same garbage on to my daughter."

Still—I could have stayed in Spokane at my hotel and visited my father at the house only when Travis was there. I didn't have to set myself up for this fear. My eyes were dry, and though I told myself that my fear was straight from my childhood when those steps would come up the stairs and pause in front of my room, when the door would open and those steps move toward my bed, I couldn't climb out of the terror which bound me against the bed and entangled me in the sum of everything that had happened between my father and me. I saw him coming toward me the evening I'd gone to my first high school dance with Lynne. I remembered the satin texture of my dress and a boy's hand on my bare shoulder, remembered my father's flushed face when I arrived back home. Though he smiled at me from his TV chair, I felt the danger: it lay between us like a tight coil that could spring up any moment.

"How was the dance, Julia?" His cardigan was unbuttoned, and his silk tie was slung low around his neck.

"All right. It was all right."

"How many boys asked you to dance?"

"Two."

"Only two? Fools. Come here, my lovely." He got up, and before I could object, his arms were around me and he was spinning me past the stairs that led up to my bedroom, into the sunroom, and back into the living room. He hummed, his breath sour against the side of my face.

"Don't." As I tore myself loose, he stumbled and caught himself with one hand on the doorframe.

"Just one little dance, Julia?"

I backed away until the knob of the front door pressed into my hip. To my left hung the gold-framed hallway mirror, and for a moment it was as if I could see my mother's reflection tilting her face under the floppy hat.

"Slut. Ungrateful child." He straightened himself, suddenly authoritative. "Go to your room. This minute."

To get to my room, I had to pass him. The week before, when he'd come home drunk, I'd locked myself into the upstairs bathroom. Though he promised not to hit me if I came out, I didn't dare believe him. After a while, I heard the splintering of wood from the direction of my room, and in the morning I found him asleep on the floor next to my bed, still clutching the hammer he'd used to demolish the bookshelf that he and Mr. Turgent had built for me.

"To your room," he repeated and came toward me. "I mean it, slut."

I darted past him and up the stairs. My brother's door was closed, as usual. He never came out to help me against my father. Still in my dress and shoes, I climbed into bed, pulled the blanket to my neck, and turned off the light on my night table. Maybe he'd fall asleep downstairs. But only too soon his unsteady steps halted outside my door. He opened it. When he was sober, he never came into my room at night, but when he was drunk, he'd tug at my blanket until it touched my chin and mumble something about me catching cold. I'd pretend to be asleep as he'd bend over me and kiss my cheek. Sometimes he'd leave then. But often he'd switch on the lamp, lift it from my night table, and bring it close to my face, turning the darkness outside my closed eyelids an aching orange until the hot bolt of outrage in my gut would burn through my fear and I'd shout at him to leave me alone, to get out of my room.

Though I kept my eyes closed as he moved closer to my bed, I felt as though I were watching the hundredth rerun of an old movie that could end in two different ways: *he leaves her room; or he beats her.* He curved over me, slobbered a kiss against my cheek, lost his balance, and steadied himself with one hand on my thigh, chuckling. My heart beating in my throat, I willed my breathing to remain slow and regular. Mumbling something about me catching cold, he pulled the blanket to my nose. I wanted to move, to wipe off that damp kiss, to get away from under his invading eyes. *In three years I'll be out of here. Forever.*

He turned on the lamp, lifted it from my night table—*a movie, the rerun of a dreadful movie in which I know which ending is going to happen and can do nothing to prevent it*—brought the lamp close to my face and held it there till I flinched from it.

He grinned at me. "See—I thought you were awake." As he set the lamp down, he knocked over a stack of books.

"Damn." I bolted up and wiped my cheek with the back of my right hand.

"What kind of language is that for a young lady?"

"Please. I want to sleep."

"Come on, have a midnight snack with your poor little father." His eyes looked yellow.

*IhateyouIhateyouI—* "I'm tired."

"At least fix me something to eat."

"Leave me alone. Please. Get out of my room."

"You get up." His voice changed. "You get up and shine my shoes. Now. This minute."

Knowing I should keep quiet. Knowing it but— "You're drunk."

"How dare you. How dare you call me drunk?" He pulled himself up indignantly. Swayed. "Liar. Ungrateful child." He struck my face with his fist. "Cunt." Pulled me out of bed. "You'll never be able to love a man." Struck me again. "Whore."

That's when I bit him—in the edge of his hand. It was the only time ever that I'd fought back. He roared—perhaps as much from surprise as from pain—and I kept my teeth clenched, afraid to let go. But he struck me down with his other hand and pulled himself free. With both arms I tried to protect my face and breasts from the heavy blows, tried to get away from him, but I tripped, fell, while his shoes, hard, kicked into my side, my stomach.

"Get up."

Through a blaze of pain I heard his voice as though it were coming from far away, and something black opened itself up to me, but I tore myself from its promise of oblivion, got on my knees, and crawled to the door, where I pulled myself up.

Arms crossed, he stood where I'd fallen. "Come back here," he ordered as if fully expecting me to obey.

I ran down the stairs and from the house, up to the corner of Shoshone and Bernard, downhill until I reached my old elementary school. It hurt to breathe. Shivering in the cool night air, I crouched behind the bushes next to the building as the beams from a slow-moving vehicle swept past me. It was too dark to recognize the car or driver, but when I heard my father's voice call out my name, I bent lower, hands and knees sinking into the soil. Finally the car disappeared, but soon it was back. I kicked in the glass of the closest window, reached through, and opened the latch. Careful not to cut myself, I crawled in and sat on the floor of the dark classroom in a cloud of soiled satin. As my eyes adjusted, the teacher's desk emerged, then rows of empty seats and the chalkboard.

"Julia . . ." From a distance came his voice. Gently. "Julia . . ."

*Why didn't he leave instead of my mother?*

*At least I fought back.*

His tires spun across the wet pavement before all sounds vanished into silence. When I awoke on the floor—aching and cold and dirty and safe—I understood that safety lay outside the home. It was a certainty that would stay with me from that day on. My first lover, Gil, would get upset with me because I'd travel to New York alone and go to theaters and museums. "It's dangerous," he'd say. "A woman alone in New York—especially at night." I wouldn't know how to make him understand that, for me, danger had only come from within the home, that no stranger had ever harmed me.

MOONLIGHT SEEPED through the upper half of the window frame and caught itself in the glass fragments on the floor as if startled by its fractured image. The chalkboard listed Brazil's natural resources: coffee, corn, rice, cotton, sugarcane, iron, mica, silver. . . . Maybe my mother was in Brazil—far away. As soon as I was eighteen, I would get away from him too. As far as I could.

I had run away before. Many times. To Lynne's house. Her brother was in his second year of law school at Gonzaga, and his mustache had filled its shadow outline. He used aftershave lotion that smelled of limes, and he'd replaced his bicycle with a motorcycle. But he hadn't offered me a single ride though I'd hinted more than once. From Lynne I knew that he had a twenty-two-year-old girlfriend who lived on the north side of Spokane and went all the way. The first time I'd appeared at their door late at night, Scott had checked his law books to make sure my father couldn't sue his family for taking me in. When he helped me put sheets on one of the three couches that took up most of the living room, his wrist touched one of my knuckles, and I felt something like a jolt, only nicer, run up to my shoulder.

"Didn't they ever call the police?" Andreas had wanted to know when I'd told him, and I'd shaken my head. "Now, I'm sure they would, but in those years . . . most people would have seen it as interfering in family matters."

I stepped across the shards of moon and climbed out of

the school window, checking for cars, but the street was empty now, and I hurried down the South Hill to West Seventh where Lynne's family rented an apartment in one of the converted Cutter mansions. I knew I wouldn't have to explain why I was here.

Mrs. Clark opened the arched front door in her watered silk robe, her frizzy blonde hair pushed back from her forehead. When she gave me a hug, my right side hurt and I moaned.

"Oh, Julia—" Taking my chin into her hand, she tilted my face and inspected me under the porch light until I felt as though my skin were made of porcelain. "You're hurting," she whispered, and took me through the marble-floored hallway with its gleaming maze of cabinets and bookshelves, into the tiled kitchen where she cleaned my face and hands with warm water as if I were a small girl.

"Is Lynne asleep?"

She nodded. "If you ever want to tell me—"

But I shook my head, mortified I'd been beaten like this.

"I understand," she said, "I do," and got me dry clothes—a blue cotton sweater and white pants from her own closet.

As I took off my mud-stained gown and put on her clothes, I saw myself wearing them home in the morning and already felt that sense of defiance that became mine whenever I walked back to my house alone after those nights, armed with the certainty that my father would not hit me while sober. *And this time I bit him.*

Mrs. Clark made us hot cocoa. Sitting across from me, her elbows on the table, she smoked a cigarette while we drank our cocoa. I wanted to touch those elbows, find out if they were as smooth as she said. A model for the Crescent department store, she massaged lotion into them twice a day. She was the only divorced woman I knew, and she had a fiancé in Las Vegas who worked as a croupier for the third-largest hotel. A stocky man who wore sun visors even indoors because his eyes were sensitive, he flew to Spokane every other month to spend a week with the Clarks. "Getting his quota of family life," she called it.

The Crescent let her buy clothes at a huge discount, and her closet was filled with silk blouses, slinky trousers, and dresses that rustled when Lynne and I touched them. Sometimes, when she had a fashion show, she'd take us along and we'd sit in the audience, trying to memorize her fluid movements for those occasions when she'd let us raid her closet and stage our own fashion show in front of the triple mirror in her bedroom. She'd become audience and announcer all at once, commenting on colors and styles, applauding while we paraded past her.

She was the one who'd convinced me to stop wearing my mother's high-heel shoes—"so unsuitable for a girl your age, Julia"—who'd reminded me to ask my father for haircut money whenever my bangs started to hang into my eyes, who'd pointed out which colors looked best on me—medium blue and most shades of green—and who'd sometimes described a sweater or dress she'd seen downtown—"It's perfect for you, and I asked them to hold it for a couple of days in case you and your father want to take a look."

When I finished my hot chocolate, Mrs. Clark yawned and covered her mouth, stretching the yawn into a funny sigh. "Tired?"

My legs felt as if the cocoa had settled there—warm and heavy. "Yes," I said.

"Scott's in Seattle for a few days." Without lipstick, her mouth seemed smaller. "If you like, you can use his bed."

I nodded. I blushed. I nodded again.

In Scott's room, I pulled down the shades before I took off his mother's clothes. The sheets were soft and smelled of lime and tobacco. And as I wondered what it would be like if he lay on top of me, I saw my wedding gown, *white lace with a scooped neckline and a long veil. I wear pink nail polish and we have a honeymoon in Hawaii and don't come back to Spokane. Our apartment is in Seattle across from Pike Street Market, where we get pastries every morning.* . . . Turning my face from side to side, I pretended kissing Scott, passionately, the way I'd seen it in the movies, but even though I moved my tongue around, my mouth felt empty, my entire body did—hollow in a way I hadn't known before—and I wished I could fill myself and believe that those hands, which grazed the bony rims of my hips and circled my scant breasts, were *not* mine.

"I DIDN'T THINK you'd ever return, Julia."

"Neither did I." When I'd hugged Lynne in the lobby of the Ridpath the afternoon after my arrival, I'd been surprised at how much she looked like her mother used to: the same high, narrow forehead; the same alert gray eyes.

"It feels weird to be back," I said. "Real weird. I'm still not sure it's the right thing."

"I didn't have any idea how much I'd missed you till you called."

"I've missed you too. Seeing you is the good part of all this."

As we walked from my hotel through the downtown area toward the Spokane River, the sun was hot on our arms. In the new park that stretched along the south bank, kids with skateboards zipped past us. Two androgenous-looking teens in floppy black coats sat on a bench with tragic expressions on their pasty faces.

"What made you decide to come back?"

"I need to ask him, Lynne—why things happened that way."

"You think he can deal with it?"

"I don't give a flying fuck."

"All right—" She grinned. "Now that we've cleared that up . . ."

"It's more like . . . if I let myself worry about how he'll deal with it, it'll become an excuse for not bringing it up at all. You think I'm being a bitch about this?"

"You know what that stands for—B.I.T.C.H.?"

"Aside from the obvious?"

"Being In Total Charge Of Herself."

"Don't I wish . . ."

"He may not be as ready for this discussion as you."

"I'm taking him to the lake for two days. I hope we can talk there."

"When are you coming back?"

"Saturday."

"Why don't we have dinner that evening? My mom wants a chance to feed you anyhow."

"I can't wait to see your mother."

"I'll pick you up on my way to her house. You may want us around after being with your father for two days."

On the path ahead of us, an old woman in a red T-shirt roller-skated briskly, a backpack slung across her shoulders, arms raised so her fingertips brushed the low-hanging leaves of the locust trees.

"Thirty years from now," I said, "that'll be us."

"Roller skates instead of wheelchairs . . . I'm all for that."

"It's a date, then."

"Thirty years . . . I'll probably need that much time to practice."

A breeze rose from the water and blew our cotton skirts around our legs. The area along the bank looked transformed: when I'd lived here, both banks had been lined with dilapidated industrial buildings; above them the clock tower of the Great Northern Railroad Depot had risen—still sound and handsome; an elevated railroad trestle had run along Spokane Falls Boulevard and across the river. A maze of bridges and railroad tracks had made it impossible to see the river and the waterfalls. Now, only the old clock tower was left and stood high at the crest of the park, surrounded by lawns where children chased one another and young couples sat on blankets.

"When did all this happen?"

"Just before Expo seventy-four." Lynne motioned to our

right where the sleek lines of a new structure rose beyond a carousel with gaudy, carved horses. "The opera house and convention center."

Part of the old riverbank had been filled in to create a lagoon where a floating stage lay anchored. We headed toward the roar of the waterfalls, which dropped nearly 150 feet here in the center of the city. Halfway across the narrow footbridge we stopped, our hands on the railing, and felt the motion of the swaying bridge rise into our bodies. Beneath us, the Spokane River plunged in white-water currents around the volcanic rocks.

"I wish it could be easier for you. Your return." Wind blew Lynne's blonde hair from her face; it was longer than she used to wear it and streaked with silver-gray.

"I think about your mother so often. . . . How is she?"

"Still engaged to the Las Vegas man. The eternal courtship. It suits her far better than marriage ever did."

"How about Scott? You see much of him?"

"Not if I can help it. He tries so hard to be understanding about my relationship with Sonja that he gets flustered around us. Then, to cover up, he comes out with the most unfortunate comments."

"Sometimes I think homophobia is the last legitimate prejudice in this country."

"Tell me about it. People who'd never discriminate against other minorities will act bizarre around lesbians and gays."

Twelve years ago Lynne had sent me a letter to tell me she loved a woman. "I only wish it hadn't taken me this long to figure out what I'm about," she'd written. I'd called her that same day to tell her I was glad for her. "You don't feel uncomfortable?" she'd asked. "Hell, no," I'd said, and after that we'd spoken quite openly—she about her female lovers, I about Andreas and, after the divorce, other men. She'd been with Sonja for three years now, and they'd bought a house together last summer.

"I wish I didn't have to be so careful at work," Lynne said as we walked to the other end of the bridge. "If the administration found out . . . You know, what pisses me off is that the other teachers come into the lunchroom, talk about trips or movies with their families or lovers, while I have to censor what I say. If I use 'we,' they ask questions. They think I have this boring solitary life—"

"No man. Poor you," I said, and we both laughed.

"If they knew how incredible our pre-breakfast sex is, they wouldn't feel sorry for me." She pointed toward a renovated brick building. "The old flour mill, remember? Full of wonderful shops and restaurants now. If you like, we can stop for a drink."

When we sat on a deck high above the waterfalls with our glasses of iced tea, I asked, "Will I get to see Sonja?" Though I'd never talked with her, I remembered her from high school—a tall girl one grade ahead of us who'd been in the drama club.

"She's in a play with the Theatre Ensemble right now. I'll ask if she wants to stop by my mom's house when you're there. You know . . ." She smiled to herself. "My mother, she figured out what was going on with me long before I had an idea. And she simply waited. She's okay with it. Quite a few people are. And the rest—I don't really want to make an effort. I used to. . . . My mother, she likes Sonja and says it doesn't make any difference to her if I love a woman or a man. As long as it's a whole person."

"Your mother has always been amazing."

"I know. So accepting . . ." She laughed. "You know where she failed me though?"

I shook my head. "Tell me."

"I didn't have anyone to rebel against when I was a teenager."

"That must have been just . . . dreadful."

"You bet."

"Remember when she taught us how to put on makeup, and we walked around with all that gunk on our faces?"

"At least we could undo that. Not like massacring your eyebrow."

I automatically moved my fingertips across my left eyebrow. Lynne's mother had shown us how to pluck our eyebrows into elegant arches. The first few times, I'd extracted each hair with her tweezer, but one afternoon I'd become impatient and decided it would be easier to go after those stubbles with Scott's razor. One of my eyebrows was gone, and I was about to obliterate the other, when Mrs. Clark entered her bathroom. "Oh, Julia," she said softly. She touched my face. Sighed. "At least it will grow again. . . . I'll show you how to use the eyebrow pencil. But it would be best not to shave off the other one."

"The eyebrow grew back again." As I glanced past Lynne at the mist that rose from the falls, and toward the rooflines of the South Hill, I felt an unexpected joy at being back in this city I'd run away from, this city I was seeing for the first time as an architect, appreciating its old residential neighborhoods that borrowed from French Renaissance, Italian Romanesque, Georgian, Swiss, Moorish, Florentine, Spanish, Elizabethan, and Gothic styles. Many of the houses were opulent, immense; they'd been built nearly a hundred years ago after the great fire, when profits from the railroads and lead discoveries in the Coeur d'Alene mines had created unexpected wealth for many in Spokane. Some of the mansions were stunning, others monuments to atrocious taste.

Kirtland Cutter, a young architect who'd arrived from the East around that time, had designed the ones I liked best. Faced in terra-cotta, red brick, Montana granite, or sandstone from Italy and Idaho, they were decorated with imported tiles and arched windows with leaded-glass filigree, cherry wood and marble in hues of red, yellow, and white. Located in Browne's Addition and on the cliffs of the South Hill, several mansions had been turned into restaurants or apartment buildings like the one where Lynne used to live.

"Is your mother still in the same place?"

She nodded. "And it's more jumbled with furniture than ever before. Have I told you how good it is to have you back here?"

I smiled at her and drank from my iced tea. "I have to make a confession . . . actually two confessions. No connection though, all right? Number one, I used to have a crush on your brother, and number two—"

"A crush on Scott?" Lynne groaned.

"He didn't know either."

"Scott? My brother? Are you talking about my brother, Scott?"

"Just because he's in your immediate gene pool . . ."

"Spare me." She raised both hands, palms toward me. "I'm glad I didn't know. It would have demolished our friendship."

"You're too hard on him."

"I guess I've never seen poor Scott as terribly exciting."

"Why poor Scott? I mean, aside from the homophobia."

"He's . . . sort of formal, I guess. Grown-up."

"God, anything but that. Grown-up?"

"You know, a corporate man with a briefcase up his ass. Goal-oriented. Stuffy. Successful . . ." She pointed to the hill below us. "Look."

Brown earth showed through the few weeds that sprouted among the rubble of stones and scraggly bushes. I made out some movement—marmots, two fat marmots whose color blended into the hill as they scurried toward the river.

"So, what's this second confession that doesn't have anything to do with the first confession?"

"I—I'm going to have a kid . . . a daughter."

Her gray eyes widened, then flickered across my body. "A baby . . . How does it feel?"

"I pee a lot."

She laughed. "That's . . . just wonderful. Tell me, is it safe to say congratulations?"

"I think so. Yes."

"You'll be great with a kid."

"Convince me. One moment I'm sure I can do it, another moment I'm terrified of messing up. I've asked myself if I'm giving her too rough a start, not being married. . . ."

"Think of the many kids who suffer through their parents' divorces. All that bitterness, the back and forth . . . At least your daughter won't have to go through that. Lots of women bring up their children alone."

"Well—at least now I won't become one of those sad women who believe themselves pregnant at age sixty or steal babies from carriages and pretend they're theirs."

"Were you afraid of turning into one of them?"

"Not really . . . but I'm aware of them. And of that longing that maybe has been there for too long and then takes a wrong turn, into the bizarre. . . . A year ago I was in a bookstore in Vermont, when this woman—white hair, meticulous makeup—stopped me and asked if I was going to have a baby. I was startled and told her no. 'Oh, I was hoping you'd have a baby,' she said, 'because I am.' With both hands she hoisted her belly up and adjusted her breasts. 'Imagine—at my age . . .' she said. One of her hands darted to my stomach before I could stop her. 'I wish you were having a baby too.' By then she was smiling and crying at the same time."

As I described the woman to Lynne, I could smell her faint perfume, see her thin body with the large stomach that stretched her silk dress.

"Have you heard of the mood-swing drug lithium?" the woman had asked me.

I nodded.

"That's what I take. I've been in and out of institutions."

"I'm—so sorry."

People pressed past us in the narrow entrance of the store and stared at us. I didn't know how to get away from her without hurting her feelings.

She brought her face close to mine and whispered, "I won't know for sure until I see my doctor, but I can feel it, that I have a baby inside me." She flung her arms around me and drew me into an embrace. "I love you."

I pulled myself free and edged toward the door. "I hope everything goes well for you."

"Thank you, sweetheart," she called after me. "Remember—I love you."

I looked at Lynne. "I felt awful, leaving her there."

"That must have been spooky. A woman here in Spokane took a toddler from a parked car and kept him for two months before he was discovered. Even then she tried to convince everyone that he was her child."

"She probably believed it."

"So—I assume then that yours is not a baster-baby?"

"A what?"

"A baster-baby. Some of my lesbian friends have their kids that way—sperm in a turkey baster. . . . The kitchen industry's improvement on nature . . ." I started laughing, and she continued, "Always erect. Even has a ball. And it works. I've been to some great conception celebrations. A couple of times I tried it myself, but it didn't take. . . . Probably for the better."

"Regrets?"

"Of course. Aren't there always once we rule something out?"

I nodded. "But not crushing."

"Not crushing. Even some relief. Still, if you don't have kids, people treat you as if you got something wrong with your life—some huge gap."

"I used to pity mothers with bratty kids in supermarkets. Clawing at cookie boxes, throwing tantrums in the checkout line . . ."

"Of course your child won't be anything like that."

As we walked back to my hotel, she asked me about the baby's father, and when I told her about Coop, she said he sounded like someone she'd want to meet. "It might last, Julia."

"As long as I don't let myself count on him." Oddly, I missed him the instant I said that.

■

THE STRIPE of light disappeared from under my door as if sucked into a vacuum. Even if my father entered my room, he could not harm me. *Not now. Not ever again.* I shut my eyes and listened to the crowns of the trees fill themselves with night wind and hold it like a long note before releasing it. At the end of the hallway my father's door closed. I imagined him climbing into his bed, drawing his own blanket to his shoulders. From his room came the muffled sound of his TV—canned laughter and voices. Tomorrow afternoon I'd be back in my hotel room where the carpeted halls blotted the safe steps of strangers, and in eleven days I would fly back to Vermont, where Coop would pick me up from the airport.

*Safe.* I sat up straight in bed. God—had the punishing father been safer than the friendly father late at night? My arms felt cold, and I rubbed my hands up and down their sides. Had it been safer to have him beat me than kiss me? I used to believe the beatings were punishment though I didn't know what I was being punished for. And even after I sorted out that he only beat me when he was drunk, I was still ashamed. What was it about me that made him beat me? When he was sober, he'd tell me he loved me and I'd feel furious, knowing he wanted to hear I loved him too; but I hadn't said it since that evening when he'd pulled me from the windowsill, that evening when I'd shouted, *"I love you, Daddy!"* Was that the reason he kept beating me—because he knew I didn't love him?

For a moment I was back inside the old, tight circle of that fear; yet, strangely, it lifted almost immediately: I no longer had to be afraid of him—it was an old fear, a superfluous fear. He'd had no right to come into my room at night. Yet, I too had invaded his room—but only when he'd been away. I'd gone through every drawer, every envelope in his room, had shaken books by their spines to dislocate hidden evidence of my mother's whereabouts, had searched his files, his medicine cabinet. Not just at the cottage but also at the house. Not just once but many times over the nine years between the day she left without a warning and the day I left after much preparation.

But except for that one photo of her, I found nothing—no letters, no other photos, no documents. If my father ever heard from her, he kept the proof in his office.

I still checked phone books for her name whenever I traveled to a new place. It had become a routine—like finding a doctor and a hardware store after moving. I would run one finger down the listings of *Ives* in hotel phone books before I'd unpack my luggage, prepared to go to her.

Outside my window, the lake rocked itself against the dock like a stubborn child, knocking about floating leaves and twigs and downy feathers from the bellies of birds. It wasn't just my father who had kept me from here for over twenty years—I'd also been reluctant to return because I would have to face losing my mother all over again. Only I hadn't known it—not until Uncle Jake had shaken the image that had served me so well all these years.

# 8

■

$T$HAT IMAGE OF MY MOTHER AT twenty-nine—luminous and young—had still been mine when we'd left Spokane the evening before, heading south on 195 to my uncle's farm in Rosalia, and it would hold fast for me until I'd carry my uncle in my arms—an old man, my mother's brother—making it absurd to remember her as a young woman. But on the way to the farm, as we drove through the Palouse in my brother's truck, I didn't have any idea yet how severely my uncle's illness had decimated his body.

I was mesmerized by the sea of wheat that rose and fell around us in miles of amber waves, divided only by the long band of road. Some of the hills carried designs of their own as if some giant had run a finger through the wheat, leaving swirls and ridges. The sun hung on one side, the moon on the other, suspended at the same height as if held on the arms of an invisible scale.

Gradually, as the balance shifted, the disk of sun descended toward the outlines of the dune-shaped fields that softened from amber to blue to purple. I would have liked to stop along the edge of the highway between the two sources of light, to gather stalks of wheat into bouquets the way my father sometimes had when we'd driven to the farm where he'd first seen my mother. She had loved the sculpted hills and open sky, had loved my father for cherishing her landscape, and yet he had taken her away from there, expecting her to carry that landscape within her.

Travis was driving fast, as though we were late. In front of the stone house, he jumped from the truck, helped my father from his seat, and rang the bell. It was windy, as often in the Palouse—the kind of wind that blows doors open and causes snow to fall in horizontal sheets. As we waited on the porch, a black dog came up to us and sniffed our shoes, but my father didn't stiffen as he used to. Even at five, I had known to step between him and any approaching dog, diverting its attention, but the Kitchendog had taken away the scent of my father's fear which used to lure other dogs to him.

The neighborhood was just as I remembered it: generous farms and towering silos that shimmered in the dusty heat; scorched pastures with horses and isolated clumps of ponderosa pines. Uncle Jake had bought my mother out when the two had inherited the farm, and she'd used the money to travel with my father. In the low hills behind the house, Travis and I would go sledding with our cousin Andy, cushioned on a truck's inner tube that was wide enough to hold the three of us. Summers we'd play in the sun-drenched hayloft of the round barn, where my mother and Uncle Jake used to play hide-and-seek, or we'd push each other on the rope swing with the deerskin seat that was fastened to the rafters. The curved roof of the barn was five times as high as its base, topped with a turret that my uncle would paint fire-red every fall after the harvest was in. We'd be tightrope walkers on the rafters, bank robbers crouched behind the arched dormers, vampires rising with a howl from beneath piles of hay. . . .

But now the turret had faded to a washed-out pink, and some of the shingles above the barn door were missing.

"I guess they didn't hear us." My father patted the dog's square muzzle and rang the bell again. Despite the heat, he wore a pin-striped suit and blue silk tie.

I pictured my uncle opening the door—not feeble, the way Travis had described him to me, but looking just the way he had when he'd visited me in Vermont. *Wearing a plaid shirt and suspender pants, he wraps me into his long arms, and we hike up the path, just the two of us, past the barn and through the upper fields, whose blond surfaces ripple with each trace of wind as if a woman were drawing a brush through her long hair. At the top of the hill—*

"Quick." Aunt Marlene yanked the door open, her lips pulled back from her teeth. "Quick. I can't—" In her ballerina slippers and lavender balloon pants she darted ahead of us through the living room and toward the hallway. Fists raised, she pounded against the solid bathroom door. Her gray braid swung between her shoulder blades. "Jake—" Her voice cracked, high and urgent. "Open up, Jake."

"Uncle Jake?" Travis rattled the doorknob. "It's me, Travis."

"We've brought Julia to see you," my father shouted.

From inside came the sound of water rushing into the tub.

"Don't you dare—" My aunt's slight body heaved itself against the door, fists flailing as if she were trying to dig her way through the wood. The whites of her eyes were showing. "Jake, if you don't open up right now—"

I caught her shoulders with my hands and pulled her toward me. "What's going on?"

She collapsed against me. The collar of her silk shirt was too wide for her delicate neck. "He says he doesn't want to live anymore."

"Stand back." As if auditioning for a part in a play, my father took three paces back and flung himself against the door. He grimaced, rubbed his shoulder, and got ready to try again.

Travis stepped in his way. "You'll hurt yourself."

"We have to get Jake out of there."

"Not like that."

"The hinges," I said, "let's get the hinges off."

Travis ran toward the basement stairs. "I'll get some tools."

My father cupped both hands around his mouth. "Jake!" he hollered. "It's me, Calven. Open up!"

"Jake?" Aunt Marlene banged one small palm against my arm. "Jake? Sweetheart . . . Goddammit, you."

When Travis and I pried the door off its hinges, Uncle Jake was standing in the filled tub, knees bent like a ski jumper about to risk the fifty-foot leap. But his bare legs were shaking— his entire body was shaking—and in one hand he held a pink hair dryer, pointed toward us like a gun.

"Stay out," he wailed, his face wet with tears. "You sons of bitches stay the fuck out of here." He'd lost a staggering amount of weight and the hair on his head was gone—except his eyebrows, which were still bushy. Folds of skin sagged from his upper arms, his stomach and thighs, making his genitals look like just one more section of aging skin. His body blocked the sunlight that streamed through the window and fanned itself around him as though his silhouette had burned itself into a bright yellow canvas.

"If you don't get out of here—" The dryer wavered in his hand. Aunt Marlene pressed her sleeve to her lips to muffle her sobs; yet, they filled the breathing gaps between my uncle's words. "—I'll drop it in the water."

My father crushed me against the sink as he pushed past me to yank the plug from the outlet—just as Uncle Jake flicked the switch with his thumb. He howled. Dropped the hair dryer. For a moment I thought it was his cry of death and brought my hands against my eyes to blot the image of his body turning blue as in horror movies. But the howl was one of fury. His frail body was shaking, his hands were shaking, while his eyes blazed with the passion to end it, all of it.

Carefully, I lifted my uncle from the tub. His long body felt slippery, light, and he didn't resist as I held him in my arms and wrapped him into a white towel like an infant, or a corpse perhaps. As if leading a procession, I carried him through the dining room past the hutch he'd built, past the guest room with the blue Jesus picture, and up the stairs. I felt the weight of my child in my belly, felt the weight of my uncle in my arms, and it was as though the two of them touched, separated only by the wall of my body. All at once I loved him more than I'd ever loved him before. I saw his mother—became his mother—carrying him in her womb, carrying him toward his death, a progression of graves, and was overwhelmed by an ancient sorrow that linked me to every woman who'd ever carried a child. I mourned the eventual death of my daughter and, for the first time, understood the wisdom of funeral processions and other rituals that connect us to the grief of others.

Followed by my aunt and brother and father, I entered the front bedroom, where I laid my uncle onto the quilted bedspread. His head lolling to one side, he lay with his eyes closed, breathing noisily, like a runner who'd crossed the finish line. Only there was no victory for him: his final spurt had ended in exposing himself. A witness to his failure, I felt implicated by his powerlessness, his humiliation. Eyes closed, he shut us out with this frail gesture, hiding himself and his spent rage from us.

I WISHED we would leave him alone, but I couldn't bring myself to step away from his bed—and it was like that with the others: my father sat down on the foot end, one hand around my uncle's shin as if trying to anchor him with his own body; Travis held my uncle's wrist in his hand as if taking the pulse; and Aunt Marlene bent over him, stroking his cheek, whispering words of reproach and relief.

As a young man he used to dive headfirst into Fish Lake from the highest cliff in one graceful arc, while she sat on a blanket far below on the sand, taking photos of him that showed him suspended high in the air as if it were his natural habitat. She taught photography part-time at Gonzaga University and took pictures that were different from our family snapshots: they held people's essence beyond the moment when the shutter clicked, and made me see them in ways I hadn't before.

The summer Travis and I stayed on the farm while our parents were in Europe, Uncle Jake took Andy and us to Fish Lake, where he taught us to leap from one of the lower cliffs. The jagged edge of stone beneath my bare feet, I made myself believe that I was Uncle Jake: I stretched up my arms and arched my body the way I'd seen him do it; yet, when I hit the surface of the water, I felt the burn through my swimsuit. Still, I climbed back up, scraping my knees. All that afternoon I kept flopping at odd angles into the water until the cliff didn't feel nearly as high as before, until I could burst the surface of the lake with my fingertips and guide my body through the gap in one sleek line. Each time, Uncle Jake applauded, his eyes the color of the sky. He had the fiercest blue eyes, the kind of eyes in which I'd catch myself: a tiny image that emerged after I stared at him for a while.

But his eyes were closed as he lay on the bed, and all at once I felt bereft of my mother's familiar image, as though my uncle had taken it from me and had given me nothing to replace it with. Nothing. She was sixty-one, only a few years younger than he, and I couldn't imagine the change in her face, her body. My hands felt numb, and that old rage rose hot in my chest.

My aunt spread a blanket across my uncle. "I could serve a snack."

"Really, Aunt Marlene," Travis protested. "We ate dinner just—"

"I'll go crazy if I don't do something." She started for the stairs. "Besides—Jake may want a little something to eat when he wakes up. He's way too thin as it is."

"Let me help, Marlene," my father offered.

"You stay with him, Calven. Please." With her flowing pants that were gathered at her ankles, she looked like an aging dancer.

"I saved Jake's life." My father beamed at me. "I pulled the cord out." His hand, draped by the blanket, was still on Uncle Jake's shin, and only the foot stuck out.

It was a bony foot with dry skin. The toenails were yellow and bent. *Toefangs.* Their tops were jagged and fine cracks ran across, as if someone had scribbled on them with the hair-thin point of a pencil. "You have toefangs, Julia," my father had teased me during my last year of high school, long after I'd stopped letting him trim them for me. He'd been trying to make me laugh, to make me look at him instead of away from him, but I'd walked from the room, my voice raspy with hurt. "I'll take care of them myself."

Suddenly I wanted to trim my uncle's toenails with my father's curved scissors, rub lotion into the callused skin of his soles and the pale, tender recesses between his toes. I wanted my uncle to feel the warmth and safety that I'd taken for granted as a small girl sitting on the kitchen table, wrapped into a thick towel, my feet in my father's hands; but it would be an invasion to trim his toenails without his consent, and it was far too late for that kind of easy comfort.

As I bent across him and kissed his forehead, I remembered how I'd evaded my father's embrace at the airport. And how cold I'd felt. *The unnatural daughter.* No. If it had been Uncle Jake who'd welcomed me there—if he were my father—I would have hugged him, long and hard.

I wished I could soothe him with a good-night story as he had soothed me that autumn night we'd stayed at his house, Travis and I in the blue room with the Jesus picture, my mother in the living room. After an hour in the back seat of a taxi, we'd arrived at the farm, jackets thrown over our pajamas. When my mother tucked me in, she knelt next to my bed and squinted into my face. One side of her face was puffy, and her eyes were mere slits.

"Don't ever get married, Julia," she murmured.

Travis fell asleep quickly, while I lay with my arms under my head, staring at the Jesus picture. The folds in his gown were the same blue as the rug and the quilts of the twin beds.

His eyes, brown and almond-shaped like doe eyes, followed me as I moved my head, as if they were alive. Cautiously, I slid off the mattress and walked over to the window, all the while watching his eyes: they kept following me—to the closet, the door, even through the door when I backed out and bumped into Uncle Jake.

"Sneaking out on us?" He lifted me to where our faces were at the same level and moved his eyebrows up and down. They were wild and darker than the rest of his hair, and I pushed my fingers flat against them to keep them from wiggling. In the living room he tiptoed past the sofa with my sleeping mother, lowered me to the floor, and draped the red and white piano shawl around my shoulders like a robe.

"Exquisite," he said. "Simply exquisite."

The silk fringes tickled my feet.

"Since everyone is already asleep—would you do me the honor of escorting me into the kitchen for something gooey?"

As he spread honey and peanut butter on the flat sides of vanilla cookies, I heard coyotes out back, but their yelps were so far away that they sounded like birds. I glanced at the gun rack which was mounted above the refrigerator, hoping my uncle wouldn't have to shoot the coyotes. He hunted them only when they came after his chickens, and then reluctantly, as if obliged to enforce some kind of justice.

"Double moons," he said and squeezed the sticky sides of the cookies together like sandwiches. "That's what Andy calls them." While we ate them and drank ginger ale, he told me a story about an elf and a pharmacist and a suitcase full of toothbrushes. Outside the window, the mounds of bare wheat fields looked purple under the chalk light of the moon.

"Julia, you look too serious," he said. "This is supposed to be a funny story."

He seemed determined to make me laugh, and he elaborated on his story, made the pharmacist stumble across the elf and orange turtles swing from the lamps until he made himself laugh, and then I, too, had to laugh so hard that my hair got into my mouth. He rinsed a linen napkin under warm water and washed honey tracks from my chin.

In the morning, the Jesus eyes were the first thing I saw, and I stared right back at them, wishing I could stay. But my mother was already folding blankets in the living room, stacking them with the sheets and the pillows on the red wing chair next to the sofa where she had slept. Though she kept her face turned away, I noticed that the skin around her eyes was still swollen, and that her cheek was bruised.

Uncle Jake put Travis' slippers on for him although my brother knew how to do that for himself; Aunt Marlene buttoned my jacket and gave my mother a loaf of pumpkin bread. On the drive home in my uncle's car, Travis and I sat between my mother and Uncle Jake though the whole back seat was empty. It felt so peculiar being out during the day in our pajamas that I was sure we would get a flat tire and that people would stare at us.

The ends of my hair tasted of honey, and I chewed on them, sucking them into my throat. Years later I would remember those sweet strands of hair on my tongue when I'd stand waiting in line at a bank and the man in front of me would scold his small daughter for chewing her hair. "Look at the nice lady behind you," he'd say. "Her hair wouldn't be that lovely if she chewed it off." And as I'd bend to the girl and whisper, "Men don't have any idea how delicious hair can be," I would be right back in that car, my brother jammed beside me, his eyes half closed, his index finger in his mouth, his middle finger up his nose—something I hadn't seen him do in a long time—and he'd refuse to take his fingers out even when he'd catch Uncle Jake looking.

As we headed downhill on Shoshone from Bernard Street, all the lights were on in our house, even in the gables where Travis and I had our bedrooms, as if somehow we were already inside the house instead of walking toward it in our pajamas. Leaves from the maple trees blew across the brick street and flagstone path. Though I wanted to run down the block to Cannon Hill Park and hide beneath the farthest stone bridge, I stayed next to my mother, holding on to her hand.

The instant she inserted her key, my father pulled the door open, still wearing yesterday's rumpled shirt and pants. His face was gray, and a speck of reddish tissue paper stuck next to the cleft in his chin. While I changed my clothes for school, I heard voices from the kitchen below: my uncle's angry, my father's contrite.

That afternoon, when I returned from school, my father was already home, preparing stuffed lamb chops, my mother's favorite dinner. Although she sat with us at the table, she wouldn't eat. She said it hurt her jaw to chew.

"I should have made something soft." My father looked devastated. "It was thoughtless of me to make chops. I should have realized—"

"I'm not hungry anyhow."

"Let me make you an omelet or maybe—"

"Nothing, Calven. Please."

My father asked me about school without looking into my eyes, and after dinner he drove Travis and me to the German bakery on Sprague, where we bought a marzipan cake. Travis ate two pieces and giggled when my father swung him around. But I didn't eat any. What I wanted was to live in the room with the Jesus picture. Forever.

After a few days my father stopped saying "I'm sorry, Lily." Soon the silence between my parents gave way to words, sometimes even laughter. My father came home every evening right from the bank, and we took walks after dinner to get ice cream. We saw a movie, took a drive to the lake cabin. *The four of us.* Together.

AUNT MARLENE set a tray with ham sandwiches, blackberry tarts, and tea on the flat half of the bed. Her back to us, she stepped up to the full-length closet mirror. "Just look at me. I'm a mess." She tucked her silk shirt into her trousers and touched her fingertips to her gray hair which used to hang to her waist in rich, brown strands. But when I saw her reflection, she wasn't watching herself; her eyes were fixed on something far inside the mirror, and her face held such raw fear that I had to look away.

"You look beautiful, Marlene," my father said. "As always."

"You don't have to eat if you don't want to," she said.

"Everything smells delicious." Travis handed my father a plate.

Perched on the bed around my sleeping uncle, whose face fell gray from the sharp edge of his nose, we balanced cups and plates on our knees. Conspirators who had kept him in the life he didn't want, we murmured across him, a web of questions and answers as solid as the blanket that covered him.

"Shouldn't he see a counselor?" Travis asked. "It's too much to handle on his own. For both of you."

"He won't go. I've asked him to, but he said he's seen enough doctors and that there isn't a damn thing—that's what he said—not a damn thing wrong with his mind."

"Would you like me to talk with him?" Travis offered.

My aunt looked small and old as she sat there in a shirt too large for her. "Yes. Thank you, Travis." Her voice sounded tired and grateful, as though she'd become accustomed to letting him help her.

"I'll give his doctor a call," he said. "He needs to know what happened."

"Would they lock him up?" she asked.

"They might want to bring him into the hospital and watch him closely."

"You're sure they wouldn't lock him up? He'd never forgive me."

"It might be a good idea to have him in the hospital," I said. "At least for a few days. Just so he doesn't try this again."

"Julia and I are going to the lake. Tomorrow, right?" My father glanced at me, and when I nodded, he reached for a blackberry tart and dropped some crumbs which Travis promptly picked up from the blanket.

"Andy was home over Christmas." My aunt looked at me and shook her head. "I haven't even welcomed you, Julia."

I came around the bed and embraced her. "I wish this weren't happening to you."

"But it's happening to all of us. . . ."

And as I held her and kissed the top of her hair, I saw my uncle *kneeling next to me in front of the trunk in my room at the cottage—an old man and a grown woman extricating the toys I've never played with as a child—fingering them, one by one, and lining them up in a circle around us on the floor. I'm certain I have to do something with those toys, but I can't figure out what that is, and as I look to my uncle for some kind of answer, I'm kneeling alone in that circle.*

# 9

■

IVE DUCKS BOBBED IN THE SHAL-
low waves in one line, the first one large and black, the others tiny, speckled brown and black. My father and I rummaged through the tin drum next to the outside sink. Inside lay chunks of bread and slices, their sides curled up from the dryness. I pulled half a loaf of French bread from the drum. Pulpy and weightless, it felt like a worm-eaten piece of wood, yet was too hard to break into pieces.

My father held out his hand for the bread. "Why don't you get a pail, Julia?" In his nylon shorts and net tank top he looked deceptively fit, like one of those joggers I'd seen outside his house.

As I headed for the wooden shed behind the cottage, my breasts felt tender, my soles tough. I would let my daughter go barefoot as soon as she learned to walk. Barefoot was better for kids anyhow, Coop's mother, Valentina, had said. She was one of those old, vital women whose bodies remain lithe and strong, whose features take on a translucent beauty. A celebrated pianist, she still gave concert performances though she was in her early eighties. She'd been forty-six when Coop was born.

"I wouldn't have been ready to have him any sooner," she'd told me when I'd worried about being too old to have this child. "Age has always worked for me. I feel better with every year, and I get more invitations to perform now than ever before."

When I opened the door to the shed, ancient smells of damp earth and rotting lumber drifted into the sunlight. Cobwebs brushed against my forehead. The boards below the window in back needed to be replaced; they were spongy, probably the result of a leak. Deflated and cracked, my mother's yellow raft lay in the corner behind the lawn mower. Garden hoses dangled from hooks on the wall; three beach chairs leaned against the side; tools cluttered a rusting metal shelf. I found an empty margarine container with a mess of washers and pushed several into the back pocket of my shorts. Under the wheelbarrow I located a metal pail.

"It'll get soft," my father said when he dropped the bread into the pail. Though his wrists looked delicate, too weak to support his hands, he lifted the pail toward the faucet.

"Let me." As I filled it halfway and sloshed the water around, I wished my father had stayed strong like Valentina. Coop had taken me to one of her concerts in New York. She was astonishing on stage, an incredible presence that challenged all laws of aging and left the audience in a hush when she withdrew her hands from the keyboard.

The day after the concert I'd met most of Coop's relatives at a party given in Valentina's honor. It was held in Brooklyn at the apartment of Valentina's brother, Luigi, a curious old man with noble features. He had a kindness about him that made him seem very much at peace with himself. When Luigi hugged me, it occurred to me that Coop might look like this as an old man.

Within minutes of arriving, I received more kisses and embraces from his family than I'd had from Andreas' relatives during our long visits to Austria. Coop's Aunt Rosina, too short to reach my cheek though I bent, planted a sequence of kisses on my elbow and said something Italian to me, while his Aunt Maria stroked my hair and told Coop he better not let me get away. As they welcomed me, I felt enveloped by their genuine warmth. In comparison my own family felt puny, bloodless.

When it came time for Coop and me to leave after the early dinner—we'd bought theater tickets for that evening— the aunts insisted on sending food with us. Though I tried to tell them we were taking the train straight to the theater, they packed huge servings of Aunt Lucia's eggplant parmesan, a thick wedge of Aunt Bellinda's cheesecake, long strips of Aunt Rosina's lasagna.

It was then that Katie, the latest newcomer to the clan— she'd married one of Coop's cousins five years before—drew me out of the kitchen. "Listen, Julia," she coached me, "you have to take their food. They'll be offended if you don't. Give it to a bag lady on the way to the theater if you have to, but walk out of here with it. And the next time you talk to them, remember to ask for the recipes."

I could tell Katie was enjoying herself, and I laughed with her while the aunts wrapped food, almost making us late for the train. After another round of hugs and kisses, Coop and I got out, lugging plastic shopping bags. In the subway station we searched for a homeless person, and even though we'd encountered quite a few the day before, we now only came across one woman on the train, who stuck her tongue out at Coop—clearly not the right candidate, we agreed, for his aunts' food. The bags on our knees, we sat in the second row of the theater, careful not to shift our weight and distract the audience with the crinkle sounds of plastic, while the aroma of garlic and tomatoes wafted throughout the theater.

A LAWN CHAIR in one hand, the pail in the other, I followed my father down to the lake, where he took off his shoes and gingerly stepped on a flat, wet rock that lay even with the surface of the lake. Rubbing his feet back and forth like a child, he nodded to himself, totally absorbed in what he was doing.

"Listen . . ." He stopped the movement of his feet, and then started again. "Now listen to this one," he said and maneuvered himself on top of another rock, shuffling his feet.

"What are you doing?"

"They sound different. Can you hear how different these rocks sound?"

"I—I guess so."

"You tell Travis. He does not believe me."

"Where do you want your chair?"

"I'll show you."

I followed him onto the dock. In the middle he stopped, put on his sunglasses, and waited for me to unfold his chair. He lowered himself, sighed, and stretched his legs. *"Calven, you have elegant toes. . . ."* They still were elegant. Long and slender, they looked younger than the rest of his body, as if they belonged to someone else.

The planks felt warm against my thighs and shoulders as I lay down in my shorts and tank top, my face toward the sun. Thirty years ago I would have seen all the wind chimes I'd built from chicken bones, twigs, and yarn, swaying in the branches of the trees above me. Now there were only leaves and, high above them, an airplane painting white streamers against the cloudless sky. If I wanted to, I could pretend I was alone. If I wanted to, I could pretend I was five years old. . . . *The bright spot way out there across the bay is the yellow raft. Soon, my mother will pull in next to the dock and shake glistening drops of water from her hair.*

I tried to remember her the last time I'd seen her, beyond the scenes I'd replayed so many times, but the old images felt stuck: *She tries on a floppy hat in front of our hallway mirror, tipping her chin so she can see her profile; she runs next to me with my kite, letting it soar high above us; she sits between Travis and me in Mr. Pascholidis' speedboat, her hair flying around her face, her mouth open with laughter; she peels an orange for me, leaving one ribbon of fragrant peel.*

What had I missed in those scenes? What details, what

clues had I overlooked? I could still see her, sitting on the edge of my bed, her hair pulled back severely, the skin below her eyes blotched. "Regardless what happens," she said, and kissed me, "remember I love you." Did that really happen? Or did I imagine it somewhere along the way? Yet, even if I had made it up—there must have been at least that one moment when she had known she wouldn't see me again, that one moment when she could say a silent good-bye to me.

*She had her good-bye. I did not.*

Sun drenched me as I lay on the dock, and I felt as though I were one of the trouble people, left by my mother on the closed lid of the wooden box, a good-luck charm to solve my own predicaments. But the wax-coated threads on my limbs had melted, fused. Shallow waves tapped a cryptic code against the pillars below me. The leafy smell of the lake swelled beyond the crowns of the trees into the glaring sky, and I wanted to climb back inside the box where it was dark and cool, where the borders were as familiar as the walls of the houses I designed. But I couldn't move, and my mother was no longer there to lift me up and return me to my box. Besides, she hadn't been the one to take me out and close the lid—I had done that myself, invoking the old ritual: *"If you take out one of the trouble people and whisper your problems to it, it will solve them while you sleep. . . ."*

Except this time I had not assigned that power to a trouble doll—I'd claimed it for myself the moment I'd stepped onto that plane to Spokane. The one outside the box certainly had to be the bravest; the others stayed inside. One left the house; the others endured shelter. One paid the price for her courage; the others paid the price for their fears. One looked for power within; the others protected themselves by giving their power away—to trouble people and gods and words.

Carefully I sat up, feeling fragile and new, as if a pod around me had burst wide open, exposing a body I needed to test before putting it to use: I submerged my feet in the water, and they didn't dissolve; I raised my arms in a half-circle, and they didn't fall off. "You left." I whispered my good-bye without moving my lips—so silent even I couldn't hear the words, though I felt them like a hum as they rose from me. "You left for whatever reasons were yours— It had nothing to do with me." And as I took long breaths, filling my lungs and releasing the air gently, I felt tired, alive.

I stood up and steadied myself against the pole on which the ospreys had built their nest that one summer. Stretching my arms above my head, I dived into the lake, which turned out to be far colder than its surface layer. I gasped as I shot up for air, then spun back and swam underwater again. Translucent bubbles disappeared ahead of me into the mysterious twilight, and I felt my unborn daughter swimming with me as I took her into these depths, into the element where she had manifested herself, insisting on planting herself within me—first in my imagination, then in my flesh. I was grateful the trouble people hadn't granted my wish to undo this pregnancy—perhaps they were wiser than I, giving me what I needed instead of what I'd asked for.

As I surfaced in the familiar space between the water and the underside of the dock, stripes of sunlight shivered through the gaps between the boards.

Above me my father's chair shifted. "Julia . . ." His footsteps crossed to the left side of the dock, then to the right. "Julia . . ."

I swam on my back, kicking my legs. My wet hair slicked back, I moved through the water with grace and agility: I did somersaults, handstands, dived to the murky lake bottom and brought up a disk of wood that felt slippery in my hands.

"Julia." My father's voice turned urgent.

I could stay there, silent in the green water glow. Freak him out with my absence as Travis and I had freaked out my grandmother.

His steps wobbled to the front of the dock. "Julia."

It was almost as if I were a child again, hiding from him in my room or behind the bushes of the school. But I was not. I was a pregnant woman, fathoming the waters I'd swum as a girl. I dived around the piles that supported the dock. My legs and arms were solid. My hair formed a cool veil around my head. When I emerged, my father's face drifted above me like an apparition—the sun stood behind him and made the outline of his head fuzzy, incandescent. As my eyes adjusted to the light, the image cleared, and his features shifted into focus. He was kneeling on the edge of the dock.

"I was looking for you, Julia." He held out one hand.

But I reached for the dock and hoisted myself onto the sun-warmed planks.

IN THE PAIL the outer layers of the bread had softened and become slimy. I tore off small chunks and dropped them into the water, where they swirled into cloudy fragments.

"I didn't know where you were," my father said.

"Just swimming."

"I heard a splash and then you were gone."

The orderly file of ducks dissolved as they swarmed around the bread. I tossed them more, watching their beaks open and close, the abrupt motion of their raised necks. A redtail hawk swooped low across the water, and the ducks drifted toward the stand of tall, hollow reeds on the far side of the dock. When I reached into the pail for a piece of bread and flung it toward them, the large duck jabbed at one of the ducklings. I pelted her with a chunk of bread, but another duckling retrieved it, and the duck immediately dashed after it. Yet, it wasn't the bread she wanted—she didn't even take it when the duckling dropped it like a belated peace offering— she just kept jabbing. Hurting. I tore off more bread. Threw it at the duck. But she didn't want it. She wanted to pursue. To maim. Kill, perhaps. As if the bread were only a pretense for getting started with the hurting.

"Look at that." My father's voice was indignant. "That parent duck hurting the little ones."

I swiveled around. Stared at him. It was as though the air had thickened around us and encased us—two figures cast forever in one of those plastic molds that contain an entire landscape and swirl with miniature snowflakes when you overturn it.

"Look at that." A frown on his face, he shook his finger at the duck that kept jabbing at the ducklings.

My throat felt as if it were filled with the slimy bread fragments. I pulled up my knees and tried to disappear into the tight curve of myself, as I had so many times as a girl when I'd sensed the danger of something about to happen. But I couldn't. I couldn't even hurl chunks of bread at the duck to keep her from hurting the young ones. "Why did you—" Words broke loose in a choked voice that didn't sound like mine. "—all those years . . ." I rocked back and forth.

"Sshhh." My father was waving both hands at the big duck. "Sshhh. Stop it. This minute."

"It was wrong."

He nodded. "Especially when there is enough for everyone. Sshhh. Go on now. . . ."

"Not the ducks . . . You—what you did." It was out. It was almost out—dislodging itself from my core like a growth that had become a part of me.

He veered his face toward me. His mouth was slack. His sunglasses had sunk to the tip of his nose.

"Why did you beat me so?" I kept rocking. Rocking.

He shook his head. Pushed his sunglasses back up with the tip of his right index finger. "I never beat you, Julia."

"But Dad—" My voice skipped. "You always beat me . . . terribly."

He looked bewildered. Injured. "When did that happen?" he finally asked.

"Many times."

He closed his eyes. "No," he said. "I never beat you."

*Liar,* I wanted to scream at him, *liar you,* while below us the duck continued to jab at the ducklings. I kicked the water and splashed her until she retreated, but the ducklings—those idiot ducklings—only followed her, and there was nothing I could do to protect them. *Nothing.* I kept kicking the water, getting it over my legs, my hands.

"Isn't it pretty out here, Julia?" My father sighed and gazed across the bay.

I couldn't answer. I simply couldn't. Bread chunks bobbed around the dock in swollen halos like pallid, uncertain vegetations that had risen from the bottom of the lake.

"You should have seen it last fall." His voice was slow. Content. He told me about the changing colors of the leaves, about the first frost, which had spared his geraniums.

I wanted to shake him, make him admit what he had done. My feet churned the water. "I love you, Julia," he used to tell me. It was the worst thing he could say because it made the beatings so much more confusing.

"I love you more than Travis," he had told me one morning in the kitchen when he'd tried to give me a hundred dollars. He'd been sitting at the table, alone, when I'd come downstairs. My jaw ached and, without glancing at him, I walked to the stove, picked up the kettle, and filled it with enough water for a single cup of coffee.

"Good morning." Incredible how much regret he managed to squeeze into those two words.

Furious tears burned behind my eyes. My back to him, I waited at the stove for the water to boil. Fifteen more months—in fifteen months I'd be out of there.

"Would you like a ride to school, Julia?"

School was a place to lie about my bruises: *"It's nothing. . . ." "I just bumped my head. . . ." "Just a bee sting . . ." "Just fell down the stairs . . ."* To tell the truth would have been even more humiliating.

I opened a cabinet and took out a cup. If only he'd go away. But his chair scraped against the floor, and his steps came to a halt next to me. My entire side felt cold.

"Julia?" He opened his wallet.

I turned and stared at him, forcing the knowledge of my injuries into my eyes. It was the one way I knew to take revenge.

He blinked. Looked away. "Why don't you buy yourself something . . ." he mumbled, "something nice," and held out two fifty-dollar bills.

To take them would have been the same as telling him it was all right to beat me. Without speaking, I shook my head as I had all those other times.

He kept the green-and-white bills between us till his hand trembled. "But I love you."

I started for the door so I wouldn't have to listen, but I could still hear him.

"I love you more than Travis."

It was then that I saw my brother in the dining room, and though he bolted up the stairs, his tortured face stayed with me like an apparition.

MY FATHER had fallen asleep in his beach chair, his mouth open, his old-man chin on his chest. White chest hairs nudged through the tiny perforations of the net shirt. *You're a liar.* My father. *Escaping into lies and sleep. I can't let you.* But I didn't wake him up. The ducklings had pulled themselves back into a single file behind the duck as if nothing had happened. Like one unit, they skirted a rotting log that jutted into the water, and steered away from us, leaving a V-shaped track that widened and flattened until the skin of the lake denied any evidence that they'd ever been there.

Shoulders taut, I walked back up to the cottage. For a moment, as I stepped from the sun into the dim living room, I felt dizzy. I sat in front of the fireplace in my damp clothes, prodded at the charred embers with the tongs, and inhaled their cold smell. *If he thinks he can get away with lying to me. . . . The bastard.* I leapt up and started for his room. I didn't know what I was looking for. Some kind of truth, perhaps—I certainly wouldn't get it from him directly.

His bedspread was pulled across the mattress, tidy, and a terry cloth robe lay folded over the back of his chair. A color TV sat on his dresser with the *TV Guide* on top and a framed snapshot of Travis and me as teenagers standing next to a meadow, pointing off toward a distant line of trees. Tourist baiting, my father had called it. It would start with him spotting birds along the road and pointing them out to us. He'd stop the car, reach for his binoculars. Usually other cars would pull over.

It became a game for him. On the way to Coeur d'Alene, the three of us would park next to a deep pasture bordered by forest. While my father would point to an imaginary spot in the trees and pretend to adjust his binoculars, we'd shield our eyes and nod. It was like being on stage with him, and even if I hadn't spoken to him in days, I'd play the part he'd assign to me and improvise from there. Within moments a car would stop behind us, and a family with two or three kids, or an elderly couple would scramble out, gesticulating toward the meadow. Soon over a dozen vehicles, most of them with out-of-state license plates, would be parked along the side of the road while people pointed toward the meadow and took photos.

"What is it?" someone would ask.

"Something big," someone else might say.

"Behind those trees."

"Where?"

My father would glance at us as if to make sure we were enjoying the game and liking him for starting it.

Travis would sometimes turn red and giggle, but I'd catch his arm. "Yeah, behind those trees ... See?" My stomach would hurt from holding in laughter. "A little more to the right."

By the time we'd drive off, the three of us crowded in the front seat even if I'd started the trip with the dog in back, others would still be stopping, trying to photograph what all those tourists were pointing at.

My father would grin at us. "Who knows," he'd say, "they may still scare something out of those woods."

*Tourist baiting.* I'd played the game with Andreas when we were first married, taking bets on how many cars we'd snare. The stakes the two of us agreed on were such that we both benefited: the winner would get one free fuck—meaning anytime, anywhere—as if we weren't already doing that.

I turned away from the framed photo, yanked open the drawers of my father's dresser: towels, underwear, shirts in the top drawers. A mess of papers and folders in the lower drawers: old bank letters, instructions for back exercises, brittle programs of plays he'd acted in, some short letters from me, newspaper clippings of play reviews, a blueprint of the cottage . . . I dug my hands beneath the papers. More of the same. I attacked the other drawer, sifted through the mess of letters and notes, and pulled out a leather album. Though I hadn't seen it since I was a child, I remembered its blue cover. A loose photo fell out—the one Aunt Marlene had taken that day at Fish Lake when Uncle Jake had taught me how to dive: my hands were already submerged, and water drops rushed toward my shoulders, forming a silver funnel through which the rest of my arched body would deliver itself into the lake, as if—suspended like that—I had waited on that square of glossy paper for over three decades.

Pasted inside the album were other photos taken before my mother had vanished, yet none of them included her. They were of Travis or me alone, of one or both of us with my father. Dried patches of glue revealed the gaps where photos had been removed—the ones with my mother, no doubt.

Many of the pictures showed me with my father: offering my father a lick from my ice cream cone, sitting with my father on my uncle's tractor, tossing a beach ball to my father, watching my father make a mess of assembling my bicycle in front of the Christmas tree—

Smiling.

Always smiling.

Such a fake, the album, documenting a happy childhood, omitting the bruises, the fear, the lies to my teachers. I couldn't bring myself to turn the rest of the pages, which would only hold selected incidents of bliss, the flip side of the memories that had stayed with me. That joy I saw there in my child-face—I didn't want to recall it. Even if I had felt it.

I shut the album. Held it in my folded arms against my chest. *I don't have to make myself look at it now.* Yet, I couldn't leave it behind. I closed the drawers, took the album to my room, and hid it in the bottom of my backpack. In the kitchen I filled a glass with ice water and drank deeply, until an ache squirmed into the spot between my eyebrows like a small starfish.

At least I had asked. At least I had come out of that silence.

From the hook by the picture window I took the binoculars and focused them on my father, who still sat in the same spot, head slumped forward, sun pounding the back of his neck and bare arms. I knew I should wake him before he got a sunburn. Travis would—the dutiful son. And my grandmother, if she were still alive, she'd rush out there now to rescue the second Calven from the sun and any other possible dangers. Ten years ago—just a few weeks before she'd died while taking a quiet afternoon nap—she'd visited me in Vermont and told me about following my father whenever he'd climbed out of his window as a teenager.

"Don't tell him, Julia. I never let on I knew he was sneaking out at night. It wouldn't have stopped him—only made him more inventive." Over the years, the freckles on her arms and shoulders had risen into her face, covering first her chin, then her nose and cheeks, until they were level with her eyebrows, leaving her forehead unblemished. "I always could tell when Calven was about to roam, and I kept close by. Just in case he got in trouble."

*Fuck it. Let him get in trouble. Let him blister—the bastard. Let him burn.*

The faucet still dripped, and I turned off the water beneath the sink. I rummaged for a screwdriver and a wrench. Pried off the cover. Whacked the underside of the handle with the end of the screwdriver till it came off. It felt great— hitting something like that. Anything. I dug out the old packing. Jammed in one of the washers I'd found in the shed. There. I slipped the packing nut back on the faucet stem. Tightened it.

In my room I changed into jeans and a T-shirt. The bamboo shades were down, letting in streaks of light that cast horizontal stripes across the walls, the dresser, even the round fishtank. One day, when Travis and I had hitchhiked back from Coeur d'Alene, we'd found both goldfish floating on the surface, bellies up, as though they'd given up on our return. I'd fed them only that morning—it was not as though I'd forgotten about them. I nudged them but they only swayed, particles of food trapped in their diaphanous tails. From the trash I got an empty orange juice can, scooped the limp bodies from the tank, and heaved them into the toilet; but even though I closed the lid before I flushed, I couldn't stop myself from seeing them: *They swirl down the porcelain basin, through the pipes below the cottage, and into the guts of the earth.* Tomorrow—I promised myself—tomorrow I'd buy new fish. But first I'd clean the tank for them. The water was cloudy with miniature turds that formed a scummy residue inside the glass.

Arms crossed, I lay on the bed now and stared at the tank—long since empty—until my eyes stung. With my questions I'd made that first slash into the Sheetrock wall, but behind that wall was such chaos that if I continued to fling the blade, I'd be crushed, washed away. I wanted to run from that pain and hide inside a fantasy—I knew how to do that—but instead I let myself feel it, wrapped my mind around it.

It was a pain that demanded all my senses and—in an odd way—sharpened them. I saw the thread inside the holes on the doorframe where the latch hook used to be, the lean shadow of the raised numerals on my porcelain clock, the hair-thin scratch along the base of the wooden trunk. I knew the smooth grain of the painted windowsill without touching it, traced the path of the wind by its sound as it wound itself through the crowns of the ponderosa pines.

But then I had to close my eyes and wind my mind even closer around the pain, wind it tightly so I'd stay with it instead of flickering into the current of the wind and escape with it. And, in a way, the reality of that pain reassured me of being here, in this room, this moment. It was something I could focus on, something that was mine alone and that nobody could take away from me.

A HAND on my shoulder—

"Julia?" My father stood above my bed. "Julia?" His face and arms were pink.

My body felt swollen, as though I were much further along in my pregnancy. I didn't want him in my room—didn't want to ever see him again. Awkwardly I sat up. The fibers of light between the gaps of the bamboo shades had nearly dissolved. "Would you please stay outside my room?"

"It is time for our lunch, Julia."

"How long did I sleep?"

"A few hours. . . . I made you some Swiss cheese on croissants. You can have some of those little pickles you like too."

I pointed toward the hallway. "Please?"

He took a step back, retreated toward the door.

"We should get ready to go."

"Can we stay until four, Julia?"

I swung my feet out of bed and slowly stood up. "I'm eating dinner with Lynne and her mother."

"We could drive back at three."

"Why don't we see how long it takes us to pack?"

He seemed to be satisfied with my answer and shuffled off. In the bathroom I cupped my hands, filled them with cold water, and lowered my face into them.

When he urged me to take at least one bite, I could barely

swallow. He cut his croissant into thirds and ate the first segment slowly. "Don't forget to pack the Mount St. Helens
ashes." He crunched a sweet pickle between his teeth and
poured dark beer into our glasses. "Look. The light, Julia—
how it shifts. Every time I see it, it's different."

A pattern of sun flared across the bay in one diagonal
swath. Tree shadows painted irregular borders onto the surface.

"I only wish you were not so angry with me, Julia."

"And I wish you wouldn't lie to me."

His eyes were confused. "I have always told you the truth.
Always."

I thought of attacking him with the news of my pregnancy—*he says something about me not being married and the child
growing up without a father, and I finish him off by telling him it
would have been better for me to grow up without a father*—but it
felt like a betrayal of my child to use her against him.

"Did I hit your brother too?"

"No." I closed my hand across the top of my glass and
pressed my palm against its rim. "You never hit him. Not
Travis."

"I have never hit you, Julia. Or anyone."

"My mother . . . you beat her. I saw you."

"I never—"

"Never when you were sober."

"But that is even worse," he shouted. "I never came home
drunk."

"Why don't you ask Travis?"

He chewed evenly, his eyelids half covering his pupils.

"Travis knows. . . . Ask him." Why did I feel like an assailant
when I was telling the truth?

But he was no longer looking at me. With both hands he
lifted an orange from the fruit bowl. Deftly moving his right
thumb below the dark star of the orange, he held it in his left
palm, turning it with the same motion he would use to screw
in a light bulb, while the peel curled away in one ribbon. Sep-

arating the sections, he offered half of them to me, and when I declined, he ate them carefully, dabbing the juice from the corners of his mouth with a cloth napkin.

"I STAYED in the sun too long," he said as we packed up to go. He took off his net shirt and prodded at the tiny pink spots on his chest. "I think we have some of that white lotion . . . the kind that keeps a burn from getting worse." He set out toward the bathroom.

I took a last glance around the cottage. The oil lamps had been extinguished, the counter and table cleared. Through the skylight a smear of sun sagged across the sofa, magnifying the areas where the velvet had worn thin. Although the fireplace was empty, the old smell of ponderosa ashes still lingered.

My fingers touched the old gouges beneath the tabletop—*LI*. I didn't want to go. I couldn't wait to leave. "Good-bye," I whispered to my mother.

"Here it is." My father returned with a plastic bottle, unscrewed the cap, and smeared lotion on his face, his arms, his chest, his thighs. An antiseptic odor drifted through the cottage. He tried to reach his back and glanced toward me as if to appeal for help.

I filled a pitcher with water, opened the latch to the breezeway, and walked outside to water the geraniums. A luminous spiderweb spanned the two logs on which the tin drum with the bread scraps rested. Ribs of light shifted across the surface of the lake, which appeared flat, as if the afternoon sun had grown too weak to penetrate its surface. The ducks were back, a tranquil cluster near the hollow reeds. In the bay floated a canoe with two boys.

As soon as I came back into the cottage, my father complained, "I cannot get this lotion on my back, Julia."

I rolled my shorts and tank top into a tight bundle, fit them into my pack, pretending I hadn't heard him. Then I stuffed in my sandals, my swimsuit, hoping he'd forget about his back. Forgetting seemed to come easy enough to him when it was convenient.

"Julia—could you?" He extended the bottle to me.

*Damn.*

"Please?"

I took the bottle. "You'll have to turn around." I tried to keep a layer of cool lotion between his skin and mine, to not touch him at all as I rubbed the thick liquid into the back of his neck, but the heat of his body sucked it from my fingers until they felt on fire. His skin had no tension to it. My fingertips sank into his flesh as they moved down the pinprick pattern of dots that extended halfway down his back to where the chair had protected him from the sun, and I was afraid for him, afraid of myself and the power of my fingers that could have torn through his skin.

# 10

■

**W**OULD YOU LIKE TO COME in?" my father offered when I dropped him off at the house on Shoshone Street.

I shook my head.

He seemed reluctant to go into the house by himself. "I wonder where Travis is. Usually his truck is here."

I took his canvas bag from the back seat. Handed it to him.

"You were so quiet in the car. . . ." He looked at me as if waiting for an explanation and then offered one himself. "Maybe you are tired. Well—" As he smiled at me, his head went into a steady nodding motion that made me stiffen my neck to keep from joining in. "Did you have a nice stay at the cottage, Julia?"

What could I do? There was no use—no use at all. "It is a beautiful spot." My voice sounded scratchy.

"I had a grand time. Except for what you said. . . ." He kept nodding. "About drinking and about hitting. That is not true."

My throat felt hot. "Why don't you ask Travis?"

The wall held until I reached my hotel. Heart pounding, I

managed to park my rental car, grab my backpack, take the elevator to the seventh floor of the Ridpath. I got myself into my room and threw myself on the bed, beating my fists against the mattress.

"You liar. You fucking bastard . . ." Tears forced themselves from me, opening my body. "You can't just deny everything. It happened— You liar . . ."

And all at once I knew what I had wanted from him—to have him say he was sorry. It was that simple. But I hadn't understood it. Not until now when I knew it wouldn't happen.

"Bastard. Liar . . ."

I didn't want to be trapped inside this rage that terrified me, swallowed me as though it had been waiting for me all those years. What if it never went away? My chest hurt from screaming. If only my fists could crash into his lying face instead of into the mattress. I should have never come back. In Vermont I'd been doing all right. I certainly hadn't hurt like this. I felt like a child again, deep inside that old torment and stuck with it—no, worse even, because now I knew that much of what I'd lost had been good.

The phone rang and kept ringing with the kind of noise that, once I noticed it, I knew had been there for a while. "Liar you . . ." I shrieked over its persistent shrilling till the sounds fused.

I couldn't possibly stay another day. As I tried to imagine myself—*packing, leaving a note for Travis, taking the next plane home to Vermont*—the fantasy wouldn't roll. I nudged the reel into spinning by remembering the texture of the airplane seat, but I was stuck. In this skin This room. This city. Myth-making—my old way of bolting from pain—was no longer working for me. In my family we all had become salt dancers, inventing our different escapes from pain: I'd soared from it with wings of imagination that removed me as effectively as my mother's physical flight; my father still eluded it with drink; while my brother cocooned himself by pretending it didn't exist. And the more afraid we were to crawl into the core of our pain as if it were a hurricane and wait there, alone, until we were ready to pass through, the more formidable our retreats had to become. Since I found myself incapable of fabricating new myths, better myths, I opted for my mother's way out: I grabbed my hotel key, crammed my wallet into the back pocket of my jeans, and fled.

THE WOMAN with the green eyelids and spiked hair sang to herself as she trimmed half an inch from the ends of my hair. I was grateful she didn't talk—I wouldn't have known what to answer. I had no idea how long I'd walked or why I'd stumbled into this long room which was lined with mirrors, only that it felt soothing to lean back against a molded basin and let this woman rinse out my hair as though everything else could be flushed out with it.

Eight customers sat in swivel chairs, one row on either side of the aisle, where a stocky teenage boy swept up nests of hair as they drifted to the glossy linoleum. Though I was used to cutting my own hair and hadn't been inside a beauty shop since the day of my wedding to Andreas, the smell was still familiar. Five hours before the ceremony I'd arrived for my appointment—plenty of time, I'd figured, to get back home and dressed—but my hair had stayed damp. Sitting beneath the hot, helmet-shaped drying contraption, I'd waited over three hours before my hair had dried enough to be arranged in stiff curls, and then I'd had to rush home, the scent of the beauty shop on my neck and scalp, and struggle into the satin gown that would turn me into a bride.

As the beautician with the green eyelids blow-dried my hair, she rotated the chair until my back faced the mirror. Across the aisle another beautician held a dryer to a woman's hair, the length and color of mine, and all at once it was as though I became that woman over there, with warm air blowing against *her* scalp, and I let *her* body sink into the chair, into an absence of passions where everything was warm and dark and without shape, where *she* would never have to take care of *herself* again if only *she* stayed in that chair, inside that void. . . .

But when the hairdresser across the room shut off her dryer and laid it on the shelf in front of the mirror, I still heard the buzz and felt the heated air—against *my* neck. Dazed, I searched for my reflection in the mirror across the aisle, and when I found it, it was attached to the competent hands of the beautician who raised strands of my hair toward the mouth of her dryer as if feeding it, and I couldn't imagine ever breaking that link with her and doing anything on my own without her.

IN MY ROOM the phone rang as if it hadn't stopped at all.

"Julia? I'm downstairs, in the coffee shop."

"Lynne?" My voice wavered.

"Are you okay?" She waited. "Julia?"

"I'm okay." I started to cry.

"I'll be right up."

"Don't—"

But she'd already hung up. The bed looked as if someone had torn it apart. I didn't have time to splash water into my eyes or pull the blankets back into place, because she knocked at the door and took one look at me and wrapped her arms around me. Her embrace only brought on a new heave of tears, and I cried into the shoulder pads of her blue shirt.

"Come here." She led me to the bed, and we sat on the tangled covers.

I found a Kleenex and blew my nose. The vile smell of my father's lotion still clung to my hands. "That liar. That son-of-a-bitch fuck-faced liar . . . You saw me, Lynne. How often did you see me, all beaten up?"

"Lots of times." She nodded and stroked my face. "Too many times."

"And he has the nerve to act as if it never happened. As if he forgot . . ."

"I'm sorry it happened like that."

"I didn't know how to bring it up with him. . . . I was afraid I couldn't. And then, this morning, we sat on his dock, feeding the ducks. . . ." I told her about the ducks, about my father's indignation. "You remember—all those nights I came to your house. . . ."

"I remember, Julia."

"Having to go to school like that . . ."

"I remember."

"And he has the nerve—" I was howling. "—the fucking nerve to pretend it never happened."

The shoulder of Lynne's blouse was soaked with my tears. "You haven't been around old people much. . . . Some of them have a way of pushing away things they don't want to remember."

"But he was there. I was there. It happened."

She rocked me. "It happened. But you've been away for over twenty years. While he kept drinking. That alone can wipe out all kinds of brain cells."

"That's no excuse."

"Of course it isn't."

"I don't know what to do, Lynne."

"Those photos in his living room you told me about . . . that's what he sees every day. That's what he believes in—the safe world he's created for you."

My head felt weightless, empty, as if everything were pouring out with the tears.

"What he did was terrible, Julia." She handed me a fresh Kleenex. "But I'm not surprised he doesn't remember."

"That's even worse. Worse than lying. Because I've had to remember it—all those years. He can't simply forget it, get away like that. . . . I want him to remember. You know, first, when I left for college, I tried not to think of him at all. Sometimes I made it a month without thinking of him. Sometimes I wished him dead. Maybe then I'd stop remembering."

"There's something real sad about him. When I see him downtown in a store with Travis, or at a restaurant, he's always so glad to talk to me about you. He'll ask if I heard from you lately, how you're doing. . . ."

"I felt sorry for him too, my first day back when I watched him with Travis, who treats him like a little kid. Part of me wanted to defend him."

Lynne brushed some damp strands of hair from my temples.

"I feel like getting on the next plane home." I sat up and blew my nose.

"You know—I like you, even if you got snot all over my blouse."

I grinned and that started another rush of tears.

"Hey—you needed to talk to him, and you did. That's what matters."

"But we barely got started. And it didn't make any difference. If only he'd said 'I'm sorry.' Something . . ."

"Maybe he isn't capable of that."

"I told him to ask Travis what happened—I better call him before my father talks to him."

"What if your father answers?"

"Travis told me he hates phones." I dialed. "Damn. I wonder where Travis is."

"You think he'll back you up if your father asks him?"

"I'm not sure. You know, when we were kids, he never acknowledged that my father drank too much. He was so goddamn loyal. . . . Blind." I glanced at the horse clock above the dresser. "Your mom's dinner—I should have been ready half an hour ago."

"She'll understand if we get together another time."

"No. I'm all right—I think. Give me ten minutes to shower and throw something else on. . . . You want to borrow a dry blouse?"

"Why?"

"Because I got snot on yours."

"It enriches the texture."

"Some people are sick. I mean, this preoccupation with snot and its effect on the texture of . . . what is this stuff? Rayon?"

"Go take your shower, Julia. I'm not taking you along looking like that." She grinned at me, but her eyes were solemn. "You'll get through this," she promised.

LATER TRAVIS would tell me he'd been at a friend's house, playing poker. When he got home a quarter before midnight, my father met him in the hallway. His voice high and urgent, he asked, "Did I beat Julia?" And I would imagine my brother's hesitation, *that moment when he can still maintain that my father has always been the father of the merry-go-round rides and the ice cream, the father from the photo album.*

"Did I?" my father insisted. "Julia said I did."

What had it cost my brother to answer, "Yes. Yes, you did, Dad"?

"Then you are a liar too. In cahoots with Julia."

"No one's in cahoots with anyone."

"Then why am I the only one who does not know about this?"

"Dad—"

"No." Tears came from my father's eyes. "I have never hit her. Or you. If that is what you think of me . . . I do not want to live anymore."

"Dad—"

"I am going to kill myself. But not like Jake . . . I will not botch it up like Jake."

"There's no reason to—"

"But first I am going to watch the *Tonight* show."

After that, Travis would tell me, he wasn't too worried. Yet, he stayed up with my father. *A bottle of Chablis next to him, my father sits in front of his large screen in his Spanish leather chair, drinking wine and laughing at the TV jokes as though he'd forgotten his suicide plans.*

"I wish you had watched the show last night, Travis. They had this fellow on—a magician."

"How was your trip to the lake?"

Without raising his eyes from the screen, my father answered, "Nice. Real nice."

"What did you do?"

"I broiled the salmon. And I made my fried potatoes."

*A few times my father dozes off, but as soon as his body twitches, he jerks himself upright, afraid to miss anything. Eventually Travis manages to get him away from the TV. When he steadies my father on the way to the bathroom, he smells the wine and mouthwash on his breath, and when he bends to take off my father's shoes, he feels furious with me.*

"How are you doing?" Travis asked when he pulled the blanket to my father's shoulders.

"Tired. And sunburned. . . . Julia liked it at the lake."

While Travis covered my father with a blanket, while my father's voice drifted off, and while Travis stood in the open door of the bedroom, wondering if he should spend the night in the chair next to my father's bed, I was still sitting in Mrs. Clark's living room, drinking the spiced tea she'd made after dinner.

"You could have had Julia as a daughter-in-law," Lynne told her mother. "She had a monumental crush on Scott."

"Our Scott?"

"That was a secret, Lynne. Besides—it was a short-lived, chaste crush."

"I'll be damned." In her black silk tunic and skirt, Lynne's mother still looked like a model though her hair had turned white. She wore it in a pale Afro. "Even I didn't spot that. And I'm usually good at that kind of thing. Right, Lynne?"

"Too good." They smiled at each other.

"But then it was just a chaste crush."

"Of course."

My cheeks hurt from trying to smile with them. I saw the large duck jabbing one of the ducklings, heard my father's indignant voice: *"I never beat you, Julia,"* and I wanted to tell Lynne's mother. But I couldn't walk into her house after all those years with yet another crisis.

"I should try to call my brother again," I said.

As I dialed, Mrs. Clark said, "Did Lynne mention that Scott is married for the second time?"

"She probably didn't want to break my heart." I waited for my brother to pick up the phone. No answer. *My father sits in front of the TV, waiting for the ringing to stop.*

"Now I liked the first wife better," Mrs. Clark said when I hung up. "She had spunk. Like you, Julia."

"Watch it," Lynne warned me. "Sounds like my mother is recruiting her third daughter-in-law."

Just then Sonja arrived, a linen jacket thrown across one shoulder. As she kissed Lynne on the cheek, her hair—long and blonde and streaked like Lynne's—swung forward, and it occurred to me that the two of them could have passed for sisters. She embraced Lynne's mother, shook my hand.

"I really admired your father, Julia." She sat down on the red sofa where I'd slept many nights. "When I was in grade school, I used to pester my parents to take me to plays, and he was in a lot of the Ensemble performances. By the time I started acting with them, your father had left . . . but people there still think a lot of him."

I thought of my father on stage in a full-sleeved white shirt and black trousers, the light on his blond hair, the spell of his voice carrying beyond me, beyond the theater, and I felt a surprising stirring of the old child-pride. But then I remembered him the day I'd left for college, when he'd insisted on driving me to the airport though I'd wanted to take a cab.

"You're doing what I did at your age," he'd said as we stood in the hallway with my packed suitcases. "Crossing the country—only you're going east while I went west. Opposite directions . . ."

I didn't answer. The evening before, when I'd sorted through my old clothes in the attic, I'd come across two bottles I'd hidden there long ago, and I'd thrown them into the trash, along with everything that no longer mattered.

"Remember, Julia, you can always come back here."

I shook my head, certain I would never see him again.

"Wait." He dashed into his bedroom, and emerged with a flat package in his hands. "A good-bye present."

"Thank you." Reluctantly, I took off the blue ribbon. As I unwrapped the glossy paper, I stared at a silver frame with a smiling eight-by-ten publicity shot of my father's face, the face I'd been waiting to get away from all those years. Despite the actor's smile, the expression had something unsettling about it—a mixture of sorrow and confusion.

I laid the picture facedown on top of the shelves next to the door. My father turned. Grabbed two of my suitcases. I followed him with my backpack and the other suitcase. Silently we stashed everything in the trunk of his car. Hands shaking, he backed out of the driveway, his face drawn, gray, and for a moment I felt sorry for him. I saw the despair in his eyes, saw a man who was passionate and frustrated, loving and possessive, an afraid-of-losing man with the best intentions, who'd spun out of control because he could no longer protect his family from the disintegration he had caused.

He drove too fast. Almost missed a red light at the corner of Third. He jabbed the brake pedal. Jerked the car to a stop. "You want to know what I had in back of the photo? Do you?" he shouted, his voice clogged, unsteady. "Ten one-hundred-dollar bills."

"Then I'm even more glad that I didn't take it."

He looked old and he looked hurt. But I had nothing left to say to him. As the light changed to green, he sat slumped, hands on the steering wheel till someone behind us blew a horn.

"HE CAME BACK about five years ago," Sonja was telling me, "just for one season to teach a drama workshop. I had a chance to study with him. He was wonderful—imaginative and perceptive—but his health wasn't that great."

Lynne glanced at me. "Same old thing."

I'd only been drunk once in my life. With Lynne. On her fifteenth birthday, when we'd snitched a bottle of rum from Scott's room. It was sweet and forbidden, and we drank it quickly. At first everything was hilarious. She walked me home, and then I walked her home, and then she walked me home. We tried stepping on every crack in the sidewalk, stumbled across some of them. "Who was the guy?" my father asked when he found me puking in the bathroom. "Who was the guy?" One arm around my back, he propped me up on the way back to my room, made me lie down. My bed kept spinning. Whenever I made a mad dash for the toilet, he was right beside me, holding my forehead, wiping the vomit off my face with a damp cloth, leading me back to my room. He said I'd feel better if I kept my feet uncovered and the light on. And I did.

"He didn't return the following season," Sonja said. "I wish he had." She got up and pulled an envelope from her leather bag. "I picked up our photos."

"Great." Lynne spread them out on the coffee table. "They're from a hike we took on the Olympic Peninsula," she told me. "We camped on Shi Shi Beach."

I bent over the photos of incredible rock formations, of a dome tent against a long stretch of beach, of orange and purple starfish, of tide pools and flats of rippled sand at low tide.

"It's an hour's hike along a forest trail," Sonja said, "and then the beach is three miles long."

"We found starfish stranded in the sand," Lynne said, "and took turns throwing them into the water."

"I want to go back." Sonja sighed.

"Now this is the woman who refused to go camping." Lynne laid one arm around Sonja's shoulders and shook her gently. "Whose idea of roughing it means a hotel without room service."

"So I'm a convert, huh?"

"Wally Steiner was the one who told me about the beach," Lynne said to me. "Did you know he has four kids, Julia?"

"Who is he?"

"Are you kidding?" Lynne turned to Sonja. "Julia and I climbed on the roof of his house to look into his room."

Sonja smiled. "And why would *you* want to go chasing after a boy?"

"Because Julia had a crush on him and talked me into coming along. She can be very persistent."

"What is this about me and crushes today?" I protested.

"He didn't look like a Wally," Lynne said.

"And what's a Wally supposed to look like?" Sonja asked.

"Oh . . . sort of nerdish, you know. With plastic protectors for his pens. But Julia's Wally—"

"My Wally?"

"—was a jock. Hunky shoulders, juicy thighs . . . on the tennis team."

"He's a district attorney now," Lynne's mother said. "His parents still live across the street from us. Even I remember you climbing on the roof. . . . Not that I saw you—I would have wrung your necks—but Lynne confessed a week later. She said the two of you almost fell off."

Through the window I could make out the shape of a house across the street in the dark, and all at once I knew it was built of brick with a steep clay-roof section below the dormers. I felt the dusty, hot tiles against my palms, felt the sudden dread shoot through my body as my feet slipped for an instant. *How much else have I forgotten?* Wally's window was open, and his rumpled bed stood right below the window. Plastic leis were draped around his tennis trophies.

"It was the summer I became boy-crazy," I said.

"And crazy it was," Lynne said. "You'd give me endless reports of how a boy had looked at you, what the look meant, and we'd plot for you to sit next to him in the cafeteria, with you so wound up that you couldn't eat your food."

"It was the year you started wearing those unsuitable

shoes," Lynne's mother reminded me. She reached across the table and took my face between her hands. It was so tender a gesture that I had to close my eyes.

*How much else have I forgotten?*

IT WASN'T until eight in the morning that I finally reached Travis, but before he informed me of my father's suicide threat, he asked, "Are you all right?" and listened to me tell him what had happened at the lake.

I was so relieved that he didn't sound angry with me. "I did try to call you," I said after he'd told me about coming home from his poker game and finding my father waiting for him. "I tried. Several times."

"He seemed all right when he got up this morning. Why don't you come over tonight?"

"I don't want to see him."

"We should talk."

"Can't we meet someplace else?"

"After last night I really don't want to leave him alone so soon." He thought for a moment. "Tell you what—you can come into the backyard when it's dark. I'll meet you there."

"That feels weird. Besides, he may come out and see me."

"Not once the TV is on."

I couldn't leave my brother to settle the turmoil I'd started. "All right then. I'll be there," I agreed, feeling as though I were playing a part in a low-budget spy movie.

When I arrived, he was stacking old tires against one side of the wooden fence and barely acknowledged me. Through the open window of the living room came the sounds of the television; its flicker ricocheted off our shadows.

"I'm sorry you got dragged into this, Travis. I didn't mean for it to spill over on you."

"Really now?" He rolled two more tires over to the fence.

"I tried to reach you last night. Several times. Warn you—"

"Was it worth it?"

"I don't know. Some of the pressure is gone, but—"

"I mean, was it worth it for *all* of us?"

"I'm sorry." I started toward the side door in the fence.

He followed me. Caught me with one arm around my shoulders. "I think it's a rotten thing that he has forgotten. Still—you should have talked with me first."

"You would have tried to stop me."

"I could have prepared myself."

"It had to be between him and me."

"But it's not. Is it?"

"I never thought he'd deny it, and when he did, you were the only person who could back me up. It's not that I'm trying to force you into choosing sides."

"It only feels that way."

"I can see where it would."

He dropped his arm from my shoulders. Strode around as if searching for another tire. Behind a rusting kitchen stove he found one, rolled it toward me, and swung it on top of the stack.

"I didn't mean to pull you in, Travis. But when he denied—"

"I don't think he's denying anything. He doesn't remember."

"He has to."

"I wish the two of you could have talked. I do. Still—" He squatted and tore out the high weeds that grew against the fence, weeds that hadn't been pulled out for years. "I hate the mess it's causing."

"Travis—I am grateful you told him the truth."

"I wonder if it's done any good though. He's not going to change."

"Last night I lay awake for a long time, asking myself the same thing—if it's done any good. . . ."

"You and your questions, Julia." He suddenly laughed. "You've always asked too many questions."

I was startled by his sudden shift of mood but tried to go with it. "I get that way," I said. "When I can't figure out the answers by myself."

"Even when you get answers, you always keep asking for more."

"Like what?"

"Oh—" He stood up, stretched himself. "I can think of at least a thousand examples. . . . Like that mean old woman next door, asking her how old she was."

"Only because she kept changing the numbers."

"So let's say she deserved those questions—"

"—which probably led to her demise and the haunting of the house?"

"Probably. But how about that handyman Dad used to hire? Short guy. Cowboy boots with two-inch heels."

"Mr. Turgent, but you kept calling him Mr. Detergent."

"Did I? Makes sense though—a handyman named Mr. Detergent. Anyhow, what you asked him the day he was rewiring that brass lamp Dad had found in Italy . . . you asked him if he wished he were taller."

"And he answered me, Travis," I said softly. "Don't you see? He answered me."

But my brother didn't hear me. He was walking away from me toward the house, dodging the mounds of clutter, while I stayed behind, clasping both arms across my belly.

# 11

 E HAS BEEN ASKING FOR
you." Aunt Marlene reached for my hands. "When are you flying back to Vermont?"

"I still have another week."

"It's just that he isn't very strong right now. But he needs to talk to you. I thought it would be good to give you a call." Her eyes looked tired, and the skin around them was dark. "They only kept him in the hospital for three days."

Uncle Jake sat by the open French doors in the living room, pillows between him and the wooden armrests of the rocking chair to hold him up and keep him from bruising himself. The maroon bathrobe made his parched skin look even paler. His eyes were uncertain, and for an instant I wished he'd been successful ending it in that last blaze of strength.

"Uncle Jake?" I laid my hands on his shoulders. His bones felt fragile, new. His smooth skull was shaped delicately. As he tilted his face and I kissed his cheek, I smelled soap and medicine. "How are you feeling?"

"Fine. Really." His voice was weak, monotonous. He raised

one hand. "Oh, what the hell— No. I'm feeling useless. Embarrassed . . . Some homecoming for you, Julia."

"You've always made this a home for me. I've missed you."

His blue eyes looked at me for a long time as if to test the truth of my words. Finally he nodded, more to himself, it seemed, than to me. A weak smile freed itself from his sunken features. "You've missed me," he said. "Despite the foolish actions of an old man . . ."

I blinked at the sudden stinging behind my eyes. And I already missed him beyond that moment, in the years to come when he would no longer be there.

"Sit down," Aunt Marlene said. "Have you had dinner?"

I nodded.

"Let me get you something to drink then. What would you like? I have coffee, tea, wine—"

Though I didn't want anything, I knew she'd offer me every item in her cupboard if I didn't settle for something soon. "Tea would be good."

"I'll make a pot," she said. "Jake, you'll want some too, right?"

He nodded and, as she turned to leave, winked at me. I sat in the red wing chair I'd claimed that summer I'd stayed with them. Legs drawn up, I would read until dusk would blur the outlines of the lush planters on the patio and the contours of the amber fields that curved along the horizon. I'd image an ocean beyond them, shifting under the moon. Here, my mother had waited for the Gypsies. The faded silk shawl still draped the piano, and I wished I could wrap it around myself the way my uncle had that one night, wished I could find my mother's glittering stones and keep death away from this house, wished I could sleep in her cave on the side of the mountain, wished I could tell my uncle about my father's refusal to admit what had happened. But how could I encumber him with my pain now that he was weak, when I hadn't come to him in those years my father had beaten me? He would have helped, but I'd been too ashamed to tell him.

My aunt returned and set a china cup against my uncle's lips; one hand supporting the back of his neck, she let him take shallow sips.

"It's getting dark in here," he said.

She switched on the rattan floor lamp. "Is this better?"

He touched her hand to thank her and turned his face toward the French doors that led to the patio. The stone planters were empty except for a few spindly remains of last summer's flowers, and a dry wind whipped through the room without cooling the air.

"Would you like to talk to Julia now?" She glanced toward me and whispered, "Remember. He tires quickly."

"She needs to know. . . ." Before my uncle could say another word, I knew it was about my mother. I knew it by the way his jaw set itself; by the way his eyes took on that old, fierce look; by the way his voice tried to invent a sense of resolution and firmness—and strangely, all at once, I wanted to stall him. Whatever he was about to tell me couldn't possibly fit the movies I'd played inside my head.

"Some people, Julia . . ." The words came from him slowly. ". . . have the kind of devotion that's difficult to bear. Your father, he adored Lily so—so totally that—" His breath was a fast pulse in his chest, moving his robe in and out.

*Stop,* I wanted to say, *you don't have to—not if it costs you that much.* But then I saw my parents dancing, looking into each other's eyes as if they were alone. I felt their arms around me as they lifted me into their dance at my aunt and uncle's second wedding, smelled the scent of my mother's hair. . . . *What have I missed? Misread? Or was it really splendid like that for a long time?*

"Lily . . . what she told us was that his love surrounded her. She tried to match it with hers, but the harder she tried, the more she felt herself lacking."

"Your mother never doubted her love for you, Julia." My aunt sat down on the arm of my chair and stroked my back. "For you and Travis."

"And your father knew," my uncle said. "It's like . . . like he kept measuring her feelings against his, seeing them diminish."

"The drinking," I said, "when he started again—"

"Lily wondered about that too." My uncle nodded. "I don't know how much it had to do with all that. All I could see was that the drinking made him close even more around her, smothering her. . . ."

*"Say you love me!"* I shut my eyes for a moment. *"Children are supposed to love their parents,"* he'd told me more than once, looking at me with such despair in his eyes that I'd felt something had to be wrong with me. Was that how it had been for my mother? All at once I was seized by an odd sense of loss at having missed out on growing up with the good father from the old photos; but it was more than loss—that feeling which settled itself in my limbs like cooling metal—it was also the fear of something I hadn't thought of in many years and didn't want to remember, something that pushed itself up inside me, confronting me with the proof of my own flawed love. I felt the Kitchendog's soft fur against my arm as he lay on my bed in the cottage, his back pressed warm against me while I read my brother's new comic book. Gently, I petted the dog's neck without waking him. In his sleep, he made small yelping sounds, and from time to time his legs twitched as though he were chasing squirrels in his dream.

But as soon as he heard my father's steps on the path approaching the cottage, his ears perked up and he leapt from my bed. Lynne's ritual of feeding him my spit obviously hadn't worked. I caught him at my door, and what happened was not something I'd planned, but rather seized me in that moment of orange-red rage when I wanted him to love me best—*only me only me me*—while he squirmed away from me, scratching at the door, tail wagging in anticipation of seeing my father. That's when I gripped his leather collar, opened the door and—as he darted forward—banged the door with deathly precision, banged it hard against his head, four times, finally trapping him between the door and the frame. His body was shaking, and so was mine when I dragged him into my arms.

"Julia?" My uncle's voice—gentle and insistent.

*"Say you love me!"* I shivered.

"Are you okay, Julia?" My aunt shook my arm.

"I want to know. About her."

"That Greek fellow . . ." my uncle said, "the one with the restaurant—"

"Mr. Pascholidis?"

"It wasn't that Lily left your father for him. . . . I'm not saying she chose the best way to go about that, Julia, but she would have stayed if your father had let her. It was the baby—"

*The baby*— For an instant I felt stunned. How could my uncle know about my baby?

"That's what he couldn't accept. That she was pregnant with the Greek fellow's baby."

*My mother in a yellow dress . . . In her bare, brown arms she holds a black-haired infant who has the Greek's laughing eyes. She looks at me evenly, then bends over the baby, smiling.*

"But I asked you." My heart was pounding. "All those times I asked you if you'd heard from her, and you said no."

My aunt rubbed the shallow spot between my shoulder blades. "What Jake said was that he would tell you if he could. He couldn't, Julia. He wanted to, but your mother said it would be worse for you to know. She—"

"I promised her, Julia. I didn't agree with her . . . but she's my sister. I urged her to fight it out in court with him, but she was too afraid of what it would do to you and Travis."

"It couldn't have been worse than leaving us behind."

My uncle watched me silently. His eyelids had sunk halfway as if he were too drained to keep them up; his breath had returned to a slower rate.

Aunt Marlene glanced at him as if waiting for him to continue, then turned to me. "Your father gave Lily a choice—a nasty divorce or to leave without a word to you. The courts, he told her, would never give her custody of you and Travis. He made her believe that she'd lose you anyhow, that it would be easier for you to deal with her disappearance than with knowing she was a slut—those were his words. . . . He made her feel so dirty about the pregnancy, Julia. Even when Jake and I tried to reason with him, he called her that—a slut."

"What happened to the baby?" I pressed one hand against my waist. She must have felt it too, my mother, that extra weight in her body, in her spirit.

"You tell her, Marlene." My uncle's voice was tired, so tired.

"She went with the Greek to his country. . . ."

*They're on a plane—no, on a passenger ship—my mother and Mr. Pascholidis, standing on the deck. They hold hands but don't look at one another: he watches the backwash that spurts from the white hull of the ship while my mother's eyes are turned toward the continent they've left. Her free hand pressed against her swelling waist, she stands in the wind as if to remind herself of the reason she had to leave.*

". . . a girl. Maria. They lived there for five years, till the Greek died. The first year we didn't hear from her at all." As my aunt leaned toward me, her heavy braid fell across her chest. "Later she told us it had been too painful for her to contact us, that she dialed your number many times but hung up before anyone could answer. . . ."

*My mother enters a red phone booth in an open market square, surrounded by stands of fruits and vegetables. Scents of flowers and garlic fuse in the hot air.* With an ancient hunger, I filled in the blanks of my inner movie, greedily, rapidly. *My mother takes a dangling gold earring from her left ear and dials a long sequence of digits. The last seven make up our old number in Spokane. She clutches the receiver against her ear—*

"I could always tell it was Lily," my aunt said, "even before she spoke. That connection from Greece had a sound to it— remember, Jake?"

"Like water rushing almost," I said, "but softer." I remembered the phone ringing, holding the receiver against my ear, trying to listen beyond the water sound and closing my eyes so nothing would get in the way. "Hello," I'd say. "Hello?" But all I'd hear through the line would be the distant current of a brook.

"She'd always ask about you and your brother, Julia. So many questions . . . Remember all those photos I took of you and Travis?"

"For her?"

"For her."

"So she had photos of us . . . knew what was happening to us, while we—" My head felt light, too light to balance on my body. "Is she—" My throat closed. *In airports, on fairgrounds, in movie theaters. Dreams of finding her. Running to catch up with her. Out of breath when I finally call out her name . . .*

The iron taste of blood in my mouth. "Is she alive?"

"In Oregon," Aunt Marlene said.

I was taken by a joy so sudden I forgot to breathe, a joy that filled my limbs, rash and hot. I wanted to go to her. See her. Now. This instant. I leapt up from the wing chair. Paced between the French doors and my aunt. Stopped to face my uncle, my hands small fists against my breasts. "Where in Oregon? What is she doing there?"

"She teaches elementary school in Lincoln City and has a house on the beach north of there . . . a small town called Neskowin."

I walked back to the French doors and stood in the half-light of nightfall. Above the arched roof of the old barn, the turret split the sky. *My mother strolls along the crest of the dune-shaped hills. Some of the fields of wheat are still green and unyielding, but most of them are golden and succumb to the currents of the breeze. I can't see her features—she's still too far away—only the banner of her dark hair, but I recognize her movements, graceful and fluid, as she leans into the wind. But then she turns around and moves away from me as all those other times—*

"Why now?" I spun around to challenge my uncle. "Why is it all right to tell me now?"

My uncle's eyelids were long and patterned with tiny veins. He looked amused. Amused and exhausted and not at all afraid of my anger. "Because it doesn't seem terribly important to keep it a secret any longer."

My aunt straightened her back. "It's an old secret, Julia, too old to guard against you."

"And Travis?"

"He never asked us," my uncle said. "We didn't feel him pushing at us to know, but you— Even your letters, the ones where you *didn't* mention Lily, they pushed at us. . . ."

"Your father never asked us either," Aunt Marlene said. "At first when she left we didn't want to see him, but that would have meant staying away from you and Travis too. Eventually, we came to accept him again—don't ask me how. . . . It was almost like he went a little crazy around the time all of that happened. It helped us to think of how good he was with you. Like when he taught you to swim—you were little still, four at most. He'd stay next to you in that raft—"

"No, that was my mother." All at once I was four again and swimming toward shore next to my mother's yellow raft. *Morning light turns the water luminous green, and my arms forge a trail of lustrous bubbles that surge against my face and tickle. I laugh. Swim as fast as I can. My mother's reflection lies on the water like a life preserver. I can swim through that ring, around the ring*—but then I peered at the features in the water, the reflection within the shape of the ring, and it was not my mother's face I saw looking at me from the raft, not her hands that pulled the oars through the water, but my father's hands, my father's face, my father's voice telling me I was his brave swimmer—

I wanted to shut off that image and get back to the one where I saw my mother's face within the ring, but I willed myself to look, and what I saw was the father who had taken me out in this raft many times, the father who had taught me to swim.

It had happened.

Just as the beatings had happened.

I saw him in the cottage only a few days ago, frying potatoes, humming . . . humming that tune I didn't remember
then but now recognized as the old Norwegian ballad he
used to sing to me when he tucked me in. *Tucked me in.* Not
the drunk father who stumbled into my room late at night
and shined the light into my eyes, but the other father, the father from *before* everything changed, the father who sat on
the edge of my bed and sang to me. . . . A rapid sequence of
other images with him at the center—they clicked faster than
I could absorb them. I felt dizzy. Leaned against the wall.
When they finally slowed down, I saw his old-man hands peeling that orange at the cottage, his thumb below the star of the
orange, but then his hands changed, became young, smooth,
and smiled as he showed me how to peel an orange without breaking the peel; one long ribbon of fragrant peel cas-
caded from his hands as he turned the orange. . . . *Not her
hands. His. All along.* And I'd even taught Andreas to peel an
orange like this: *"My mother showed me. . . ."*

"Are you sure he was the one who taught me to swim?" I
had to ask though I already knew.

"He started you slowly," my aunt said. "Just around the
dock. He'd get right in the water with you. Once he fastened
a rope to the straps of your swimsuit—remember that, Jake?"

My uncle smiled. "We took turns standing on the dock,
holding that rope like a fishing line while you swam. You
could never get enough of the water."

"Even when your lips got blue," my aunt said, "you'd still
want to keep going. After he bought the raft, he took you out
into the bay and let you swim back while he stayed next to
you."

"He was so patient with you," my uncle said.

"All this time . . . I thought my mother was the one." *What
else have I turned around in my memories? Where else have I substi-
tuted her?* I was overcome with a sudden longing for this father my uncle and aunt had summoned, a longing that was
forceful and confusing.

"About once a year," my uncle said, "we drive to the coast

for a few days and stay with Lily. She's only been back here twice . . . when I wasn't doing so well last spring, and then a few weeks before you came here. Now that Maria is grown, she lives alone."

"Maria—" The name felt foreign on my tongue. My mother's other daughter. The daughter she had *not* left behind. The daughter who was ten years younger than I. "Does Maria live close to her?"

"She went to law school in Houston and works there now," my aunt said.

"I have so many questions. . . ."

"I wish we could have told you when you first asked."

"Does she know I'm here? That you're telling me?"

"No," my uncle said, his voice suddenly firm again. "I don't have a hell of a lot of time left, and I don't want to spend it fighting Lily on this. She is a powerful woman, your mother. . . . A lot like you." He pulled at his eyebrows. "We listened to her once, and I don't think it was the best decision."

My aunt reached into the pocket of her flowing pants and handed me an index card. *Lily Ives, 17 Pershing Lane, Neskowin, Oregon.* A phone number with a 503 prefix. It was almost too easy. For a moment I wished I didn't know. Then I wouldn't have to do anything.

*I still don't have to—*

But then that in itself would become my choice.

I traced my aunt's blue ink handwriting on the card. "I always thought if I found out where she was, I'd drop everything . . . go and see her immediately. Part of me still wants to. But also—I don't know. It was her choice not to see us. She may not want to hear from me."

I wished they'd contradict me, but they sat in silence. It felt as if, by passing the secret on to me, they had freed themselves from its encumbrance, and it was all mine now—not entirely the joyful discovery I'd imagined so often, but a risk: the risk of having my mother turn from me once more; the risk of finding a stranger who couldn't possibly match more than thirty years of fantasies and distorted memories.

"Neskowin is a nine-hour drive from here," my uncle said. His arms rested on the pillows that held his body safe within the chair.

"Eight with the new speed limits . . ." Aunt Marlene smiled. "We didn't want to wait till your last day here before we told you. In case you'd want to see her."

"Whatever you do—" Uncle Jake said, "give us enough time to call her . . . to tell her that you know."

When I got ready to leave, he insisted on standing up. Aunt Marlene and I helped him from the chair, and he hugged me with surprising force, his thin arms like steel bands around me, his fists digging into my back. We held one another for a long time, and when we let go, we both tightened our arms once more in an embrace. I promised to visit him again before I returned to Vermont. As we stepped back, our hands still on each other's arms, his eyes were lucid; in their fierce blue I reached for my image, but instead I saw the child-me who used to emerge in his eyes long ago, as if she'd stayed there, with him, a long-limbed child with a mouth too wide, and it felt as if he were releasing her to me.

ON THE DRIVE back to Spokane, I pictured myself calling Travis. It was almost physical, that longing to hear my brother's voice and take both of us back to that time when our family had still been whole. As soon as I closed the door of my hotel room, I reached for the phone, but it rang under my hand, vibrated, and I picked it up, half expecting to hear my brother.

But it was a woman's voice, faint, hesitant. "Is this—Julia?"

"Yes."

"This is your— This is . . . Lily."

I sat down on my bed. Tried to say something—what, I didn't know—but couldn't bring anything out. Finally I managed to say, "Yes. This is Julia."

"Marlene called me. I—I'm not sure . . ."

I cleared my throat.

"This is hard."

I nodded and then realized she couldn't see me. "For both of us," I said.

"Is it all right that I'm calling you? Would you rather if . . ."

I felt her waiting as if already preparing to leave me again, become elusive, hang up as she had all those times she'd called from Greece without identifying herself. Only this time she would disappear for good. "No," I said quickly. "I want to talk with you. It's just that . . . I feel sort of numb right now."

"If you want to see me it's up to you and if you don't want to I'll understand that too." She rushed the words together as if she'd rehearsed them and was afraid to stop.

"What about you?"

She didn't answer.

"What do you want?"

"This is so sudden."

"I think I want to see you, but . . ."

"I am sorry." Her words sounded insufficient.

I closed my eyes. *Mother, I wish you had fought for me, that you had taken me into your shame with you. It could not have been as bad as leaving me behind.*

"Have you told your brother?"

"I was just about to call him."

"It's the same for Travis. If he wants to . . ." I heard the pain in her voice. "If you had any idea how— All those years."

There was something so unreal about speaking with her that I felt overwhelmed by a deep tiredness which took hold of my limbs, my heart. I could barely hold the receiver in my hand.

"Julia?"

I wanted to crawl into bed, pull the blanket to my shoulders, sleep. . . . "I'll talk with Travis. Would you like me to call you in the morning?"

"I'll wait for your call. And—" Her voice trembled. "Julia?"

"Yes?"

She was silent. Finally she whispered, "It wouldn't be appropriate to say. Besides—you'd probably find it difficult to believe."

I pulled my legs up on the bed. Rested my forehead on my knees. *Is she trying to tell me she missed me?* I wasn't ready to hear this from her—not after she'd left me behind. "I'll talk with Travis . . . and call you."

"Till then," she said and hung up before I could say anything else.

I felt exhausted—too exhausted to call my brother. In a minute, I told myself as I lay down on the bed in my clothes. *In a minute.* Twice I woke up and reminded myself to call Travis, but before I could rouse myself, I drifted back into a dense sleep that left my body sweaty and aching when I woke up at dawn, crying from that familiar dream of running down a long corridor after the tall figure whose face was blank. I lay there, trying to will my mother's features into that blank oval, and when I couldn't even recall what she looked like, I turned on the light, took her photo from my wallet, and ran my fingertips across its creased surface as if to memorize her through touch.

I WAITED until seven before I called Travis, and we arranged to meet for breakfast at Lindaman's, just a few blocks from our old house. I arrived first, got a cup of coffee for Travis, a cup of tea for myself, and claimed a table next to the brick wall that displayed eight exquisite sketches, charcoal nudes on parchment. Through the window I saw Travis walking down the hill and crossing Grand Boulevard.

"Have you been waiting long?" He slid into the molded chair across from me.

"I know where she is," I blurted. I'd meant to prepare him—not to come out with it like that.

He stared at me, his eyes dark surfaces in his pale face. "Who?" he finally asked, though I could tell he knew.

"Lily—" I laughed, a forced laugh. "Now I'm calling her that. Our mother. She's in Oregon."

A moment of unbearable yearning passed across his features, then vanished. "How did you find out?"

"She called. Late last night. She wants to see us . . . if we want to."

"That's—great." He stirred his coffee. "Just great." His spoon kept clicking against the inside of the cup. "So she called you. Just like that. Tracked you down. The right hotel and everything."

"Aunt Marlene told her."

"And did the two of you have a nice chat?"

"Travis—"

"Listen . . ." He pushed his cup away. "I can't stay long. I have to get to that church to pick up the damn dishwasher. It's not worth it, bickering with that minister. He's been at me every day, threatening. . . ."

I caught him by the wrist. "Please? Let's just talk."

He jerked his arm away. "I've lived here all my life, and you come back for two weeks. Two lousy weeks. Sure enough, it's you she calls. Always you. Not just for him . . ."

"What do you mean?"

"He even told you."

"Told me what?"

"This is too embarrassing. Childish." He tried to laugh. "All right. I'll say it— That he loved you more." *My brother's ashen face in the hallway, my father's voice: "I love you more than Travis."*

"But I didn't want it."

"He was always trying to please you—Julia this, Julia that— cooking your favorite meals, giving you presents."

"I didn't want it. Any of it. The beatings *and* the presents. Maybe if you'd had the guts to stand up to him . . ."

My brother raised his chin as if to ward off a blow. His eyes were angry slits.

"You always took his side. The wrong side, Travis."

He studied me, sadly. "There was no wrong side, Julia." And then he laughed, and kept laughing while people at other tables stared at him. Most of them wore suits—power suits, Coop called them—and seemed on their way to air-conditioned offices. Travis pushed up the sleeves of his flannel shirt. "There was no right side either. It was a fuckup, a total fuckup, whatever way I looked at it. But somehow you managed to get yourself out of it. Away from here. Somehow—" He finally stopped that awful laugh. "Somehow I'm the one who got himself elected to take care of him, listen to him brag about you, admire photos of you. . . . Some trophy I got myself, eh?"

"I didn't tell you to live with him. You—you like fussing over him."

"Someone had to look after him."

"He can take care of himself. You should have seen him at the lake."

"Ah yes, your wonderful stay at the lake. When you brought him back, he was ready to kill himself."

"You know he didn't mean it. You said so yourself."

"That was a dirty shot. I'm sorry."

"Has he talked about it again?"

"No, just that one time. I'm sure he's forgotten."

"He was a lot more independent at the lake though."

"Then why don't you take him back to Vermont with you?"

"Why are we doing this, Travis?"

"I could stand on my head . . . but you'll always be his favorite."

"No." The skin on my face felt stretched. "I don't want it, Travis. Any of it."

"Seems to me like you're stuck with it."

"Do you have any idea how humiliating it was?"

He looked stricken.

"It would have been even more humiliating to take his presents, eat his meals. . . . Travis—I couldn't. I simply couldn't."

"He barely noticed me." Travis rubbed his index finger

across his wristwatch. "And now . . . even she—she calls you."

"Because I've been asking questions. Uncle Jake—"

"Don't you think I wanted to know too?"

"Did you ask?"

"I couldn't."

"I told you as soon as I knew. . . . Travis, he kicked her out, Travis."

My brother's head jerked up.

"She was pregnant."

He stared at me.

"Remember Mr. Pascholidis who had that restaurant on the other side of the lake? She went to Greece with him when Dad told her he'd fight her for custody . . . that she was a slut, that he'd tell us she was a slut and—"

"It's a marina now."

"What?"

"The Greek restaurant. Someone bought it ages ago and turned it into a marina."

*Has he heard anything I've said to him?* "She has another daughter, Travis."

"I rented a sailboat from the marina once. . . ." He was gazing past my left shoulder. "They have a floating snack bar at the end of the pier. You can get pop and beer there, corn dogs. . . . Dad really likes those corn dogs."

"Travis?"

He blinked like a man who'd just entered a brightly lit room. "Where in Oregon?"

"Neskowin. On the coast. Come with me, Travis."

"I can't."

"Please? We could leave tomorrow morning. Today if you like. Or the day after tomorrow."

"It's you she called."

"She asked about you."

"Big fucking deal."

"I promised her I'd talk with you."

"You've kept your promise—you've talked with me. All right? If she wishes to see me, let her come here."

"You want me to tell her that?"

"She's the one who went away. At the very least she ought to visit her brother before he dies."

"She's been there."

"Lately?"

I nodded.

"Good for her. And for Uncle Jake. And for you. I guess she has her priorities."

"Christ, Travis, I'm scared. I don't want to go alone. I have no idea what she's like. All those years . . . I've wanted to find her, but now that she's waiting for me—"

"It's not working, Julia."

"What?"

"I won't let you con me into coming along because you're afraid."

"That's not what I'm doing."

"I have to go." He stood up.

"Travis—"

"If you want to talk more, come over for dinner tonight. We'll get some Chinese food."

I hesitated.

"You've avoided him ever since you came back from the lake. Eventually you'll have to see him. And if you take off for Oregon tomorrow, there won't be that much time left."

"All right," I said. "I'll pick up the food on the way. You still like pork fried rice?"

He nodded and started for the door.

"Wait." From my pocket I took the index card with my aunt's handwriting. As I copied my mother's address and phone number on a paper napkin, the letters ran out and swelled as if they'd been held under water. "Here." I stood up, slipped the folded napkin into the pocket of his shirt. "You may want to have this."

"We'll see you tonight."

"Travis—when I learned how to swim. . . . who took the raft out and stayed next to me?"

"Dad. He taught both of us like that. Why?"

I didn't want to think of the father who'd taught me to swim, who'd peeled oranges for me. To remember him was more threatening than memories of the bad father. I knew what to do with those memories—they were familiar and kept me from feeling his loss.

I had grieved the loss of my mother.

And I was afraid to dive into the grief for my father.

The grief for myself.

I wanted to tell Travis, but there wasn't enough time—not when he was hurrying away from me.

# 12

HE WINDSHIELD WIPERS PAINTED
a relentless fan pattern against the glass. I'd been in the car
for almost five hours, on my way to a mother who had become
less real for me ever since I'd found out that she existed. But
as long as I was in the car, moving, as long as I didn't get
there, I could still try to envision her any way I wanted to.
When I'd set out early in the morning, I'd felt excited, impatient, but soon after I crossed into Oregon, I thought of turning back.

*"If you want to see me it's up to you and if you don't want to I'll
understand that too."*

I pulled over and stopped. Tumbleweeds, soggy with rain,
lingered on the edge of the highway instead of spinning in
lacy patterns across it. To my right, the Columbia Gorge
dropped steeply and ascended on the other side of the river
in sand-colored layers that trembled as the rain coated my
windows. The air in the car felt cold, damp. I tried to evoke
the ghost mother of the faded movies, but she wouldn't come
to me: the frayed celluloid had finally snapped, and the reel
spun madly without revealing her. All I sensed was her pres-

ence behind the voice on the phone, shapeless and constant, not the luminous image of my fantasies.

"You and Travis are welcome to stay at my house," she'd said when I'd called her yesterday after meeting Travis for breakfast.

"It looks like I'm coming alone."

"I see. . . . Let me give you directions then."

This was happening too fast for me. "Would it bother you if I stayed at a hotel?"

"There's an inn just a ten-minute walk from my house." She sounded relieved. "The Blue Heron. I could reserve a room for you."

"Thank you. Yes." So formal. So polite. So frightened.

"If you like, we can meet in the dining room."

Rain seeped down the car windows, enveloped me in a safe, gray atmosphere, rendered me invisible. Ironically, I'd found my mother, had come across her when I'd least expected it—after I'd said my good-bye. But she was no longer twenty-nine, and I was older than the image I had carried of her. *I might not recognize her. And she has no way of knowing me.* The longing that had kept me fused to her had dissolved, and I felt separate. Terrified.

As I thought of her waiting in Neskowin, perhaps even more terrified than I, perhaps regretting her invitation, I pictured myself taking a U-turn, driving back: *I cross the Columbia at Umatilla, take Route 395 through the semidesert past leaf-green signs that list the names of parched, yellow towns—Connell, Lind, Ritzville. . . . At the Formica counter of a roadside cafe I order a bowl of thick soup, warm my hands along its sides, eat careful spoonfuls that dislodge the chill from my stomach.*

But as my eyes probed the space beyond the rain, I saw the Rousseau painting of the lion and the sleeping Gypsy woman. If the lion nudged her, hard, the Gypsy might roll away from him and down the slope of that barren terrain—to disappear forever—but then again she might awaken, sit up, and reach for that mandolin under the blue-ringed moon of the desert landscape.

Carefully, I turned the key in the ignition. The windshield wipers exposed a spread of lush trees and meadows, so different from the countryside of the painting, and I eased the car forward into the stretch of glistening road.

IT HAD FELT awkward being around my father yesterday. My knowledge of Lily's whereabouts lay between us like something concrete, and I felt as though I were the one keeping things from him. It was absurd—after all, he was the one who'd bullied her into leaving, who'd encumbered my brother and me with the mystery of her disappearance.

He opened the door before I could ring the bell, as if he'd been standing there, waiting for me to arrive. "Look," he said, and thrust a blue flashlight at me. "Look what Travis bought me for the cottage."

He seemed delighted to see me, while my body felt stiff as soon as I got near him. It was hot in the house, hot and stuffy and not quite clean. His face and hands still looked red from our stay at the lake, and the skin on his nose had begun to peel in dry flakes. For him, nothing seemed to have changed between us. *I never beat you, Julia.* Was he acting? Pretending? Or had he really forgotten?

Throughout the meal—egg rolls and moo goo gai pan and pork fried rice I'd picked up two blocks from my hotel—his eyes, the faded yellow eyes of an aged cat, kept darting between Travis and me. The two of them had spent all afternoon at an estate sale—my father in a black suit as if attending a funeral, Travis in his usual attire—and had returned with a couple of dented trunks, a wooden icebox with black moisture rings, and six boxes full of knickknacks, musty books, and rusting ice skates, all still in the living room with the other junk.

"You should have let me buy that clock," my father complained. The collar of his white shirt looked stiff and new, while his hair was damp with perspiration.

"It was overpriced," Travis said.

"I would have paid for it. I pay for everything else." He

turned to me, his voice agitated. "The neighbors, they give Travis hell for that mess out there. I bet your house does not look like that."

"The next sale should take a lot of the stuff out," Travis said. "You know that."

"I bet Julia earns ten times as much as you. In a real job." He smiled at me as if expecting his show of approval would enlist me in whatever plot he was working on. "Would you like to see a movie tomorrow, Julia?"

"I'm going away for a few days."

"But I want to—" He stopped, a vacant expression on his face. His right hand found the stem of his wineglass; he blinked and brought the glass to his lips.

What if I told him, *I'm visiting my mother?* Would he react with a sudden expression of guilt like those villains in old Perry Mason movies, who always confess at the last moment in court as Perry moves closer for the final interrogation?

"Take this," he said, as if he'd just discovered what he'd misplaced and gave me his gold fountain pen. "I want you to make a list, Julia."

"A list?"

"I want you to write down everything you want to inherit from me."

Travis set down his fork. His wide hands lay flat on the table.

"I can't do that," I said.

"Paper. Of course, we need some paper for that." My father looked around as if waiting for some stagehand to appear with paper. Even now he had to be theatrical. "Did you bring some paper, Julia?"

"I don't want to do this. It feels strange."

A shiny coating of sweat stood on his upper lip. "Because you live so far away. The list. And because you never visit."

"I really don't want anything."

"Nothing?" His shoulders sagged.

"Some kind of peace . . . I guess that's what I hoped to find with you when I came back here."

He looked startled. His hands fluttered up as if to wipe away a confusing image. "And . . . did you find that, Julia?"

I stared at him. The back of my shirt felt soggy. I slung the question back at him. "What do you think?"

"Yes." He looked as though he were trying to tear through some dimness of his own. "Yes . . . I think you found that."

The air shifted, pressed itself closer around us. My usual way of confronting was never going to resolve anything with my father. I could either hang on to this forever or find some way to let go of it.

"There's one thing I'd like to take with me if you don't mind." I felt my brother waiting, watching. "A photo album I found— I mean, it was at the cottage."

My father's voice was quick and hopeful. "We can drive to the lake and get it for you."

"It's already at my hotel."

"Oh." He looked from the pen to my face and then back to the pen, this old man with the delicate wrists—my poor little father, as he used to call himself—trying to mask his disappointment that we wouldn't make a trip to cottage, but it showed in the line of his jaw, in the carefully hooded eyes. "You are welcome to keep the album, Julia. Of course you are."

"Thank you."

"A movie," he said, as if he'd just discovered what he'd misplaced. "I want to take you to a movie, Julia. . . . Travis can come too."

"I won't be here."

His face took on a discouraged expression, and it was as though I saw two men at once—the one in the raft who'd taught me to swim, who'd remained next to me and called me his brave swimmer, and this old man with the bone-white hair who ate cautiously, who kept touching his napkin, whose wineglass was already empty. *What if he really can't remember the beatings? But I want him to remember. To feel the torment of those memories.* Yet how could I expect him to remember anything when I couldn't trust *my* memories?

"Where are you going, Julia?"

"The coast."

"An old friend," Travis said with a warning glance at me. "Julia is visiting an old friend on the coast for a few days. Isn't that right?"

I wanted to blurt out the truth, wanted to accuse my father of driving my mother from us.

"An old friend from college," Travis added.

If I didn't stop him, he'd pretty soon make up a name for this old college friend, give her children, a job, a husband . . . like those stories we'd made up that summer at the lake, inciting and outdoing one another with details.

I looked straight at Travis. "A dear old friend. Marie-Louise Bencham. She works for a hypnotist in Seattle. Travis knows all about her."

Travis giggled. He actually giggled. Then his face smoothed over and his eyes locked with mine. "That's right. A real gutsy woman. Make sure you tell Marie-Louise how much I admire her for having that baby . . . at her age."

I stared at him. How dare he play my secret like that?

But he only raised his eyebrows as if astonished I'd missed my turn. "Without a husband too. But then she's always been very . . . self-reliant, wouldn't you say so, Julia?"

"More than you could possibly know."

"Remember, Dad, we met her a couple of years ago when she came through Spokane and looked us up?"

My father blinked, then nodded hesitantly.

"Blond hair." I leapt back into the story. "Gorgeous blond hair. Down to her waist."

"Down to her tailbone, actually. She lost most of it though." Travis clicked his tongue. "A boating accident."

"It got wound around the motor blades."

He rolled his eyes as if to say, *some lame attempt,* but he picked right up. "Her fiancé had to cut off her hair to save her life, and it never quite grew back again. Good old Marie-Louise Benchman."

"Bencham."

"Right." He busied himself tucking a napkin between the top two buttons of my father's shirt. "Dad—why don't you move a little closer to the table."

"It was all rather tragic," I said.

"Extremely tragic. And devastating," Travis said, and for a moment that old childhood radiance was back in his face.

When he walked me to my rental car after dinner, I said, "Some storyteller you are."

"We've done better."

"I was ready to kick you under the table."

"I didn't break any confidences."

I laughed. "Just made me squirm a little, right?"

"I wish you lived here. Without all the old . . . mess. Just live here. Make up bizarre stories the way we used to. Be twins again."

"Twins." I slid into the car and rolled down the window. "Come to Oregon with me, Travis."

"I hope it goes well for you." He reached into the car and messed up my hair. "I honestly do."

"I'm scared shitless."

"So? When has that ever stopped you?"

THE SUN was out when I arrived at the Blue Heron with two hours to myself before Lily would meet me. I thought of walking to her house, appearing on her doorstep and startling her with my presence—a pregnant foundling—but instead I took off my sandals and set them beneath the brass bed, toes pointing out. Someone had laid a fire in the brick fireplace. After I stripped off my clothes, I sat cross-legged in front of the flames that flickered rapid shadows across my belly and breasts as if to cast mirror images of the child curled within me. I felt her sweet, languid heaviness in my flesh as though every cell in my body were slowly stretching itself to adapt to her growth.

I stared into the blaze until my skin began to glow, and all at once I wished I could cup my hands around Coop's flamingo mug of hot chocolate, say his name aloud between sips, and believe that the potency of the hot, sweet drink would surpass that of the prescribed water, and that the old test of romance from 1802 would last. *Forever kind of stuff* . . . I shook my head.

Only ten days ago—the evening before I'd left for Spokane—Coop had cooked spaghetti for us at his cabin. The only light had come from six mismatched candles stuck to saucers in the middle of the table. He'd washed his hair before I'd arrived, and it was still damp on top, but the ends had sprung into reddish golden curls.

"I'm scared, Coop. I'm so fucking scared."

He came around the table, knelt next to my chair, and rocked me in his arms, listening without interrupting me as I flew at him with my doubts.

"What do I know about bringing up a child? I'm not willing to stay home. Aside from that, I can't afford to stay home. What if I feel stuck always having to consider someone else . . . ?"

My eyes closed, the side of my face pressed against his chest, I went on, "My father's brother died as an infant because he caught his head between the slats of his crib."

"They build cribs differently now. All kinds of safety standards."

"What if she is in my way?"

"I'll bring her to my place then."

"It wouldn't be fair to her."

"And why not?"

I raised my head. "You may not even be there when you tell her you will."

"I'll work on it."

"You even forgot the ultrasound."

"I told you how bad I felt about that. . . . You'll be good with the kid. I know you will."

"Sometimes I know it too. But other times . . . What if I just got trapped by Claudia's biological urge?"

"By what?"

"I may have made a terrible mistake, Coop. I don't even know what to do with a child. I mean, I know more things that I *won't* do—like leave her or hit her. I know I won't touch her or kiss her while she's asleep. I'd never want her to look at me with the disgust I felt whenever my father did that."

"Come here, you." Coop stood up, drew me from my chair, and held me an arm's span away from him, his hands steady on my shoulders. "Look at me," he said. In the dim light, his eyes appeared slanted, secretive. "You'll figure it out," he said slowly. "Once she's here. You'll surprise yourself with how much you already know—deep in your gut. Besides, she'll learn from you—just by the way you are."

I took a deep breath.

"She'll learn to go after what she wants," he said, "even if others discourage her."

"And she'll get clobbered in the process."

"Sometimes. Sure."

"I'll be too old. By the time she graduates from high school, I'll be sixty."

"You'll be sixty anyhow. Think of my mother."

I thought of his mother. And then I thought of Coop's other relatives—that wonderful clan—who'd surely welcome my daughter with the same warmth they'd welcomed me.

"Listen," Coop said, "here's something you can do for this child of ours. . . . Teach her how to fret. You're good at that."

I had to laugh. "If only that were enough. Don't you ever get scared about having her?"

"Remember now, my dear," he said in a Bogart voice. "Men can always bail out."

My shoulders went stiff under his hands. "That's not funny."

"No, it's not. But it's what you expect from me—that I won't be there for you. Or her."

"You haven't done anything to assure me otherwise."

"And I won't knock myself out trying to. You'll have to

come to that on your own." He pulled me close and held me. "I'm here right now."

WHILE THE claw-foot tub filled with steaming water, rapid gray clouds obscured the sun and pinched the light from my room. From the tub, I could see the beach: an endless succession of ashen waves whirled from the mist like dervishes and leveled themselves on the sand as if looping back into the ocean below the ground through some mysterious passage. As the chant of the sea mingled with the sound of my bathwater, I felt lulled as though the only things that mattered were that chant and the cycle of the waves.

After I'd finished soaking in my bath, I tried on every item of clothing I'd brought. Nothing looked right. How could anything possibly match my mother's memories of me? I finally ended up in the baggy cotton slacks and purple shirt I'd worn on my drive here. It was six o'clock when I brushed my teeth—seventeen strokes—and took the stairs down to the dining room.

Everything in the room was mauve: the tablecloths and curtains, the fanned cloth napkins, even the stems of the wineglasses. The only other guests were two women—both of them too short to pass for my mother—finishing their dinner at a table by the wall. They looked like sisters with their careful curls and round faces. If they lived in Neskowin, they possibly knew my mother. I walked past them to a table by the window and ordered a glass of orange juice from a stocky waiter, who wore a calligraphic name tag, *Allen,* on his mauve shirt.

Twenty past six an elderly couple arrived in wet raincoats. The woman was far too old to be my mother. I straightened the ragged edge of a fingernail with my teeth and wished Travis were with me. Perhaps Lily had changed her mind. After calling me to drive for nine hours, she had fled the state, the continent. Surely I would be able to feel it if she were nearby.

But then she was the kind of woman who inspired waiting. She'd never been one to arrive on time, especially when she used to leave Travis and me with babysitters. Sometimes, if my father got home from the bank before she was back, he'd decide to surprise her by taking all of us out to dinner. He'd dress Travis and me up and, if it was warm outside, sit with us on the front steps, waiting for my mother in a crisp white shirt and dark suit, reading a magazine while we'd leaf through picture books. He'd glance at our pages each time we'd point something out to him, but all along he'd be scanning the street as if rehearsing with us for all those days he and my mother would pull us into that awful wait for each other—she silent at the dinner table, afraid he'd stopped once again at a bar instead of coming home; he anxious for her to return from those afternoons that made her look beautiful.

Once or twice he'd step to the curb and search both ends of the street as if to postpone the moment when it would become evident that she was late. "Something must have come up," he'd say as he'd walk with us to the store on Monroe Street to get some kind of treat for us—ice cream bars or lollipops—that always left my stomach hurting. But if my mother came home while we waited, we'd run to the curb and stand aside while she'd park the car and emerge with packages or, perhaps, a new hairstyle which, soon, she'd change back to the way that suited her best: straight and parted on the side with one wave across her forehead. It would feel like a celebration—*the four of us* dressed up for our reunion.

THE RAIN had stopped, but the air was still silvery and heavy when a black Jeep parked next to the entrance. The dome light flickered on, but not long enough for me to see the driver. When a woman in a fisherman's sweater and jeans got out of the car, I tried to find reasons why she couldn't be my mother: this woman did not move with the grace I remembered; this woman had limbs that had thickened; this woman had gray hair and looked like someone's grandmother. *My daughter's grandmother.*

I shrank back from the window. To get to my room or the bathroom, I would have had to cross the lobby. I thought of pretending I was someone else, but as I stared toward the arched door of the dining room, waiting for her to transform herself into that eternal Gypsy, she stood already there, shielding her eyes as if blinded.

*What if she expects me to take care of her from now on?*

I felt ashamed. Stunned by this thought I hadn't expected. And yet I saw *a wheelchair, legs too frail to support her, fingers that tremble as she tries to bring a spoon to her mouth—* Absurd. The woman who was coming toward me seemed rugged and competent, as if she'd always looked after herself. I set down my juice glass. Stood up as if pulled by a string.

She stopped at my table, looked at my face and then out of the window as if to make sure her car was still there. *The getaway car.* As I stretched out one hand, she grasped it with both of hers: they were the size of mine, but coarse, as though she were used to hauling nets or stacking crates, and her fingernails were clipped like those of a man; between her right middle and index fingers, the skin was stained yellow brown.

"Would you like a drink? Something to eat? If you want—" I pulled my hand free. "I'm rattling."

"Why don't we both sit down?" She smiled, edgily, and let herself down. Her gray hair was too short to swing around her face the way it used to, and it gave her entire body a solidity that simply didn't fit her.

Silently, we sat across from one another. From time to time we scrutinized each other, then looked away like twelve-year-olds on a first date arranged by their parents. Her cheeks were broad and tanned, the kind of tan that deepens with age and comes from being in the wind all year. Her eyes were taking me in, hungrily almost, absorbing each detail about me, and I wondered if, like Travis, she could tell I was pregnant.

I picked up my fork. Turned it in my hands. "Did—"

"How—"

We both laughed—abrupt, uneasy laughs.

"One at a time." She took out a pack of Camels.

"You first."

"Did you have a good trip?"

"Long but good, yes." My voice was hoarse. *By now Travis regrets that he hasn't come along. He wonders what she looks like, what we're talking about.*

"I'm sorry I'm late."

"It's all right," I lied.

She gave no further explanation.

I tried to think of something to say. "It looked like the sun made it out for a while at least this afternoon."

"That's the coast for you, always changing—sun to rain to sun—often within minutes."

I couldn't believe it: we were talking about the weather; I was sitting here with my mother and we were talking about the weather.

"So different from Spokane," she was saying. "Once you get weather there, it stays. For weeks . . . Do you mind if I smoke?"

"Go ahead."

"You don't—"

"I quit. A couple of years ago."

"A filthy habit." She inhaled deeply. "I like it. How did you stop?"

"Well . . . I promised myself if I still wanted to smoke at age seventy, I'd let myself."

"That's amazing. It would never occur to me to plan that far in advance."

Again, we sat in silence, a silence I wanted to plug with words because I sensed her slipping away again, becoming remote. *"Pleasant dreams,"* she used to tell me when she tucked me in at night, and if she forgot, I'd call her back from the door. *"You didn't say 'Pleasant dreams.'"* But I could no longer coach her in what to say.

I turned my head in a sudden panic. "The waiter, I wonder where the waiter is." If I could order something for her, weigh her down with food, keep her here . . .

We got through several minutes by flagging down Allen with the mauve shirt and ordering a glass of Burgundy for Lily, another glass of juice for me. Travis had been right: I should have stayed in Spokane with him and let her come there if she cared to see us. My mouth went dry with anger. She had been thirty-five minutes late, and she hadn't even asked about Travis.

As if she'd read my thoughts, she asked, "Travis—he couldn't come?"

For a moment I considered making up an excuse for him, but if we were to talk, it had to be without evasion. "I think he'd want to see you if you came to Spokane."

She looked out the window and, after a while, back at me. "I want to hear about you, Julia. About your life. Your work . . ."

"The abridged version?"

Her gaze was level. "Whatever version you choose to tell me."

"I didn't mean to jump at you."

"It's all right."

"I'm behaving like a brat."

"Maybe you need some food."

"Maybe." I had to smile. "Aunt Marlene's remedy."

"For everything. But they do have good scallops here. You—you used to like scallops." She reached for another cigarette. "You must have questions."

"If I ever started, I might not stop." I felt her eyes wanting to dart away, just like mine, but we held each other's gaze, stubborn, as if locked into a staring contest.

"So . . ." she said softly. "Start then."

"Just like that?" Heat rose into my neck and face. Maybe she was already sorry I was there. I certainly wouldn't blame her.

"Just like that. Yes."

I didn't know what to say to her. There was too much. Not enough. I'd only had nine years of my life with her. A long, long time ago. To ask her questions felt like betraying the luminous mother of my memories and letting this imposter in on something that had nothing to do with her. I leaned forward. "I guess—all those years I thought of you the way you were *before* you disappeared. Not that I don't believe it's you . . . But it feels like I'm with someone I don't know." And then it struck me: *I'm still waiting for a ghost though I'm sitting here with her, my mother, am actually sitting across from her.*

I tried to laugh, but what came out sounded like a sob. "It must be even weirder for you. I mean, I was a kid when you left—while I knew you at least as an adult."

Her eyes filled with tears. "For me the strangest part is realizing you don't need me. You're grown-up. Independent. Successful . . . Even though Jake and Marlene kept me informed, it's different seeing you. . . . What I've felt worst about all those years is leaving you and Travis when you still needed me."

"Then why did you?"

She placed the cigarette between her lips, struck a match four times before it lit.

"Why did it all change so?"

"It was better this way, Julia."

"How can you say that?"

"It would have been harmful for you to know."

"Not nearly as harmful as losing you without a word. Wondering all the time . . ."

She laid her cigarette in the ashtray and inspected her hands; they were still slender though the rest of her body had overlapped the silhouette that used to define her.

I wanted to tell her I was glad I'd found her, but I didn't

feel glad. I felt cruel. Powerless. "Your other daughter—?"

"Maria . . . Her name is Maria."

"You see her often?"

"She lives in Houston now. She's getting married in September."

"And you're flying out for her wedding?"

She nodded, closed her eyes for a moment, and I wondered if she, too, was thinking of my wedding when she hadn't been there. Just as she hadn't been there for my graduation or hundreds of other occasions—significant and ordinary—since I was nine.

"Does Maria know about Travis and me?"

"It was better for her not to know."

"Better for her . . . better for us . . . How about you?"

She reached for her glass. Held it between both palms as if keeping it from bursting apart. "I made some decisions back then that were—difficult, Julia. . . . Extremely difficult. And not very good. I was younger then. Afraid."

"Of him."

"Yes. . . . His power."

"Then why did you leave us with him?"

"He was good with you."

I felt as though all the blood were rushing out of my body. "Oh no," I said. "No. He wasn't."

She grasped the bridge of her nose between her forefinger and thumb as if to steady herself.

"He beat me."

Her lips were paler than the rest of her face and made her appear defenseless.

"I had to go to school with bruises on my face and arms . . . lie to the teachers. . . ." My voice was flat. *Why do I have to do this—assault her with what happened to me? She knows what it's like to be beaten.* And yet I told her, had to tell her—aiming each incident at her like a weapon. From time to time her lips opened. But she didn't speak until long after I was finished.

"I believed you were safe with him, Julia. . . . I really did."
Her face seemed to have aged since she'd entered the dining
room. "God, I'm so sorry. Maybe I should have known. He—
he beat me. Several times. Those last years."

"I would have come with you."

"He'd only have taken you away."

"Not if you had fought for us."

"I would have lost you in court . . . and you would have despised me even more."

"I never despised you. Besides, the courts wouldn't have
taken us from you. Unless a mother is totally irresponsible—"

"Perhaps I was totally irresponsible then."

"No—" My voice had risen. "Not you."

"Your father would disagree with you." She propped her
sturdy arms on the table. "At the time, I believed him when
he told me I would lose you in court. He is a powerful man,
Julia."

"Not anymore. He's getting old."

"So am I."

"The drinking . . . He's become very slow. Not just physically. His mind, too."

She frowned at this unfamiliar image of my father—old
and slow—and for a moment she looked confused, as if she
saw herself dancing with him on the patio beneath the paper
lanterns, the April breeze skimming across his hair. . . . And
I—somewhere deep inside—I still wanted them to reach for
one another and dance with the lightness and joy I remembered, wanted that dance to undo three decades of separa-
tion, wanted them to draw me into their embrace and across
that line of salt where everything would be intact again.

When she spoke, I felt as though I still hung suspended between them, my feet flapping high above the land. "There
were days, Julia . . . after I had to go away, many days when I
couldn't even get myself dressed." The words came to her
slowly—as if she were discovering them for herself. Often she
wouldn't get up because she wouldn't know where to start;

each day would loom ahead of her, empty, yet crowded with insurmountable details. She'd stay in the safety-prison of the warm bed. "Safety in not moving. In not making the wrong decision." She'd press her eyes shut and lie on her side, her body curled tight, holding her warmth captured within the circle that would expand as the new child within her ripened. To stay like this. To stay like this and forget all else. To pretend that her already-born children were in the next room, asleep, and that soon we'd wake up and eat breakfast with her.

"You used to talk in your sleep," she said, her tall body motionless, "you and Travis. One of you would say something and then, within minutes, the other would call out . . . the first words clear, then slurred as if—linked within your sleep—you were communicating a secret code." Awake at night next to the Greek, she'd strain for the sounds of our voices. She'd pull herself from that illusion uncountable times when our voices would not reach for her, when the fear of a future without us would rush at her and she couldn't bear to think of even one more day. That physical separateness from her children—it was a wound that could not heal because each morning she had to mount the raw edge of her loss and forfeit the veil of scab that had formed overnight.

As I let myself be absorbed into my mother's suffering, I began to understand how she had made herself function, balancing each hour, each day. Simple motions took as much concentration and effort as if she were performing them for the first time: making the bed, letting in the bathwater, washing a blouse, pouring a cup of coffee. She'd forget about the bath until the water had cooled, find herself with a cup of coffee in her hand without remembering that she'd poured it. *Motions.* She'd discover herself standing in front of the mirror in her slip, brushing her hair, unable to recall having picked up the brush.

And the new child—though it was miraculous to touch her—frightened her. There were too many ways to lose her, hurt her without meaning to. *Yes,* I wanted to say, *I know that fear, I already know what that's like,* but I didn't want to break out of the current of her words that carried me into the strand of life she'd led without me. There would be enough time to tell her about the child I would have. I saw her with Maria in her arms, *stroking one thumb across the downy cheek, choked by the memory of using that same gesture to soothe Travis and me,* and I saw myself, *holding the red-haired infant I'd nursed in my dream and comforting her just like that.*

"I thought it would stop once she reached the ages you and Travis were . . ." my mother said, "that I'd stop recognizing you in her, comparing— But it almost got worse." So aware was she of the years she had missed being with us that she kept imagining us not only through those years but beyond—into ages she hadn't known us. And so she lived both lives, feeding her memories and visions of us while draining her existence with her new daughter and her new husband, whose olive faces and dark eyes made her feel as though she'd been traveling toward both of them since that day she'd seen the tents and horse-drawn wagons in the Rosalia school-yard.

"Neither life was whole." She would do what she needed to do for Maria—feed her, bathe her, soothe her—but every moment of joy would hold its mirror image of sadness. Often, she couldn't bear to touch this child, who was not just Maria but every child she'd birthed, and she'd press her into the arms of her baffled husband and run from the white stone house that belonged to her Greek father-in-law.

Alone, she'd climb up the cobblestone road that twisted to the top of the Peloponnesus hillside. High above the town, which clung to the rugged slope in the same shape as the scar above her first husband's eye, she'd look west across orange and cypress trees; west past the maze of red and amber tiled roofs and the shallow waters of the sheltered harbor, with its tangle of fishing boats; west toward the open sea of the Mediterranean and the boot of Italy, too far away to be discernible, and further yet, past Spain and Portugal; west across the wide sweep of the Atlantic and the bulk of the North American continent. . . . And if she had been able to push them aside—those masses of land and water that stretched between her and her children—push them aside or shrink them, she surely would have done so as she stood on the cliff beneath the bright sun, wearing the vibrant clothes of her new country.

"Some days," she said, "up there on that hillside, my body would be so heavy with tears that I couldn't trust myself to return to the house and be around others."

"I think I saw you once," I whispered, "on that hill. Was there a stone wall—a wide wall, piled high with gray rocks?"

The skin at her temples looked thin, translucent. She nodded.

"An orange tree . . . and lichen, patches of lichen on those rocks?"

"Yes."

"You caught me. I jumped and you caught me. One of my—my daydreams, whatever you call them. You wore a dress with embroidery down the front, and you caught me when I jumped. . . ." I closed my eyes and felt it again then— my daring leap into her open arms, the jolt of our bodies merging and reeling into the tall grass, even that yearning to taste the dark seeds of earth to stall the inevitable moment when my body would be severed from hers again.

But when I opened my eyes, expecting to see her, the woman across from me was no longer the mother of those fantasies which had replaced her, spinning off each other, snaring me with vivid and convincing images. The real mother couldn't win by making herself fit into those fantasies—but she could shatter them with her presence, with the solid shape of her body, the real scent of nicotine, the gray in her short hair.

"Sometimes I hated you for not being there. . . . Other times I felt you right next to me."

She nodded, slowly. "I was."

My eyes burned. "I used to believe you had disguised your-self. . . . I'd get into trouble staring at people to see if they were you. To check their voices, I'd ask them stupid questions."

"I'm so sorry, Julia."

As I looked through her eyes at myself, her grown daughter, I could feel her anguish so acutely, as if I were being pulled inside her—far deeper than any leap into her arms could have ever taken me; and though I fought to stay separate from her pain, it was already becoming mine as if all the losses I'd ever endured had merely been practice sessions.

AFTER MY MOTHER drove off in her Jeep, I walked to the back of the inn. The chill of the sea breeze shifted through me as if my body had lost any substance. My surroundings—sculpted dunes and the vast expanse of ocean—felt as though they didn't belong here: they belonged in my father's childhood, in another time when he had slid down those slopes of sand. There was a trick to it, he'd told me, and when I was six, he'd shown me what it was: our heels high off the ground to prevent them from digging into the sand, we'd glided down those hills, clouds of amber sand dust billowing around us. "Those dunes—" he'd said one summer vacation when we'd looked from the kitchen window of his mother's house toward the ocean, "they feel so alive . . . all that shifting sand. And yet there's such a feeling of death about this place."

The tide was out now, and in the mist I felt bewildered, adrift without the old purpose of chasing after my mother. I'd found her, but I'd relinquished the fantasy that had served me for over thirty years. A trade of sorts—though not even. Still, a better trade, perhaps, than the one she'd made: her seclusion in return for her brat daughter. I was ashamed for pushing at her with my words. She, too, had been beaten. She, too, had paid a tremendous price. And when she'd fled, it had been in weakness and fear. As I kept sifting through every word of our talk—a talk I'd imagined in countless versions since the day she'd left—I wasn't sure how much of it was hers and where I had embellished what might have happened.

My arms felt cold, and when I rubbed them, the flats of my hands felt even colder. A sea anemone clung against the lower side of a rock formation that was crusted with mussels. As I touched its green sepals, the anemone drew into itself, and suddenly I felt that panic I'd only known in the old dream of chasing, chasing down the unending corridor after a tall figure without features, and it was as if this was the moment I'd dreamed all those years—a premonition come to full term. I recognized the sting of breath in my throat, recognized the walls of that nightmare corridor. I felt the sweat of the dreams, that damp, cold sweat, and understood that— once the figure finally turned—the face would no longer be the blank, tight oval of skin. I felt a pounding in every fiber of my body. The figure was my father, had been my father all along, though I'd tried to impose my mother's features.

My hair and face were damp. All those years he'd been a distressing presence in my life, but I had taken that presence for granted—the one parent whose place in the world I knew—and though I had feared him, ignored him, detested him, I had never been without him. I had returned to confront him, but instead had found—no, torn free, excavated, resurrected—someone I hadn't expected, the other father, the one I hadn't let myself think about, the good father whose memory I had killed in order to survive.

My lips tasted salty. I shivered. And saw my father kneeling on the end of our dock, extending one hand to me, and it was my response—the decline of his help as I pulled myself onto the sunny planks—that kept coming back to me throughout that night, snatching me from shallow spans of sleep.

# 13

∎

HEN LILY OPENED HER
door the next morning, she seemed more at ease, this tall
woman I might have evoked with my child-sorcery. *Lily Ives.*
*LI.* Add an *E* and it becomes *LIE*. But why was I here if I wasn't
willing to trust her?

As she stepped aside to let me in, that old grace manifested itself for a moment, even though the shape of her
body had changed. "You look tired."

"I kept waking up." My stomach felt as skittish as during
the early months of my pregnancy when I'd soothed it with
bland crackers and peppermint tea.

She looked at me, closely. Waited. Her eyes were clear. She
wore jeans again and a blue cotton shirt, tucked in loosely.

"I'm all right, really. How about you?"

"I'm making French toast for us. Why don't you lie down
until breakfast is ready."

"I'd rather help."

"You still like strawberries on your French toast, Julia?"
She was saying my name as if relishing it, as if amazed to say it
aloud to me.

"Yes, I still like strawberries."

"Good. That's good."

I followed her through her living room, which contained few pieces of furniture and hardly any pictures on the walls, as if she wanted to be ready to pack and move at a moment's notice; yet, the things she had were striking, elegant in their simplicity, and matched the colors of her rug, a white dhurrie with a symmetrical, slate-blue design. Western light slanted through the sliding glass doors that faced the beach.

"It suits you," I said. "I like it." And yet, somehow I must have imagined her house the way we'd had ours when I was a girl—filled with furniture my parents had collected on their travels.

Next to the kitchen phone hung a Georgia O'Keeffe calendar with my name entered twice: Thursday for dinner at six and Friday for breakfast at nine. Last night after meeting me, she must have come home, picked up a pen, and written my name on the calendar for breakfast.

"Coffee, Julia?"

I shook my head. "You have any juice?"

She pointed to the refrigerator. "See what you like."

At the blue-tiled kitchen counter I sliced strawberries while she flipped thick triangles of batter-soaked bread in the pan—just like other mothers and their grown daughters working side by side in countless kitchens. I had seen them over the years, those women who had no idea how fortunate they were, had envied them again and again when they'd turned their necks toward one another with a comment or an easy laugh.

As I poured cranberry juice, I felt grateful to be performing these ordinary tasks in the same room with my mother; and yet, I had a sense of it not being quite real, as if I'd stepped for good into a strand of life I'd only flitted through in my fantasies, at the cost, perhaps, of leaving the reality I'd built for myself in Vermont. I didn't want to choose: I wanted all of the strands to continue and merge so that I'd never lose anyone again; I wanted those strands to come together like the jumble of silver-gray lines on the screen where I'd first seen my daughter—a mouth, a femur, a heart—and I was impatient for that instant when those lines would shift into focus and reveal the entire pattern; I wanted to recognize it by myself, this design, wanted it to align itself around me and hold me in perfect balance.

"Travis is on his way."

I glanced up, alarmed. "It's too soon."

"He's in Portland." She lifted two browned wedges of bread from the pan and set them on a plate with a paper towel. "He called. Just before you got here. From a car rental place at the airport."

"How long—"

"About two hours from there to Neskowin."

"Are you ready for another first encounter? If Travis is anything like I was yesterday . . ."

She looked at my face as if to gauge my mood and then grimaced. "I would have preferred to get both over with at the same time. Or skip them altogether—"

I drew in my breath.

"—and go right on to second encounters."

I smiled. "They do seem easier."

"Much easier. Let's eat, Julia."

But all I felt was an urgency to talk with her alone before Travis arrived. I had no time to get into this slowly, carefully, no time to waste anticipating what I wanted to hear. As we sat down in the breakfast nook, two speckled birds pecked at sunflower seeds a few inches away from us in a compact, wooden A-frame that was mounted to the outside of the window and covered with clematis vines.

My mother spooned strawberries on my French toast.

I came right out with it: "I'm pregnant."

She set down the bowl. Her eyes held me, encouraged me to go on, and all at once those words that hadn't been there the day before rushed from me: I told her about the baby, my divorce from Andreas, the office I'd opened with Bob Elling, the Kitchendog's death, my relationship with Coop, the tonsillectomy I'd had in fifth grade, the design award I'd won in my senior year of college, my marriage to Andreas . . . and with each moment I was aware of my brother getting closer to Neskowin, his hands on the steering wheel, leaning in our direction. *I don't want him here. Not yet.* It was too soon to share her with anyone else. How could I possibly pack thirty years into two hours?

Whenever I asked her questions about herself, she brought our talk back to me again, and I was as starved to tell her about what had been happening to me all those years as I was to find out about her. There was an urgency too in her listening, as if she knew that once Travis was here, it would change, become his and my shared history—not mine alone. Right then, I resolved to give the two of them time to talk without me.

WE LEFT the food on the table and took our juice into the living room, where we settled on a sand-colored canvas sofa that faced the glass doors. Low shelves with books lined the bottom three feet of the other walls.

I told my mother about Claudia's Aunt Edith. "She's already looking forward to taking care of the baby while I'm at work." I described her to my mother, that slight, soft-faced woman with the lush Bronx accent, who had fabulous stories of her girdle-fitting days, yet looked like the principal of a girls' school in her tailored suits and fitted blouses. "Aunt Edith thrives on cooking and fussing around Claudia's house. And whenever Claudia tells her she doesn't have to do all that work, she insists it's like a vacation."

"You're lucky to have her for the baby."

"They'll adore each other. I can already see the two of them wearing a path into the lawn between the two houses."

The sea was still, one surface of ripples too low to sustain white crests; hoops of morning sun flitted across it as if an athlete were hurling discuses from a far distance.

"Feeling better, Julia?"

"Eating helped." I took off my sandals. Tucked one leg beneath me, and sat sideways, facing my mother. "Why didn't you contact us later? After we'd left home. When we were older. . . ."

"I thought of it. You don't have any idea how often. A few times I came very close—" She suddenly smiled as if she'd been caught at something. "I was at your graduation."

I stared at her.

"Jake and Marlene told me where it was. I stayed way in back. With opera glasses. I'd bought them just for that. You looked—so determined, so focused . . . as if you were doing exactly what you wanted to do. I felt proud of you."

How could she sit there and smile? I felt stunned. Angry. "Why didn't you come up to me?"

"I wanted to—so much, Julia. But I'd promised myself before I traveled out there that I wouldn't. A condition I made to myself."

"Was that the only time?"

"That I saw you? Yes. But I sent things through Jake. You were told it was from him and Marlene. That woven shawl for your wedding—"

I saw myself wrapping the shawl around my neck, felt the soft fabric against my skin, and was struck with the waste of all those years without her. My eyes stung. "I still have it. I covered my window seat with it."

"Those hand-painted dishes on your thirtieth birthday . . ." Her anguish was deeply etched into her features. "In a way I was there . . . a rather dissatisfying way."

"I wish you'd made yourself known."

For a long time we sat there silently. "So do I. Now. But then . . . Eventually it became too late. It felt like a—a mountain of botched-up chances. Too high to climb across. It was better to leave it behind."

"No," I protested. "No, it wasn't."

"I was afraid if I contacted you I'd be doing it for selfish reasons, Julia. I really believed it would be better for you and Travis if I didn't unsettle your lives again." When she'd found out from Jake that Travis had enrolled at the University of Oregon, she'd called the registrar's office for a copy of his class schedule. Twice that day she'd seen him from a distance as he walked from one building to the next, but when she'd returned four weeks later, he had already terminated his studies.

"At one point—you may not like to hear this—it became easier not to contact you. It isn't that I forgot you and Travis. . . . Not for one day. But it was behind me. Along with the rage I used to feel toward your father. That gray dog," she said, "remember? The one that got your father? He never had a chance to get away from it. His drinking was like that . . . waiting for him. It wasn't enough to try and keep it away, to be aware of it. . . ." She looked out toward the beach, the light full on her face, and I was moved by her compassion for my father and wondered if she, too, had an image of him as a small boy, stumbling as that sleek dog fell upon him and bit into his face and into the waves that fused above him, shutting out the screams and aching sun.

"Much of what he did came out of pain, Julia. I hurt him too. But I started feeling that rage again . . . after you told me he'd beaten you. If I had known——" Her voice snapped, and suddenly she looked as angry as that New Year's Eve when she'd taken the car, stranding my father at a party where he'd been playing the clown for everyone, jabbering away and laughing. She'd finally reached across a lamp—a yellow lamp with long silk fringes—and had slapped him once, hard, before walking out with Travis and me. I tried to imagine her in a room with my father now. He'd be no match for her. It would be like punching a pillow—no resistance. He'd blink, shake his head, mutter a sentence or two.

"If I had known——" she said again. Her face and neck were blotchy, and all at once I found myself hoping that Mr. Pascholidis had treated her well.

"Mr. Pascholidis . . ." I started, prompting her to talk about him, but she remained silent. *His rings flare in the sun as his hands turn the wheel of his boat. He throws back his head and laughs aloud into the wind.* I wanted to ask my mother a dozen questions about him and finally settled on the one that encompassed all the others: "Did you love him?"

She thought for a moment as if surprised I'd come right out and asked that, and I didn't think she'd answer me, but then she said, "When I first knew Niko, it was infatuation . . . as with the others. You may as well know. Maybe you already do. It's not something I'm proud of, but there were—" She drew her shoulders up. "Before Niko. Two others. They—they gave me the illusion of being myself entirely. Your father, he is— He can be very possessive. . . ."

I heard my uncle's voice: *"Some people, Julia—have the kind of devotion that's difficult to bear . . ."* and felt my father hugging me just a bit too long.

"With the others I didn't have to fight to stay separate. I always was. And that made me separate from your father at the same time. Can you understand?"

I nodded.

"I came to care deeply for Niko after we'd lived together for a while. He was a decent man, Julia. . . ." Her words drew pictures of a life far simpler than the one she'd led in Spokane, a life much closer to her early years on the farm in the Palouse. "If it hadn't been for Maria, I wouldn't have gone with Niko. Even then—when I first knew I was pregnant—I was trying to keep our family together. I offered your father an abortion, but he wanted me out of your lives.

"Now— Now when I look at Maria, I'm so grateful I didn't have that abortion. She doesn't have your courage, Julia, your toughness, even though she made it through law school. Underneath she's a rather timid girl. I fed her my sadness with my milk, and there was nothing I could do afterward—when I was stronger again—to make up for it. . . ."

She told me of taking Maria to swimming lessons. "All the

other girls would run into the shower, rinse off, and then swim. Maria would drag me along, stand with her arms clasped around herself and cry if I didn't turn on the shower for her, if I didn't stay next to the pool while she swam. I'd get so cross with her. She always hung back where other children moved forward . . ."

"I want to meet her."

"Eventually."

"Eventually . . ."

"When the time is right for her, too." My mother lit her first cigarette since I'd arrived. "Maybe I would have been in a better position to fight for you if I hadn't been pregnant, but either way, I had to lose someone—in this case you and your brother. . . . And I'd come to accept that. At least I'd convinced myself of that until Marlene's phone call. It opened everything up again. And now I'm doing things I didn't expect."

"Like seeing me?" I rested my arm on the back of the sofa.

"Yes. . . . Calling you. Sitting with you in my house. Talking with Travis on the phone. It shifts everything. Do you really want to know why I was late yesterday? Do you? I couldn't back my Jeep out of the garage. I forgot how to. Ridiculous, isn't it? But I was in that garage a quarter to six, and when I turned on the ignition, I didn't know what the next step was. Simply blanked out. I've had that damn Jeep for years, and I sat in it for half an hour, trying to figure out how to get it into reverse. . . ."

She tried to smile, but her lips trembled. "I finally dug the owner's manual from the glove compartment and followed step-by-step instructions." She took a couple of deep draws from her cigarette. "When I used to look at the rest of my life, Julia, it didn't include you. . . . You or Travis. At least not during the last ten years or so. Even though I thought about you every day, I didn't expect to be with you again. Until then I used to fantasize reunions—God, did I ever—but it was too painful to keep going with them."

"I did that," I said, "kept going with my fantasies. I was sure you'd come back."

"Things are good for me. Here. I'm teaching in a school I like. I have friendships. . . . Part of me is resistant to things changing. As they will. That is if you—"

"Of course I do. But how about you? What is it you want?"

She looked at me for a long time. Even though her face had filled out and sagged a bit around the jaw, the high line of her cheekbones had persisted. "I haven't quite figured that out."

"We could meet halfway between here and Vermont."

"Or I could visit you there, yes. . . ."

I saw her in my house in Proctor. *We sit down for dinner at the kitchen table. It's already dark outside, and the light from the Tiffany lamp encompasses us in a saffron ring.* . . . I wondered how I'd feel about this tall woman with the gray hair and the clipped fingernails if I met her for the first time, say if she moved into the clapboard house across the street from me, a stranger. I'd feel drawn to her independence, to the way she took responsibility for her mistakes.

"Denver would be about halfway. Or maybe Minneapolis." She laid her hand on my arm, which was still stretched across the back of the sofa.

At first I nearly pulled it away—her touch set off something like an electric shock that ended in the side of my neck—but I kept my arm there until I only felt the warmth of her hand. "How are you with letter writing?" I asked.

"Not bad. How about you?"

"Usually the phone is easier."

She tilted her head. "He's here. Travis is here."

And then I heard it too, the sound of a car in the driveway, and when she looked at me, it was with an expression of loss that was out of proportion for the moment.

SHE OPENED the door for Travis, and they shook hands with the same awkward formality that had hampered my first encounter with her. In one arm he held a gift-wrapped package. Although the paper was new, the silver bow looked crushed, as though it had been reused on at least four occasions. *"Look, Mama, look at me jump. . . ." "Look at me climb. . . ." Showing off for her.* Even now. While I hadn't even thought of bringing her something.

His eyes were deep-seated with exhaustion, and his expression was so raw and guarded that it seemed indecent to witness their reunion. Feeling his uncertainty as though it were mine, I walked over to the glass doors and stood with my back to them. Mist had settled again over the ocean, and though its surface was still calm, it appeared to shift in almost imperceptible designs as if an immense creature were holding its breath at the bottom of the sea.

Their words came to me in mumbled patterns, too low to discern, and formed a natural background sound to the motion of the waves until it was as though I were listening to their long-ago voices and saw my brother in his striped play-suit, holding on to my mother's leg as she opened the front door.

"Stay home, Mama."

"Travis—" Her eyes were shining as they strayed past him to my father, who leaned quietly against the wall next to the gold-framed mirror. "I won't be long, Travis." She wore perfume and high-heel shoes that matched her red dress with the shoulder straps.

"Where are you going?"

"To a concert."

"Come on, Travis." My father moved forward and lifted Travis up. He took my hand into his. "Let's cook dinner, you and Julia and I."

"Good night then," my mother called out from the door, her voice too cheerful.

But my father turned without answering and took Travis and me into the kitchen.

■

"I SHOULD have come with you." Travis stepped next to me. A trace of beard smudged his cheeks. He'd dressed in a blue suit and white shirt that made him look like someone else's brother.

"What made you change your mind?"

He gave me an embarrassed grin, and all at once I did feel glad that he was here.

"We can drive back together," I suggested.

"Hey . . . I just got here."

I laughed. "All right. No rush."

"How long are you staying?"

"I don't know yet."

"Maybe we can drop my car at a local agency."

I looked over my shoulder. "Where's our— Where's Lily?"

"In the kitchen. Making coffee. I brought her one of those old wooden coffee grinders, and she wanted to try it out. I got it at an auction in Colville. She can grind spices in it too."

"That's . . . thoughtful. How did you manage to get away from—him?"

"I left Dad plenty of groceries. The piano teacher across the street promised to check in on him."

"What if he walks off by himself?"

"He never has before."

"What if he hitchhikes to the cottage?"

"What is this? Calm down."

"If he starts to remember . . . Those questions I asked him. Would he do something foolish?"

"Are you going to feel better if I call? Now?"

"You know he won't pick up the phone."

"I'll call Mr. Curtiss."

As he headed toward the phone, I could see us already, racing back to Spokane in my rental car and finding the front door of my father's house wide open. *The TV blares, but the lights are still off though it's turning dusky outside. He's no longer there. Not in the living room, not in the kitchen or his room or*

*the rest of the house. The piano teacher hasn't seen him since early
that morning when my father brought him three cinnamon rolls for
breakfast.*

*"He baked them himself." He shows us a plastic-covered plate with
one and a half cinnamon rolls as if offering them as a substitute for
my father.*

*Once more we search through every room and the yard, but it's im-
possible to determine how long my father has been gone: it could
have been half an hour or all day.*

*"Tell you what—" Travis says, "I'll drive through the neighbor-
hood, and if I don't see him, I'll take off for the cottage."*

*"It's probably too soon to call the police."*

*"We'll find him." Travis gives me a brief, hard hug. "All right?"*

*"I'll check around Cannon Hill Park and then stay here in case
he comes back."*

*In a few of the houses, lamps have come on, outlining the leaded
panes and arched windows. None of the other neighbors has seen my
father, and after I knock at several doors, I run down the brick street
and into the park that lies deserted while normal families sit around
dinner tables.*

*In the shallow water, twigs and pinecones drift about. Reeds,
skinnier than those at the lake, grow in irregular clumps. A dog has
left one paw print in the mud. High among the leaves and branches
of the largest weeping willow hovers a slow shimmer of white. Grass
brushes my toes through the straps of my sandals. Two swans, their
wings nearly touching, glide across the pond. I stop. Turn back to
the white up there in the willow, wishing I could hold on to something to steady myself because there—on the highest limb that over-
hangs the water—stands my father, almost hidden by the leaves. The
tail of his white shirt has slipped from his trousers, and he stands
with his head tipped as if listening to the slow pulse of the pond that
rocks itself against its swampy edges.*

*Careful not to startle him, I move close to the trunk and step be-
tween the ridges of the raised root system. "Dad? Don't move, Dad."*

*Branches crackle as the shimmer separates into two sources—my
father's shirt and hair. His face hangs way above me as he peers*

*through the web of leaves. "Julia," he exclaims, as if he'd walked in too early on his own surprise party.*

*"Don't move."*

*"What are you doing here?"*

*"I was looking for you."*

*"Come on up then."*

*I check around the trunk for a way to hoist myself into the tree, but the coarse bark offers only slight indentations. The trunk is massive and dark, too thick to embrace for even two people. Gnarled limbs swirl off at odd angles and billow into a spacious crown. Some of the thinner branches arch across the water, forming half an umbrella, their long leaves touching the surface. As a girl I climbed to the top of this tree and most others in the park, but it seems higher now and not nearly as safe.*

*"How did you ever get up there?"*

*"I—I don't know."*

*I look around for help, but the park is still empty. "Can you make it down?"*

*Fragments of bark and leaves drizzle around me as he shifts his weight along the branch. The reflection of his shirt bobs on the water as though a drowned man had risen to its surface.*

*"Slow," I yell. "Real slow."*

*Above me, his breathing hangs harsh and belabored as though he'd always been here—part of this evening, this tree—even when my mother carried me on her shoulders around this pond, even when I caught turtles here with Lynne, even when I rode on the handlebars of Scott's bicycle. Always here, my father, rehearsing his part in my nightmare, waiting for his cue to turn around and reveal his features to me.*

*"Just stay where you are, okay? I'll get some help."*

*"Don't go, Julia——" He sounds frightened.*

*"Try and sit down. . . . Good, you're doing it. . . . Careful. Hold on." I kick off my sandals. Reach up to link my hands across the branch closest to me. Pressing my feet against the trunk, I let them grasp their way up the bark until I can hook them over the branch. My breasts are in the way and my arms ache with my new weight as*

*I hang there by my hands and feet like a crazy, pregnant baboon.*

*My breath comes in quick bursts as I maneuver myself to where I can sit on the branch. I don't dare look up or down, only at the next branch. While my father watches me, I pull myself higher and higher until, finally, I straddle a branch about six feet below him. My thighs are trembling, my palms sore. Smells of grass and stagnant water reach for us, pull at us.*

"It is pretty here, isn't it?" *My father gazes across the stripe of moon that sways on the pond.* "I do not know how to get down. I have been trying. Before you got here . . ." *He sounds embarrassed.* "Old men do not belong in trees."

"Neither do pregnant women."

*He touches the cleft in his chin, which looks softer, less defined than when I was a girl.*

"Someday you can tell my daughter how we got stuck in this tree."

"Stuck in this tree," *he repeats to himself, and smiles toward the shadow outlines of houses on the other side of the park.* "I do not like this . . . getting old."

"Why don't we stay here and rest awhile?"

"I am not tired."

"It's a good place to rest."

*Brisk air rises toward us and cools our faces as we look down at the black mirror image of the tree's branches that lies on the pond as if tempting us to climb into its depths.*

*Slowly, my father extends one leg and lowers it.*

"Wait—you'll slip in those shoes." *I reach up and untie his leather shoes, tug them from his feet, and toss them into the grass far below. I peel off his socks and grip his ankles while he attempts to lower himself to my branch.* "Grasp with your toes," *I say.* "Pretend you have monkey feet."

"Monkey feet?" *He looks at me with the gold-flecked eyes of the father I used to know.*

"That's right. Monkey feet."

*Though his movements are cautious, they take on an almost elegant symmetry as his body tries to traverse the gap between us. His hands still span the highest limb of the willow while his feet angle for some hold, and for a moment there—just before I can position his bare feet on my branch—I'm certain we both will fall, my fingers around his ankles, teeter off and drop into a night-tunnel-dream scene, spin and shatter into a thousand pieces. But my father holds on. He holds on though I can no longer make out the limb that supports him or the branch that awaits him, and it is as though he levitated in the tapering light.*

"Mr. Curtiss saw him half an hour ago." Suddenly Travis is back next to me.

*Wind rushes through the leaves in a coarse whisper, flicking their long, pointed ends against our faces.* "What?" I asked. "What is it?"

"The piano teacher. He saw Dad half an hour ago."

*On the moss-green pond far below us, the swans make their wide, graceful sweeps as if choreographed.* "And here I was rushing back to Spokane and getting him out of a tree."

"A tree?"

"Coop—the baby's father—he says I always need something to fret about."

"Fret-of-the-day. I know that only too well."

"I'll have to remember to tell Coop. Fret-of-the-day. He'll like that."

"Tell him it's our grandmother's legacy."

"Are we that bad? Tell me we're not that bad, Travis."

He laughed. "Not that bad. Maybe because you and I can divide her capacity for fretting between us."

"So . . . what do you think of our mother?"

"She— She's different. Not just older. Different too."

"Be easy on her." I opened the sliding door.

"Where are you going?" He sounded worried.

"For a walk."

"You don't need to leave."

"I had time alone with her. Now it's your turn."

Barefoot, I walked north along the beach. If I kept going, I'd eventually reach Canada. Alaska. The end of the world. I had touched him—had touched my father, even if it had only

been in my fantasy, even if I still didn't know what to say to
him. It had been easier to accuse him. Before I'd remembered . . . A fine drizzle moistened the air. Close to the water,
in the darker sand, my bare feet left a lengthening string of
deep imprints. I thought of Lynne and Sonja rescuing
starfish. But there was nothing to rescue here, and even if
there were, I had no one to rescue it with. All at once I had to
laugh. *High drama at the edge of the Pacific.* I could whip it into
more of a pitch. Like those howling dervish waves I'd seen
yesterday from my bathtub. I could even add some self-pity—
*no one to rescue starfish with, for crying out loud, Julia.*

Far ahead of me, a bulky mass jutted from the sand. Probably a rock, I thought, but after I waded through a cold stream
that ran across the beach into the sea, I saw that it was an immense tree trunk. Its base lay buried beneath layers of sand
and shells as though it were growing right out of the sand.
But of course that was impossible. Some of its broken root
ends stuck out from the ground, and barnacles grew all over
its bark. In its hollows, pockets of sand had settled. A shallow
tide pool had collected around its base, sustaining a micro-
cosm of life. It was a different kind of growing—not the usual
way a tree grew, not the expected beauty of a tree—yet magnificent, sheltering.

I wished I knew how to sketch so I could take an image of
the tree back with me to Vermont. It reminded me of Lily:
she too had been marred; she too had survived. I walked
around the stump and touched the bleached wood where it
fused with the sand. There had to be thousands of tree
stumps on beaches, but I'd never looked at one this way.
Would it stay on this beach? It must have been under water
for a long time. Now it was here—flawed and splendid. Until
when? Maybe it didn't matter. Maybe all that mattered was
that, for now, this was the best place for it.

I bent and, with both hands, picked up a glistening stone
and hurled it into the waves. Salt particles clung to my palms,
and I rubbed them together until the friction made them

warm. Then I chose another stone. And when I threw it, further, the arc of my arm encompassed the sky.

As I APPROACHED the back of the house, I could see my
mother and Travis sitting on the sofa, faces turned toward
each other, but they didn't notice me till I stood on the deck
and brushed the sand from my feet. The sky was clearing
once more as the sun outlined mounds of clouds with gold,
forcing shafts of brightness through the gray in even streaks
that looked as artificial as those fingers-of-God panoramas in
religious pictures.

Travis opened the glass slider for me. His hair was brushed
back, exposing a few gray threads at his temples. It didn't
seem right—Lily's youngest child graying before me. But
then he wasn't the youngest; not anymore. Maria was nearly
ten years younger than we were.

Barefoot, I sat on the dhurrie rug and told them about the
tree stump. "It felt strange being around it . . . peaceful."

"I know the one you mean," my mother said, "but I've
never thought of it like that."

"Makes me want to head out there," Travis said. On the
table stood his coffee grinder, the deep brown wood buffed
to a rich sheen.

"Maybe we'll take you there this afternoon." My mother lit
a cigarette, and dropped the match into a ceramic ashtray.
"When are you going back to Vermont, Julia?"

"My plane's leaving Tuesday."

"From Spokane?"

I nodded.

"That gives us a few more days." She looked exhausted, yet
oddly content. "Can you stay longer?"

"I'd like to, but I have some projects waiting. Last week we
were selected to do a school library and—"

"We'll see each other soon," she said softly.

"When?" It shot out so abruptly I startled myself.

"Let's talk on the phone sometime next month." Her smile

was uncertain. Was she planning her getaway before we dis-
cussed her arrival? "We can probably do something during
my winter vacation. I have two weeks in December."

*Probably.* I wished that could be enough for me, but it
wasn't. I wanted guarantees. Assurances. After three decades
without her, I was not about to settle for something as vague
as the possibility of a visit. "How—" It felt dangerous to ask
this from the woman who hadn't even let herself be pinned
down for the next moon-walk. "How would you feel about
making definite plans before I take off?" I tried to laugh, to
make it sound less important. "I want to mark your date of arrival on my calendar and—" My voice closed off. My throat
felt liquid. . . . My entire head did.

Travis' eyes raced between her and me—as helpless as all
those times he'd tried to invent his flimsy peace between me
and my father.

To my dismay I started to cry. "You just fucking left us
there with him. You—" A swell of fury and panic choked me.
I tried to stop, tried to remind myself of her suffering, but all
I saw was her too bright smile as she stood by the door in her
red dress with the shoulder straps, eager to get away. *Leaving.
Always leaving.*

"You just fucking left us there with him. . . ." I kept saying
it through my sobs.

She looked devastated. This was what she must have been
afraid of before she'd let me come here.

"You just fucking left us there with him. . . ."

Travis got up and walked to the slider, where he stood with
his back to me; but my mother gathered me against her, cautiously at first as though I were brittle, dangerous even, while
my sobs echoed through the room. I felt small, incredibly
small, as if my old belief—that children always stayed that
way—had finally turned out to be true. Only I was no longer
riding on my mother's shoulders in the night wind, and I
didn't think I'd ever feel that safe with her again.

When I finally managed to stop crying, I couldn't bear to

look at her or Travis. "I'm sorry," I mumbled and tried to disengage myself from her, but she tightened her arms around me. It took effort to keep my eyes open. We stayed like that for a long time, silent, her arms around me, the only sound the choppy pattern of my breath.

"Here, lie on the sofa." She took my elbow, helped to get me settled, and spread a blanket across me. I turned my damp face toward the canvas back of the sofa and let the steady rhythm of the sea fill my head. I felt weightless— awake and asleep, there in the living room, yet out on the beach next to the tree stump. I touched the barnacles, inhaled the briny mist, and saw myself from a distance, stretched out on the sofa, a blue afghan covering me.

"Rest," my mother whispered. A hand, her hand, brushed my cheek with the suddenness that used to distinguish her movements, and for the instant it lingered on my skin, I felt treasured in a way I hadn't known before.

TRAVIS AND I stayed at her house for three days, and there were moments when fragments of that long-ago magic broke through layers of time and reached for us, held us as if to reward us for waiting all those years.

We dropped off his rental car, picked up my bags at the Blue Heron, and moved us in—Travis into the guest room, me into the living room with its view of the ocean. While brief showers chased strings of rain across the ever-changing sky and floods of sun dried the sand, we looked at photos that Aunt Marlene had sent my mother, photos of Travis and me as recent as the year before. And we talked—talked almost incessantly—even when we took walks or cooked or played my mother's tapes of flute music.

Travis and I urged her on with questions about her years in Greece and her return to the United States, where she and Maria had lived in Fort Lee, New Jersey, within walking distance of the George Washington Bridge. She'd taught school there as a substitute teacher, and they'd stayed a few years.

Gradually, they'd moved across the country—a year in Ohio, two in Iowa, six months in South Dakota—packing up and heading west again until the dunes and ocean had stopped them, sustaining my mother with familiar hills and endless skies.

Though I didn't want to miss a single word she said, I kept drifting into brief naps as if my body were restoring itself after a long illness.

"You look like you slept in your face," Travis greeted me Sunday after my second nap. He sat down on the edge of my sofa.

"That bad, huh? Thanks a lot." I ran both hands through my hair. "Where have you been?"

"We sat on the deck, had lunch. . . . It feels good to be here—with her and with you." His voice grew sober. "It's always been with me, the not knowing. I never said anything— still . . ."

"I know."

When I slept, it was without retaining dreams, and I'd wake up, my body warm and soothed. Monday morning we said good-bye to my mother, and I felt her palms solid against my back as we embraced. For an instant I had to fight the old habit of fear that I'd never see her again; and yet, I felt prepared to go, to be a mother now that I'd become a daughter once more.

She, too, seemed ready to send us on our way though she walked next to the car in the rain as I backed out of the driveway, her hand on the edge of my open window. "Come back soon and stay longer."

"I'll try." Travis reached across me and covered her fingers with his.

"About some of those things I said to you . . ." I started. "I'm sorry."

"I kept waiting for one of you to say them. I'm relieved they're out." Her gray hair was plastered to her forehead, her face and sweater wet. "And I'll visit you. All right? But it's too soon to say when."

I nodded though I wanted her to bring her calendar out here, flip the pages to December, and write my name on the first day of her Christmas vacation. But then I looked into her wide, tanned face, and it had already become more familiar than the film I'd carried within me—yet it had not erased it, merely superimposed itself.